**Sophia Williams** lives in London with her family. She has loved reading Regency romances for as long as she can remember and is delighted now to be writing them for Mills & Boon. When she isn't chasing her children around or writing (or pretending to write but actually googling for hero inspiration and pictures of gorgeous Regency dresses), she enjoys reading, tennis and wine.

**Also by Sophia Williams**

*How the Duke Met His Match*
*The Secret She Kept from the Earl*
*When Cinderella Met the Duke*

Look out for more books from Sophia Williams coming soon.

Discover more at millsandboon.co.uk.

# THE DUKE'S CHRISTMAS FAKE FIANCÉE

Sophia Williams

MILLS & BOON

First published in Great Britain 2025
by Mills & Boon, an imprint of HarperCollins*Publishers* Ltd,
1 London Bridge Street, London, SE1 9GF

www.harpercollins.co.uk

HarperCollins*Publishers*, Macken House, 39/40 Mayor Street Upper,
Dublin 1, D01 C9W8, Ireland



ISBN: 978-0-263-34543-8

11/25

FSC
www.fsc.org
MIX
Paper | Supporting responsible forestry
FSC™ C007454

This book contains FSC™ certified paper
and other controlled sources to ensure responsible forest management.

For more information visit www.harpercollins.co.uk/green.

Printed and Bound in the UK using 100% Renewable Electricity
at CPI Group (UK) Ltd, Croydon, CR0 4YY

To Charlie

# *Chapter One*

*Cecily*

*Sussex—December 1814*

Lady Cecily Carlow stared in horror at her Aunt Jane.

'The Earl of Steed?' she repeated.

'Indeed.' Her aunt bared her teeth in the closest approximation to a smile she ever achieved when addressing Cecily. 'A wonderful match for you. I am quite overcome.'

Cecily was overcome, too.

'I can't,' she said baldly.

'Cecily!' Her aunt's teeth disappeared and her mouth pinched together. 'Surely I do not need to remind you that you *have* to marry and that at your advanced age you are unlikely to get any other offers. You are four-and-twenty years old, Cecily.'

'Aunt, the Earl is old enough to be my grandfather and he is habitually rude to me and all others he deems his inferior.'

'Cecily, he is an *earl*. And extremely wealthy. And soon you will be his Countess. A rich earl must be allowed his idiosyncrasies.'

Cecily took a deep breath. 'Aunt. I believe that his rudeness goes far beyond mere idiosyncrasy.'

'This coming from a young lady who exhibits clumsiness, talkativeness and over-friendliness amongst her many defects. You would do well to reflect on your good fortune. Your uncle has told the earl that you will of course accept his offer. He dines with us this evening. I know that you will not reject the earl's hand. You would not wish to force your uncle to cast you out.' Her aunt picked up her skirts and executed a magnificent departure from the room.

As the door closed behind her aunt, Cecily sat down with a thunk on the threadbare divan behind her. Her aunt had spoken particularly viciously. Cecily had a strong feeling that the threat to cast her out was not an idle one; she was sure that her relatives had been looking for an excuse to get rid of her for a long time. Which meant that it was likely that by the end of this evening she would either no longer have a home here with her aunt and uncle, or she would have agreed to marry an elderly ogre.

She didn't *enjoy* living with her aunt and uncle, but it was the only home she'd had since her parents' deaths when she was seven and she did at least have a roof over her head, and was adequately fed, and had friendships with the servants and the few local acquaintances she was able to meet on the occasions her aunt allowed her to join the rest of the family for social events.

What would life be like married to the Earl? She pulled her shawl around herself, suddenly cold.

Her aunt was of course right; it did seem that Cecily was peculiarly unlovable, and she had no dowry, so very few men would choose to marry her, as evidenced by the fact that she had never before received an offer. Her aunt and uncle were not particularly well-off, and what funds they did have they preferred to spend on themselves and their own two children, so Cecily had not had a London Season, her aunt believing that she would be able to marry her off to someone like a desperate local squire (in her aunt's words). No local squire had, however, yet been desperate enough.

So it was understandable that her aunt and uncle would wish Cecily to accept the Earl's offer. But horrifying.

And such bad timing. The Earl lived nearby and had surely known of Cecily's existence for many years, and it was at least five years since the death of his last wife (possibly his third, perhaps his fourth; Cecily couldn't remember), so it did not seem that he had until now been in any hurry to marry her. If only he had waited a little longer. In about three months' time she would be coming into a sum of money—about which her aunt and uncle knew nothing—sizeable enough to allow her to buy herself a cottage and live independently, so she would then have nothing to fear in rejecting the proposal.

She heaved an enormous sigh before standing up. If this were to be her last day of relative freedom, she shouldn't waste it moping. Her aunt had been so excited by the news of the proposal that she appeared to have forgotten to give Cecily any list of chores for the day. It was still only eleven o'clock in the morning and she therefore had several hours ahead of her before dusk. She should make the most of her aunt's lapse and go for a long walk, firstly because she very much liked the freedom of walking alone and secondly because if her aunt couldn't see her she couldn't tell her to do anything. And thirdly because one's thoughts roamed more widely when one was walking outside and perhaps she would be able to think of a solution to her problem.

Twenty minutes later, she had walked herself briskly out of sight of the house, taking a well-practised route that put a copse of trees between her and the back of the house so that if anyone should choose to look out of a window in that direction they wouldn't see her. She skirted the copse, continuing to make sure that she didn't come into view of the house again, before finally breaking cover and heading over the hill that marked the border of her uncle's property and the neighbouring property, owned by Felix, the new Duke of Garth, who was a good friend of hers and would always welcome her on his land.

It was so good to be here in the open air. If she *did*, heaven forbid, have to marry the Earl, she would at least, as his Countess, be able to walk to her heart's desire, she presumed; surely he wouldn't find as many mundane household tasks for her as her aunt did. She would also hopefully be at greater leisure to pursue friendships with other ladies living locally. And she would almost certainly be able to avoid her aunt and uncle quite largely. So there *would* be some advantages. But none of them would compare to the bliss of living alone in a cottage of her own.

She had agreed with Miss Holland, her cousins' old governess, with whom she still corresponded very regularly, that Holly—as she fondly called her—would come to live with her in the cottage, and she knew that they would go on very well together.

She stopped walking, the better to listen to the chatter of the birds around her, and closed her eyes, raising her face to be warmed by the December sun.

'Cecily!'

She hadn't been expecting to hear anyone call her

name and gave a great start, which caused her to trip over her own feet.

'Sorry,' the Duke of Garth said, as he jogged over to her, his long legs covering the ground easily. 'I shouldn't have surprised you like that.'

'No, no, it was my fault.' Cecily put her hand in his so that he could pull her upright. 'My aunt accused me only this morning of being too clumsy for anyone to wish to marry me, and while it wasn't *kind* of her, it was certainly accurate.'

'*What*?' asked Felix, his brow furrowing.

She nodded, before explaining, 'She pointed out, again, my defects as a marriage candidate. Because—terrible news—apparently the Earl of Steed has offered for me.'

'Steed?' Felix's frown deepened. 'What do you mean?'

'Apparently the Earl called on my uncle this morning to tell him that he intends to propose marriage to me and wishes us to be wed as soon as possible, before Christmas.'

'But—' Felix's handsome face screwed into an expression of disgust '—the man must be at least five-and-seventy years of age.'

'I know.' Cecily began to walk again and Felix fell in beside her. 'He is, however, extremely wealthy and of course well-connected, and were we to have a son—' she was unable to suppress a shudder at the thought of engaging in the act of creating a child with the Earl—she had learnt about the relations between men and women from some of her aunt's housemaids '—he would be the next Earl and my aunt would be his proud and no doubt very interested great-aunt, and if I were to be married off my aunt and uncle would no longer have to provide for me. And if I refuse his proposal, I will apparently be cast out by them.'

'Good God. Barbaric. Do you think they mean it?'

'I wouldn't like to put it to the test. I feel that they have been looking for an excuse to get rid of me for a long time.'

Felix nodded, which was a relief, because Cecily was not in the mood for polite pretences that things weren't as bad as they actually were. One of the many things she enjoyed about Felix's friendship was that he never bothered to sugar-coat unpleasant facts.

'This is so dreadfully timed,' he said. 'It's only about three months until you will receive the payment for your novel.'

Cecily had confided in Felix the year before that she had written a romantic novel and that, without wishing to be boastful, she was quite proud of her own work. Felix had asked if he could read it and she had at first demurred, but then had suddenly decided that she would like a second opinion beyond Holly's. Holly had said that she believed it to be excellent, but she was always fiercely protective of Cecily and would never criticise her work, so her opinion could not really be relied upon in this regard.

Felix was the only true friend she had outside Holly and the servants' quarters, and honest with his opinions but never unkind, so he was the ideal critic. She had shown him the first chapter, and he had told her that he loved it, so she had allowed him to read the rest of it. He had been so impressed by the whole that he had suggested that he approach a publisher on her behalf, and now—to Cecily's continued immense joy and near disbelief—the book was to be published anonymously in the new year and Cecily was to receive a lump sum payment from the publisher by Easter.

Once she had discovered the sum that she would receive—greater, she was sure, because it had been negotiated by an influential duke—she had determined that she would purchase a cottage for herself. Holly, one of the few people who had been truly kind to her, had immediately confirmed that she would be extremely happy to live there with her. Cecily had told Felix of her plans and he had said that he would help her find an appropriate property.

'I know,' she said. '*Such* bad timing. I have been trying to think of solutions to my problem. I will of course try to postpone the wedding for a few months, but presume that the Earl will refuse a delay, given that he was so specific about wishing to marry before Christmas. I wondered whether I might perhaps marry him and then divorce him, but I'm not sure whether a lady can instigate a divorce, and in the meantime I would have to…be his *wife*.'

Felix was shaking his head.

'I really don't think you can or should rely on a future divorce as your solution. Why do not I advance you the funds?' he said. 'And we can search for a cottage immediately.'

'That's very kind.' Cecily wished so much that she could accept his offer, but there were so many immediately obvious reasons that she couldn't. 'But I can't. I couldn't take your money.'

'It would be a loan from one friend to another, and I would be extremely happy to make that loan; and it would not inconvenience me at all.' He was, Cecily knew, extremely rich, but that wasn't the point.

'Thank you—and indeed I am very grateful for the suggestion—but I don't think it would work. It would still take some time for me to find somewhere to live and as a single lady with no other family I would not be able to stay anywhere else while I looked, so would still run the risk of having no roof over my head by tomorrow. My aunt would be incandescent with fury, I'm sure, at the thought of her ungrateful niece embarrassing her by retiring to a cottage rather than marrying the Earl. And there are *many* other reasons that your suggestion wouldn't work.'

'What are those other reasons?'

'Well, they're all quite nebulous in my mind, but I just have a very strong sense that it could end very badly for me.'

'Yes.' Felix bent for a moment to pick up a stick. 'I do think that it would be risky for you. You need to be protected from your aunt's wrath until you have your own home.'

'I do,' Cecily agreed. If only such protection were possible.

'Perhaps we could find you somewhere to stay immediately.' Felix prodded the ground with his stick a couple of times, as though disturbing the earth would cause good ideas to emerge. 'Perhaps with a relative of mine.'

'We can't do that. It would look so particular, as though you had an interest in me.' Cecily loved the fact that she could always speak so frankly to Felix. She didn't love the twinge of longing that had accompanied her words, and she should ignore it; she was very lucky to have him as a close friend, and of *course* he did not and would not ever have any romantic interest in her.

'Hmm. What you need—' Felix did some more ground prodding '—is actually for someone other than the Earl to genuinely show an interest in you. You need to be affianced to someone else.'

Cecily rolled her eyes. 'Well, yes, that *would* be ideal, but very unfortunately palatable fiancés do not grow on trees.'

'Hmm. Maybe…*maybe*…we could *find* a palatable fiancé for you.'

'Er, because actually they *do* grow on trees? What do you *mean*? There are no palatable fiancés available to me. That is the whole sad point.'

'Shhh.' Felix prodded the ground yet more as they turned along the path of a low wall and began to follow the wall up a hill. 'I think I'm having a good idea. Don't disturb me.'

Cecily glanced sideways at him, sure that he *wasn't* having a good idea, because it didn't seem as though there were any to be had, and then looked over at the sheep hugging the hill a few hundred yards from them. Sheep were lucky; they didn't have problems like this. Although it would probably be boring to be a sheep.

'Would you like to be a sheep?' she asked Felix.

'Definitely not,' he said, apparently not needing to think about it at all. 'Such dull lives.'

'They all look happy, though?'

'Only because they don't know any better.'

'Do they ever get sad, though?' Cecily pursued.

'Probably, a bit, I suppose, but I imagine not as

much as we do. If we were never sad, though, we would probably never experience true happiness either.'

Cecily looked at his profile, suddenly very serious, and reached out for a moment to squeeze his hand. 'I'm sorry,' she said. She hated to remind him of the loss of his wife. Felix was six years older than Cecily. His bride had been a year younger than him. They had married very early, and his wife had died three years later, in childbirth, leaving Felix a very young widower with a toddler and a newborn baby. His sons were now eight and six, and from what Cecily had seen he was an extremely devoted father.

He shook his head. 'Don't apologise. Many people experience tragedy, and I have been very fortunate in most ways. I don't want people to feel they have to be cautious in terms of what they say to me. And we are straying from the topic of *your* misfortune now, which I am determined to reverse.'

'I would be very pleased if you were able to reverse it, but I don't think it's possible. I must hope that the Earl proves himself to be an agreeable husband.'

Felix looked at her and the gravity in his eyes caused her to swallow.

'I don't think that is very likely,' he said. 'From what I have heard.'

Cecily swallowed again.

'However—' Felix grinned at her suddenly '—I have the perfect solution.'

'You do?' Despite her horrible predicament, Cecily found herself smiling back at him; his smile was almost impossible to resist.

'Yes. It's very simple. You and I will temporarily pretend to be engaged, just until you have your money. Once you have it, and I have used the funds to purchase a cottage on your behalf and you have arranged with Miss Holland when she is able to join you, we will tell the world that you decided that you prefer not to marry me. That is to say, you will jilt me. It will do me no harm; as you know, I do not wish to marry again, and, if I did, it would make no difference because I am a duke and I can't really think of *anything* I could do to deter Society's matchmakers if it were known that I was on the lookout for a wife. And it cannot harm you either, because your only alternative is marriage to the Earl, which would be worse.'

'We can't!'

'Why not?'

'Because…' Cecily looked at Felix's wonderfully-familiar, handsome face. It was obvious why not. 'Because it's preposterous.'

'Why is it preposterous?'

'I don't know,' she said weakly.

'Precisely. I don't think it *is* preposterous. I think

it's an excellent idea. You are one of my very closest friends. I wish to help you. I believe that this *will*, indisputably, help you. And it will be at no cost whatsoever to me. So why would we not go ahead with it?'

Cecily frowned a little as she thought. Instinctively, it *did* seem preposterous. But she couldn't actually fault his reasoning.

'Erm…' she said.

'Is that a yes?' Felix was grinning again and her lips were, of their own volition, widening again.

'I'm not sure,' she said, knowing already that she was going to acquiesce.

'It's *such* a good idea,' he said.

'I'm beginning to think it is.' She thought—for one tiny moment—of how lucky a young lady would be to be *genuinely* affianced to Felix and nearly sighed out loud.

It didn't seem likely that he would remarry—indeed he had on one or two occasions stated explicitly that he felt that doing so would be a betrayal of his late wife—but as his good friend she had to hope that he wouldn't remain lonely for life. She hated the fact that he was still clearly so sad from the tragic early loss of his wife a few years ago; it was horrible to think of his misery and loneliness, which he kept well-hidden the majority of the time, but which were occasionally still quite evident.

Although, if he *did* remarry, it would mean that their friendship had to change, perhaps, even—horrible thought—cease. She had been barely out of the schoolroom when he had lost his wife; as their friendship had developed into one between adults, rather than that of a little girl hero-worshipping the older boy next door, she had been conscious more than once of the thought that the friendship could not have happened if he had still been married.

If she was also occasionally conscious of noticing how particularly attractive he was, she pushed those thoughts away. He was her best friend, and best friends did not think of each other in that way. And *he* clearly didn't think of *her* in such a way, or he would have demonstrated that by now.

Which was not surprising, because, as her aunt had pointed out by both word and action, Cecily was just not particularly lovable. A man might perhaps briefly one day think he had fallen in love with her, but he would soon discover her unlovability, and it would be awful if that happened with Felix; her friendship with him was one of the best things in her life. So it was *ideal* that it was clear that he would never have any kind of warm feelings towards her.

And, apparently, nor would anyone else.

She heaved a sad little sigh at the thought of how very little she had to recommend her as a bride.

'Cecily? Please do not feel that you have to fall in with my idea if you really aren't convinced that it's a good one. I *do* think it's a good plan, but I don't wish you to feel that you have to do anything you don't wish to do.'

Cecily shook her head to clear her stupidly morose thoughts—she should really bear in mind how lucky she was to have a friend like him and to be due to receive the payment for her book in only three months' time—and smiled at him.

'If you're entirely certain that you are happy with your plan, then I am almost persuaded,' she said.

'Capital.'

'We must agree now, though, that if for any reason you wish to stop the charade, we will stop immediately,' she told him.

'I will not wish to stop it.'

'We must still agree that, however.' Cecily put her hand out. 'Can we shake on it?'

'I am happy to shake, but there is no need.' Felix clasped her hand in his and Cecily found herself relishing the feel of his firm grip, the way his larger hand fitted around hers. Had they ever shaken hands before? She wasn't sure. She hadn't *felt* his touch like this before, all the way to her stomach. Perhaps it was because, with their conversation about their fake betrothal, she had, for the first time ever thought—allowed herself to think for longer than a second or two—about him in the guise of someone's suitor—obviously not hers.

Her hand was still in his and they were looking directly into each other's eyes as they spoke. No one shook hands for this length of time. And no one noticed how very fine their best friend's eyes were and felt so very warm inside because of their touch. She wriggled her fingers a little and then pulled her hand away.

'Thank you,' she said, not having any other words.

'It's my…pleasure.' His voice sounded much gruffer than usual.

And then they stood and continued to look at each other for a long moment, which was very…odd.

Felix broke the silence. 'I should accompany you back,' he told her. 'We must announce our…betrothal…as soon as possible. Better to forestall the Earl than to tell him that you can't accept his offer because you will shortly have another announcement to make.'

'You're very good at planning,' Cecily told him, attempting to make her voice light and joking, to break the strangeness of the moment.

'I certainly am.' Felix bowed deeply before her and she laughed, relieved that the strangeness had now dissipated.

'Shall we go?' He held his arm out and she took it.

And they turned round and walked back in the direction of Cecily's aunt and uncle's house, to announce—really quite unbelievably—their fake engagement.

# *Chapter Two*

*Felix*

'Thank you again,' said Cecily as her aunt and uncle's house came into view. 'I am most grateful for your kind suggestion, but I would like you to know that you really don't have to go through with it; we can pretend the conversation never happened and bid each other farewell now.'

She had provided a stream of inconsequential chatter as they walked back, but Felix had noticed occasional lapses in her memory of what she'd just said; clearly she had been distracted and worrying about her situation.

'Certainly not,' he said. The thought of Cecily marrying the Earl was quite repulsive. The man was more than fifty years her senior, and his reputation was appalling. Felix's father had been of similar generation to the Earl and had been vocal in his disapproval of him; a lot of men treated women badly, but—if the Earl's boasts were to be believed—he surpassed most in his poor behaviour.

'Really?' She stopped walking and turned to face him.

'Really.' He studied her features for a moment. She was very pretty—beautiful, even—and very easy company. Had she had the advantage of a Season, she would, he was sure, have received an acceptable proposal, even without any dowry. Not every man was in need of bolstering his coffers via marriage; many wished to wed someone with whom they thought they could be happy, indeed love. As Felix had himself, with his late wife. 'I must admit that I would in fact enjoy helping you pull the wool over your aunt and uncle's eyes.'

His weak joke had the desired effect: Cecily laughed. He knew that she knew as well as he did that her uncle was not the most reasonable of neighbours and that Felix had at times been driven to near fury by him.

'In that case, thank you very much; we both have something to gain from it,' she said, still smiling.

She was very unlucky indeed that her aunt had barely even taken her into local Society; with that smile alone, she would have attracted any number of suitors, Felix was sure.

'Let us go, then.' Felix held his arm out—she had

been holding it for a while earlier in their walk but had dropped it to bend to look more closely at a winter berry-laden bush—and she took it again. 'Let us march straight into your aunt's best saloon and ask to see both of them together.'

Perhaps fifteen minutes later, Felix and Cecily ascended the steps to the front door of Cecily's aunt and uncle's house.

'Your Grace.' The butler, Tramkin, bowed very low in Felix's direction, not sparing even a glance for Cecily.

Felix glared at him. He had never liked Cecily's aunt, Lady Milton, who he knew had not provided the happiest of homes for her niece, and on the rare occasions he entered the Miltons' house, he was always deeply unimpressed by the way in which the butler seemed to join in the Miltons' disdain of Cecily.

He knew from her that the other servants were kind to her and that she counted them as friends, but that in itself was very sad. She was a lady and her best friends should not be servants; it wasn't as though she could live properly amongst them. And the butler, the most senior of the servants, demonstrated no respect for her at all. It was a miracle that Cecily had retained the sunny nature she exhibited whenever he saw her.

He drew Cecily's hand firmly through his arm,

which earned him a look of open astonishment from Tramkin.

'Lady Cecily and I would like to see Lord and Lady Milton,' he told the man in freezing tones—how *dare* Tramkin look at Cecily with such insolence? 'We will wait for them…'

'In the blue saloon,' supplied Cecily.

Tramkin marched very rigidly ahead of them into the room and then stiffly retreated, leaving the door wide open.

Cecily, her eyes dancing, whispered, 'This masquerade will be worth it just to witness the outrage of Tramkin that I might have had good fortune.'

Felix smiled at her, not, however, finding it remotely amusing that she had to live in such a hostile environment.

'Don't worry,' Cecily said, clearly correctly reading his thoughts. 'Mrs Wilson, the housekeeper, is a very good friend of mine, and perpetually at war with Tramkin, partly because of his disapproval of me.'

Well, that was something.

They were interrupted by Lady Milton entering the room.

'Your Grace,' she simpered.

'Lady Milton.' Felix bowed and—in the face of more simpering—decided to come straight to the point. 'I have something of great import to discuss with you and Lord Milton; I wondered if he is at home this afternoon?'

'Oh!' Lady Milton stared at him for a moment and then said, 'I collect that it is a matter of business, or perhaps politics. My husband is engaged with the Earl of Steed at present; we expect to announce happy news from that quarter imminently.'

Felix heard Cecily give a small gasp beside him and said, 'What a coincidence. I am not here to discuss business or politics; I have happy news of my own…and Lady Cecily's…to announce.'

Lady Milton opened her mouth and then closed it, goggling at him all the while. 'Happy news?'

'Yes.' Felix smiled blandly at her.

'I…' She goggled a little more and then stepped forward, picked up a bell from a side table and rang it.

Tramkin appeared suspiciously quickly—he must have been hovering very close to the door—and then, on Lady Milton's instruction, bustled away to ask Lord Milton if he would be so kind as to join them.

As soon as he had left the room, Lady Milton said, 'I am intrigued, Your Grace, as to the import of your news.'

'Indeed.' Felix was not going to tell her about it without Lord Milton present; he could see no benefit in having to repeat himself. 'I look forward to sharing it with you and your husband.'

Lady Milton glared at him, appeared to do battle

with herself, and then said, 'It is a most beautiful day, is it not?'

'Yes,' Felix agreed. 'A sunny, frosty day must always lift the spirits.'

Lady Milton's spirits did not look particularly lifted.

They stood in silence until Lord Milton entered the room, followed by the Earl of Steed.

Once greetings had been exchanged, during which Felix made sure that he stood very close to Cecily as the Earl pressed her hand and smiled at her far too warmly, Felix rushed into speech to forestall any other announcements.

'Lord and Lady Milton, I must apologise for any irregularity in my comportment; I should perhaps first have sought your approbation—' their consent was not required given that Cecily was of age '—but I was overcome by emotion and could not prevent myself from speaking immediately. In brief, I would like to announce my engagement to Lady Cecily.'

There was a stunned silence before Lord and Lady Milton and the Earl all spoke at once.

'I beg your pardon?' Lady Milton said.

'Nonsense,' Lord Milton said.

'Lady Cecily is *my* fiancée,' the Earl said.

Felix looked at Cecily, who was wide-eyed and appeared to be speechless. Then he looked at the others, who were mainly drop-jawed.

'I'm sorry; perhaps I spoke indistinctly,' he said. 'I have just announced my engagement to Lady Cecily.'

The other three all began to speak at the same time again, and for a moment it was hard to hear what anyone was saying, until the Earl's voice rose to prominence.

'Lord Milton and I have just agreed that Lady Cecily is to marry me. Unhand my fiancée, Sir.'

Felix opened his mouth to reply and then became aware that Cecily was trying to make herself heard.

'I think we should allow Lady Cecily to speak,' he said loudly over the others, who all fell silent.

'Thank you.' Cecily had her hands clasped in front of her so tightly that her knuckles were showing white. 'I am of course of age and it is therefore my own decision whom I marry.'

'Nonsense,' Lord Milton repeated. 'You are my ward, and I have agreed that you are marrying the Earl.'

'I am no longer your ward.' Cecily's voice was impressively steely.

'Nonsense,' Lord Milton said again.

They all stood and looked at each other for a long moment, Felix grappling with *how* to conclude this conversation in the face of Lord Milton's bizarre intransigence. He didn't wish to leave Cecily alone with her lips-pursed aunt and the purple-in-the-face Earl, but he did wish to understand exactly what it was that was causing Lord Milton to be quite so set on the Earl as his niece's future husband. Presumably he had agreed to pay an enormous sum—perhaps settle all Lord Milton's debts, which were reputedly very high—and Lord Milton feared that Felix would not be so generous.

Felix had to admit to himself that he would enjoy witnessing the Miltons' impotent wrath in three months' time when Cecily jilted him and retired to her own cottage with Miss Holland, leaving them not a penny better off.

'I am afraid that it is not nonsense,' Felix said.

'Lady Cecily is my fiancée and we are to be married this week,' the Earl stated.

'That is correct,' said Lord Milton.

Lady Milton had been standing in silence with her eyes swivelling between the different participants in the conversation, before finally refinding her voice.

'Perhaps you would like to join us for dinner at the end of the week?' she suggested to Felix.

Lord Milton nodded vigorously. 'A marvellous idea. You would be most welcome.'

'That is very kind,' said Felix. 'I will of course, I trust, be seeing my fiancée before then.'

'Good God, fellow,' the Earl said. 'I knew your father. Your impudence knows no bounds. The lady is my fiancée and when you next see her she will be my wife.'

Felix couldn't quite believe what he was hearing; it seemed highly likely that if he didn't take further action now Cecily would be forced into immediate marriage with the Earl. He glanced at her, to see that she was looking in his direction, wide-eyed and definitely paler than she had been a minute or two ago.

He was going to have to get her away from here today, he realised. But how? He couldn't ask her to stay alone with him in his house; if he did so then he would *actually* have to marry her, and very soon.

If only his mother-in-law, who usually resided with him, hadn't gone to visit her sister for two nights.

Perhaps they could invite another chaperone.

It still wouldn't necessarily be ideal for her to be under the same roof as him with only one chaperone, though.

His Aunt Davinia!

He should have thought of her before. She lived in his London house with an elderly female cousin and two of his great-aunts. It would be quite unexceptionable if Cecily were to go and stay with them.

He could then perhaps host a large house party for the Christmas period, with Cecily and his aunt and other relatives included, so that he could continue to keep an eye on her safety, while not having actually to marry her.

That seemed like the perfect solution. Especially since, during a recent walk while discussing her future purchase of a cottage, Cecily had mentioned that she had never before visited London and hoped to have the opportunity to go there one day.

He cleared his throat. 'Lady Cecily has agreed to leave today to stay in London with my Aunt Davinia, the Countess of Bradstock, and her cousin, Lady Ariadne Marsh, together with two of my great-aunts, until we are married.' He glanced at Cecily to see the beginnings of a smile on her lips. 'Indeed,' he continued, 'we must make haste before nightfall, so we must bid you farewell now. Cecily, will it take you long to pack?'

'I can be ready within a very short time,' she told him, her smile growing. 'I have very few possessions.'

'Excellent. Perhaps—'

'Lady Cecily isn't going anywhere,' the Earl interrupted. 'Her uncle and I shook on our deal this morning.'

'I'm afraid that it is not within Lord Milton's power to determine whom Lady Cecily should marry,' Felix said.

'Indeed,' Cecily said. 'Thank you for all your kindness to me, Aunt and Uncle. I have accepted the Duke's proposal, and will bid you goodbye when I have gathered my belongings.' She smiled at them all and swept out of the room.

Felix wanted to applaud her.

Apparently the Earl did not; he stepped forward and said, 'You will meet me for this, Your Grace. I believe that you were not intending this London visit until just now.'

'Meet you?' Felix could hardly believe his ears. Duels being largely a thing of the past, and his behaviour rarely giving rise to offence, he had not previously been called out.

'Name your seconds, Your Grace.'

'I am not going to meet you,' Felix told him. He couldn't fight a man over forty years older than him.

'Oh, I see. You're scared.' The Earl drew himself up—to much less than Felix's height—and puffed his chest out. 'You have heard my reputation. Three men killed in duels in the last century.'

Felix laughed out loud. 'Yes, I am very scared,' he said sarcastically.

'There will be no duels sullying the name of my niece, the new Duchess,' Lady Milton suddenly intervened. Felix could almost *see* her mind working; she had obviously decided that they could not reasonably prevent his marriage to Cecily and was clearly imagining herself moving regularly in ducal circles in the future, as a duchess's aunt.

'We must discuss what financial settlement you wish to make,' Lord Milton said.

Felix eyed him. Were he actually marrying Cecily, he would not wish her relatives to embarrass her and would be prepared to make a small settlement in order to achieve that. He would not, however, wish to reward them in any way beyond the bare minimum; they had made Cecily's life a misery for the entirety of her time with them. Since he was *not*, however, genuinely marrying her, he did not wish to tie himself to any promises; he would not like her uncle to be able to sue him for a breach of contract.

'My man of business will deal with any such matters,' he said.

'Not good enough,' Lord Milton protested. 'I wish to discuss a settlement now.'

'I collect that you wish to disclose the extent of Lady Cecily's dowry?' Felix said, one eyebrow raised.

Lord Milton glared at him. 'You will not be difficult, I trust.'

'Never,' murmured Felix.

Cecily made very good time in packing her belongings together and was back in the room with her worldly goods—contained in an extremely shabby-looking, and very small, portmanteau—before the rest of them had had more than a few minutes in which to stand in awkward—or angry—silence.

'Excellent,' said Felix extremely heartily when he saw her. 'Let us…'

Oh. He had of course come here on foot. It would

take a long time for them to walk back together and they would then not be able to make the journey all the way to London in one day.

'I should be very grateful if you would lend me a carriage for the return journey to the castle,' he said to Lord Milton.

'Certainly not,' said the Earl.

Felix raised an eyebrow and said nothing.

Lord Milton spent several seconds looking between Felix and the Earl, clearly trying to work out who would be angrier if he failed to oblige them, before coming down on the side of the more senior aristocrat and his closer neighbour—and his niece's newly announced fiancé—and saying, 'Of course.' He rang for Tramkin and instructed him to ask for a carriage to be brought round to the front of the house, and then said, 'Let us go outside.'

'Goodbye,' Cecily said to her aunt and uncle.

Her aunt dabbed underneath her entirely dry eyes, saying, 'I declare I am quite overcome. My little niece becoming the Duchess of Garth. We will of course visit you in London.'

Cecily smiled faintly at her and said nothing, before mounting the carriage steps.

As the carriage began to move, she opened her mouth and then closed it again, before mouthing, 'The coachman might hear us if we speak.'

Felix nodded and mouthed, 'Very true,' in return,

before saying loudly, grinning at her, 'I count myself the luckiest man alive.'

'And I the luckiest lady,' Cecily replied, laughing. She leaned to look out of the carriage window. 'I can't believe that I won't see these lanes again for some time. I haven't travelled further than Lewes since I came here when I was seven.' Lewes was the nearest town.

'You will enjoy visiting London, I'm sure. There is much to see.'

'Oh, yes, I'm sure I will, if I am able to visit attractions and places of interest.'

'You will certainly be able to do so. While I am in London, I will escort you myself, and when I am not there I am sure my aunt will be more than happy to accompany you.'

'Felix, you must not feel obliged to do so,' Cecily said extremely earnestly. 'I should not have said that; I will enjoy it even without visiting the attractions. Just walking around the streets will more than suffice.'

'I will not feel obliged; it will be my pleasure. It is always enjoyable to see sights through the eyes of someone who has not seen them before; it is too easy to become over-accustomed to them.'

'Well, thank you very much. I am much beholden to you.'

Felix indicated in the direction of the coachman

with his head, and then said, 'Not at all,' before continuing with, 'It is a beautiful day for December, is it not?' to avert any incriminating conversation while there was the possibility that the coachman might overhear.

They arrived shortly afterwards at the castle, and he directed his butler to organise refreshments to be provided for Cecily, a maid to be asked to pack to accompany them on their journey, his valet to pack very speedily for Felix's stay in London and his groom and own coachman to ready his mother's old, but extremely luxurious and comfortable, travelling chaise, while he removed to his desk in the library to write some notes to his man of business and then to the nursery to tell his boys that he would be travelling to London but that he would be back very soon and that in the meantime they must behave very well for their nurse and their grandmother, his mother-in-law, his late wife's mother, when she returned home tomorrow.

He had a nasty feeling that things were going to be more complicated than he had originally thought when he'd had the idea of how to save Cecily; at least one of his aunts and cousins would presumably mention the fake engagement to his mother-in-law, and his boys might also therefore find out about it, and he needed to do something about that, but he really didn't have time to address it now if they were to arrive in London before nightfall; he would have to think about it later.

When he returned to the small sitting room where Cecily was waiting, he found her sitting in a chair near the window, nibbling a macaroon and idly studying the family portraits that adorned the walls.

'I hope you haven't been bored,' he said, lowering himself into the chair opposite her and taking a macaroon himself. 'I had a couple of matters to attend to, which took a few minutes longer than I had expected.'

'Not at all,' Cecily replied. 'I've been enjoying myself greatly sitting here. I can't tell you what a wonderful treat it is for me to be able just to *sit*, in a warm room—' she gestured at the fire in the hearth to her left '—and with no feeling that someone is about to scold me or send me off to do an unpleasant errand. Also, these macaroons are *delicious*.'

Felix laughed, because clearly her comments had been intended light-heartedly, but he didn't *want* to laugh; he wanted to ride straight back over to her aunt and uncle's and tell them how unacceptable their treatment of their niece had been.

'Who are the people in the portraits above the mantelpiece?' Cecily asked, apparently unaware of his internal struggle not to express his fury with her relatives.

'My parents as children with their families and then as adults with their own children.'

'They're very happy-looking pictures.'

'Yes.' Felix studied them himself for a long moment. Much like not seeing London through the eyes of a newcomer when accustomed to it, one rarely studied the portraits in one's own house. 'You're right.' He smiled, thinking of his parents, and then glanced at Cecily, feeling guilty. It was clearly a long time since she had felt that she lived in a happy environment. 'One is lucky if one has a happy family,' he said.

'Indeed.' Cecily took a sip from her glass of ratafia. 'And the converse might be that one is unlucky if one does not. However, luck changes.' She looked at him for a moment. 'You…' She didn't finish her sentence, but it was clear that she was alluding to the loss of his wife. Felix really didn't want her to continue with that train of conversation. She bit her lip for a moment and then clearly decided that it was too difficult a subject to broach more overtly. 'And I, now, today, all of a sudden, have been very lucky.'

Felix raised an eyebrow. 'That's a very positive way of looking at what has happened.'

She shook her head. 'No—it is factually correct.

I'm free of my aunt and uncle, and I'm going to London.'

She smiled up at him and Felix found himself drawing a sharp breath, suddenly very aware of how entirely reliant she now was on him.

He should really have thought a little more carefully about what he was undertaking when he gave in to his immediate impulse to save her from the Earl.

No, that wasn't true. Any amount of thought would have led him to the same conclusion; he had had no choice but to help her.

It did, however, feel like a great responsibility that could have some quite unpalatable consequences.

# *Chapter Three*

*Cecily*

Felix's face had just altered most comically. With a jaw as square as his, there was no point at which he did not look strong and determined—not to mention quite ludicrously handsome—but his brow had suddenly furrowed and his eyes held an arrested look.

'Have you…have you just realised the import of what we have done?' Cecily asked. '*Please* do not feel that you have to continue with our charade if you do not wish to. I can easily return to my aunt and uncle and agree to marry the Earl, and it will just be as if today had never happened.'

As she spoke, she did her best to produce a nonchalant smile to disguise the fact that the mere thought of returning to her aunt and uncle and then marrying the Earl was filling her with cold dread. She needed to think positively. Perhaps she could continue with her writing and leave the Earl once she had received her money. Would that really be feasible, though?

Felix's voice cut across her increasing misery. 'Certainly not. I am extremely pleased to help you and it will not inconvenience me in the slightest. Indeed, I was already planning to visit London very soon.' He rose to his feet. 'We must in fact leave as soon as possible. Are you ready to go?'

'Yes, I am.' Cecily rose too, almost overcome with relief that he was happy to continue with their charade. 'Thank you so very much.'

'I have an important request to make,' Felix said as they left the room together. 'You have to stop thanking me.'

Cecily laughed. 'Very well. Th…'

Felix tsked. 'You very nearly thanked me again.'

'But I stopped myself, for which I believe I should receive great credit.'

'I will allow you that credit.' He smiled at her and she caught her breath. It was a *good* smile; his lips were so well-shaped and his teeth so perfect. She'd always loved it. And now…it felt—in some way—as though the smile was just for her, as though their secret—the intimacy of the secret—somehow added an intimacy to, well, everything.

'Thank you,' she said, aware that her voice sounded a little shaky.

'No, no, no.' Felix shook his head sorrowfully. 'No more thanking, remember? You have already failed.'

Cecily managed to produce a fairly unshaky laugh. 'I'm sorry. I will try much harder.'

'Yes, indeed. See that you do,' he said, twinkling at her.

The twinkle only made him look even more handsome. Which was not at all what she should be thinking. She and Felix were *friends*, and he was a still-grieving widower. It *was* acceptable to acknowledge his handsomeness in the way that she might note that the view from the window was particularly pleasant, but it was *not* acceptable to feel so, well, *breathless* when she thought about it.

Usually, when they were together, on their walks, she did of course occasionally think about how very handsome he was and how very much she enjoyed his company. But she was nearly always able to carry on behaving perfectly normally. He was just her very handsome best friend.

Today, however, she was finding it much more difficult not to think about him in *that* way.

It was probably understandable, though. Obviously she was just a little flustered from the extremely surprising turn her day had taken; that was all.

'I have asked Lizzie, one of the maids here, to accompany you and act as your lady's maid while you are in London,' Felix told her as they walked out of the house together.

'Oh, good gracious, I don't think I need a maid.' She had never had one; indeed she had often been required to act almost as a maid herself, in assisting her cousins when they dressed for evenings out.

'I think you do.' Felix suddenly looked almost stern. 'I will instruct my aunt to assist you in acquiring a wardrobe suitable to allow you to participate in everything that London has to offer.'

'Oh, I…' Cecily adored clothes, and colours, and fabrics. She would *love* to have the opportunity to own just a few nicer gowns than the brown and grey ones she habitually wore courtesy of her aunt. She clearly couldn't allow Felix to pay for clothes for her in addition to everything else he was doing for her, but perhaps she could take some money from him as a loan. There was no reason, after all, that she couldn't spend just a little money on herself in the future when she had the means to do so. 'I *would* enjoy being better dressed. If you are able to, I would be very grateful if you were able to lend me some money so that I can buy clothes for myself, and then I will pay you back when I receive my book money.'

'Yes, of course.'

'Are you sure that it won't embarrass you financially to loan me the money?' Cecily didn't want to assume too much. She had on more than one occasion overheard her uncle saying that Felix was rumoured to be one of the richest men in England, but rumours were not always correct.

'Certain,' he said very firmly. 'I think the easiest thing will be for you to buy whatever is necessary and for my aunt to arrange with the various seamstresses and haberdashers and whomever else from whom you purchase items that they send the bills on to me. I will then keep a very careful record of them and deduct your expenses from the amount that you earn from your novel.'

'That would be wonderful. I apologise for breaking our agreement, but I must thank you.'

'You have nothing to thank me for beyond a small loan,' Felix told her. 'So there must be no more thanking in this regard.'

Cecily laughed. 'I will not thank you any further but I will say that I am most grateful. I will very much look forward to a shopping expedition.'

'I imagine that you will need to undertake more than one expedition; you are likely to need to make many purchases.'

'Oh, I hope so. Assuming that Lady Bradstock will not mind.'

'She will be positively delighted. I know that she very much enjoys shopping.'

Cecily could barely suppress a shiver of delight

at the thought of the experiences in store for her in London.

'Here we are.' Felix indicated the carriage ahead of them. 'You will not mind if I ride alongside the carriage, I trust.'

'Of course not.' Cecily was a little horrified at the shock of disappointment she'd just felt at discovering that he would not be inside the carriage with her and Lizzie. Truly, she was behaving very oddly today. It was, again, clearly due to the very strange situation in which she found herself.

'I should have asked before now: do you have a book with you, or would you like to take one from my library to read?' he asked.

'I do very much enjoy reading, but I think I would like to look out of the window today.' Cecily had not travelled outside Sussex—and hardly at all *within* it—since she'd arrived with her aunt and uncle when she was seven; it would be a great luxury just to watch the countryside go by, and then of course as they entered London there would be countless sights for her to devour with her eyes.

The scenery proved to be delightful, and Lizzie no less enthralled by it than Cecily, and soon they were in a very fair way to becoming as firm friends as people of different stations might be. Cecily had often thought it a great shame that ladies were not supposed—indeed not really allowed—to be on very friendly terms with housemaids, because her aunt and uncle's servants—other than Tramkin—had been much kinder to her than the family had ever been.

And, when you were kept in what was to all intents and purposes very straitened circumstances, like an unpaid and also unwanted companion, with dozens of unpalatable chores daily, there really was little *point* in being a lady. Cecily was quite sure that she would have been much happier as a governess, for example, if she had had the good fortune to be one with a kind employer. And she might even have been happier as a maid, had she had good friends amongst the other servants in whatever house she might have been in.

'Oh, we're stopping,' she said after they had been journeying for an hour or two. They were entering the courtyard of an inn.

'His Grace will wish to stop for food and to change his horses,' Lizzie said wisely.

Barely had Lizzie finished imparting her wisdom than the carriage door opened and Felix said, 'I thought we might partake of a late nuncheon; the inn at which I would usually stop in this area is closed for refurbishment following a flood, but I am sure this one will be more than adequate.'

'Certainly,' Cecily said, delighted to be experiencing a meal in an inn for the first time.

'I have procured a private parlour for us,' Felix told her. 'Lizzie, I have asked for provision to be made for you.'

'Yes, your Grace; thank you,' said Lizzie, scrambling to curtsy.

'Apparently it is your fate in life to be thanked,' Cecily remarked to Felix as they began to walk across the courtyard together towards the inn's entrance.

'The thing is,' he said, 'I had the great good fortune—by sheer chance—to be born to this position, and firstly it is *easy* for me to help people, because I am surrounded by servants and wealth, and secondly I have a moral duty to do so; if I perform my role correctly I will assist people in less fortunate positions. I perform that duty willingly, but it is a duty, and I should not be thanked for it. I should rather thank my servants for looking after me so well.'

Cecily nodded. 'Very true. Not every peer is as dutiful as you, however, and your servants and tenants are fortunate to have you.' Her uncle certainly expected to be thanked most fully by those less fortunate than himself to whom he gave help—a relatively rare occurrence. She suddenly had a nasty thought and gasped. 'Oh my goodness. You felt that it was your *duty* to help *me*.'

'No, no.' Felix shook his head. 'I have no duty with regard to you beyond that of a fellow human being.

You are a good friend and I would always choose to help my friends, but it is a choice. Certainly not a duty. I am extremely happy to help you.'

'Oh, yes.' Cecily nodded sarcastically. 'When you woke up this morning, the first thing you thought was that you would like to enter into a fake betrothal.'

Felix laughed. 'Fair enough; I did not actively wish or expect to enter into such a charade today or any other day. However, I assure you that I am more than happy to participate in it. I enjoy helping my friends on the occasions I am able to do so. And, frankly, the entire charade is worth it just to have witnessed the Earl trying to challenge me to a duel, not to mention thwarting your uncle.'

Cecily laughed too, and then said, 'I enjoyed that too. I will not thank you again. Instead I will tell you that I am very much looking forward to our nuncheon.'

Felix smiled at her. 'As am I. Apparently engaging in such a charade makes one very hungry.'

They were interrupted by a man—presumably the tavern's landlord—hurrying out of the front door and saying, 'Your Grace, my lady,' as he bowed so very deeply that he was in danger of toppling over. 'My name is Muston.'

'Good afternoon, Muston,' Felix said.

'Allow me to show you into our best parlour, Your Grace.'

* * *

The walk from the front door of the inn to the parlour was not long, but by the time they had reached the parlour, Muston had, by Cecily's estimate, said *Your Grace* and *my lady* at least twenty times each. It was hard not to compare the treatment that she received as Felix's companion to that which she had received when trailing behind her aunt and uncle on the very rare occasions she went out with them.

She really shouldn't mention it.

The second Muston had bowed and Your-Graced and my-ladied himself out of the room and closed the door behind him, however, she found herself saying, 'It is quite remarkable to me how very much respect a duke receives.'

Felix nodded. 'I fear that I don't notice it as much as I should, because it is rare that I travel without people being aware of who I am, but, yes, one is certainly placed upon a pedestal.'

'I wonder whether it's that *you* are placed on a pedestal,' Cecily mused, 'or that it is your wealth and position that are.' She saw Felix raise his eyebrows and cock his head to one side as though waiting for the outcome of her thoughts. 'I think it's both,' she decided. 'You do of course have great largesse to distribute, which must very frequently invite sycophancy, but you are also an object of curiosity. Most people very rarely have the opportunity to meet persons as august as dukes. Indeed you are almost as much of a curiosity as a prince.'

Felix laughed. 'I am grateful to you for putting me in my place. I had not thought of myself as a curiosity, but now see that I was wrong. Perhaps you think that people might pay to see me, as they would to attend a circus.'

'Oh, yes, I'm quite certain they would,' Cecily agreed. 'Although not *too* much, because you in yourself are not particularly unusual—' that wasn't really true; he was quite the most handsome man she had ever met '—so people would feel most hard done by if they paid more than a very small sum to view you.'

'You are quite abominable. You inform me that I am a curiosity, but only a very low-value one.'

'That's right,' said Cecily, grinning at him.

'Well, I take leave to inform you that as my companion and current fiancée you are equally a curiosity.'

Cecily nodded, considering. 'I think you're right. You were merely born into your position, while to the outside observer, I was chosen by you. All while wearing the drabbest robes imaginable.'

Felix nodded, very seriously. 'People should certainly pay more to catch sight of you than me, then, as an even greater curiosity.'

'Yes, indeed they should.'

As they smiled at each other, there came a knock on the door.

'If I mistake not, that will be our luncheon,' Felix said.

'I am very much looking forward to it,' Cecily told him. 'This is the first time I have ever eaten in an inn; I feel very fortunate to be having so many new experiences. And not just accompanying a curiosity and becoming one myself. I have already greatly enjoyed the journey here. The scenery was quite beautiful.'

'Yes, it is. Sussex is a very scenic county. We are very lucky that the skies are cloudless today. I should say that *I* am very lucky that the skies are cloudless, so that you have something to marvel at other than my curiously ducal self.'

Cecily's laughter was interrupted by a second—truly thunderous—knock on the door.

'Come in,' Felix called.

Two serving girls entered bearing a large number of dishes between them, and uttering very frequent Your-Graces and my-ladies.

When they had nearly finished depositing the dishes on the table in the middle of the room, Muston entered, saying, 'Your Grace, my lady, we have done our poor best to serve you a meal befitting of your station.'

'This looks quite wonderful,' Cecily assured him with her biggest smile. 'And it smells delicious too.'

She and Felix both waited until Muston had gone and then stared at each other. The table was *covered* with plates.

'This looks good,' Felix said. 'But I fear we will disappoint Muston as we cannot possibly even *sample* all the different dishes, let alone finish any of them.'

'I'm very worried that the people out there will have nothing to eat,' Cecily said. 'No one knew that we would be coming today, so, unless Muston keeps copious quantities of food just in case people of quality happen to enter the inn, he must have diverted supplies from other people's tables. I hope that they will not be dining on soup and bread alone today.'

Felix nodded. 'With all my talk of duty, I should have thought of that sooner.' He frowned. 'I'm not sure what we can do about it without offending Muston.'

'There must be something. What about—?' Cecily was interrupted by a knock on the door, followed immediately by the entrance into the room of one of the serving girls who had brought them their food.

'Begging your pardon, Your Grace, my lady,' the girl said breathlessly. 'I forgot to say Mr Muston wants you to know that he killed one of our chickens this morning when we heard your Grace was passing and hoped you would stop here. With an axe. He wanted you to know how fresh it is.'

'We are most honoured, and it looks and smells delightful,' Cecily said, smiling at the girl.

'Thank you very much.' Felix smiled too, and she curtsied. 'We are indeed honoured.'

'Thank you, Your Grace, thank you, my lady.'

As the door closed behind the girl, Cecily said, 'Oh my goodness, this is awful. That poor chicken was going about its day and then all of a sudden its head was chopped off just because we were *perhaps* coming. Otherwise it might have lived for several more weeks. And it would probably have been entirely eaten when it did die. We can't let it go to waste. But we can't eat it all. And, also, think about all the people in England who don't have enough to eat. Although at least the other people in the inn should still have enough, given that the chicken would never have been done for them.'

Felix picked up the carving knife and fork that had been laid on the table. 'I do agree that we shouldn't let all this food go to waste. One must hope that Muston has an eye to his business and uses the dishes that we can't finish to make soup or pies tomorrow.'

'I wonder whether we could ask that anything we can't eat be packed up into baskets and distributed to any local people who are in need,' suggested Cecily.

'That is an excellent idea.' Felix stuck the carving fork into one side of the chicken and removed the breast very cleanly. 'Perhaps we might just share this part of the chicken? And taste enough of all the other dishes to make it clear that we have sampled them, without making ourselves ill from over-eating? And then state that it was all quite delicious and we would like others to be able to share in our good fortune?'

'That sounds very sensible,' Cecily approved.

'Allow me to serve you a little of all the savoury dishes to begin with?'

'Thank you.'

'I will allow that *thank you*,' Felix said as he placed chicken on her plate, 'due to its being more of a social requirement than indicating heartfelt gratitude.'

Cecily laughed. 'I will endeavour to continue to keep any genuine heartfelt gratitude well-hidden and certainly not acknowledged with any thanks.'

'Thank you.'

Cecily raised her eyebrows and said, 'Your *Grace*. You have broken your own rule.'

Felix smiled at her and said, 'Apologies,' before beginning to place a little of each dish on to Cecily's plate.

They both began with the chicken, which was deliciously tender. The next dish, lamb and haricot beans, was also tender, and wonderfully flavoured.

'What is that?' Felix mused out loud.

'I think sage, with a delightful sweetness from caramelised onions,' Cecily told him.

'Yes, I believe you're right. You have very good culinary knowledge.'

'I have always spent as much time as I can in the kitchen. It's very warm in there; it's very interesting learning about household management, which might of course stand me in good stead in the future; and it got me away from Aunt Jane.' She grinned at him and then wished she hadn't spoken when she read pity in his eyes. 'There is no reason to pity me,' she said firmly. 'Many people experience far greater hardship than I ever have. And a small amount of hardship serves to make one appreciate nice things, like this luncheon, which I am very much enjoying.'

'You're making me feel that I take far too much for granted.' Felix said nothing for a moment, and then asked, 'When you weren't in the kitchens, with whom did you eat at your aunt and uncle's house?'

'I usually ate in the nursery, or sometimes alone. Or with the higher servants, which was my favourite, as long as Tramkin wasn't there, which he rarely was. He deems himself vastly superior to even Mrs Wilson, who is the housekeeper if you remember.'

Felix put his cutlery down as his mouth straightened into a stern line. He remained silent for a long moment and then said, his tone much milder than his expression, 'That will not be the case in my house. You will of course eat with my aunt—and myself when I am there—and any other family members or guests. I will consider you a most valued guest.'

Cecily *knew* that her life at her aunt and uncle's house had been more difficult than that experienced by many people of her station; her cousins, for a start, were treated much more kindly than she was. And she had thought that she had become so accustomed to it that she almost didn't mind any more; it was just the way it was. But when presented with the prospect of being treated like a 'most valued guest', she was, she realised, almost breathless with pleasure.

Felix was looking at her with one eyebrow raised and lips part-relaxed from the sternness into a small smile.

'Rather than thanking you,' Cecily said, 'I shall tell you that I am greatly looking forward to eating delicious food with your family and I am full of gratitude.'

'As previously stated, no gratitude necessary. Now—' Felix indicated the table '—can I serve you anything else?'

'I'm not sure that I can manage too much more,' said Cecily, with real regret. 'Particularly since I understand that they intend to bring a second course.'

'You do need to save yourself for that if you enjoy puddings,' Felix said, as though it was an extremely serious matter.

'Yes, I do.' Cecily had a very sweet tooth, which

her aunt's cook had indulged quite regularly when she visited the kitchen.

'You might have to sample the dishes on my behalf; I am not particularly fond of sugary dishes.'

'It will be my great pleasure.'

'Why, thank you,' he twinkled at her, which made her smile. He had already twinkled like that earlier in the day; it was truly lovely.

They had never eaten together before; Cecily had rarely been invited to dine with the rest of the family when they had guests. In fact, while she and Felix had spent a lot of time together walking, she wasn't sure that they'd ever really been inside together. It was nice to think that she would get to know him better, indeed already had begun to do so; he was someone whose company she very much enjoyed.

'I don't think I can manage any more,' she said a minute or two later, placing her spoon next to her unfinished bowl of trifle with reluctance.

'I'm not surprised,' Felix told her. 'You've had a *lot*.'

'I've had a busy morning,' Cecily pointed out. 'It made me hungry.'

Felix laughed and then said, 'Are you now ready to re-continue our journey, do you think, so that we might reach London before nightfall?'

'Yes, of course.'

There was a knock on the door, followed by its immediate opening and the entrance into the room of the girl who had served them before.

'You've eaten a lot,' she said in astonished tones. 'Mr Muston didn't think you'd eat anything much at all, but he wanted you to know that he was making a big effort for you.'

'It was all quite delicious,' Felix said.

'Indeed it was,' agreed Cecily, smiling warmly.

The girl's beam of gratification was so wide it must almost have hurt her cheeks.

When she'd closed the door behind her, Felix said, 'I presume that you are now going to tell me that the young lady's joy at our appreciation was more because it was ducal appreciation than because she wished for acknowledgement of the effort they had put into preparing the dishes.'

'Well of course,' said Cecily, laughing.

'I hope you're impressed by my quick learning; I am already fully recognising of my status as a curiosity and nothing more.'

'Well done.'

'Hmmm.' Felix smiled at her and then pushed his chair back. 'We really should go now, I think.' He stood up and then moved round the table to assist Cecily with her chair.

'Thank you.' She could easily begin to enjoy such unnecessary help, she realised. It was delightful; it made one feel…cosseted.

He held his arm out for her to take and they proceeded in stately fashion out of the room, through the inn and across the courtyard, accompanied all the while by much bowing and scraping, and peered at throughout by a great many eyes.

Mr Muston was waiting with his wife next to the carriage to bid them farewell.

'Thank you so much for your wonderful hospitality,' Cecily said to them. 'The food was all quite delicious. Would it be possible to ensure that the dishes that we were unable to finish might be distributed to nearby people in need?'

'Certainly.' Mr Muston nodded and smiled as he bowed.

'You'll make a lovely duchess,' Mrs Muston told Cecily as Felix handed her into the carriage.

'Thank you,' Cecily said, smiling at her.

She was of course never going to be a duchess, but she was having such a lovely day and Felix was such delightful company that it was very easy to imagine that it would be a great pleasure to be his Duchess.

Which of course she never would actually be, so it was silly to have such thoughts. Once she got to London, she would definitely banish them from her mind.

# *Chapter Four*

*Felix*

Felix almost snatched his hand away from Cecily's once he had her firmly established within the carriage. For some reason her touch had awakened something in him that he didn't want to think about.

He did from time to time still—of course—feel desires such as those he had felt for his late wife, Aurora, but not for virginal ladies of quality, not for ladies who might challenge Aurora's position in his heart. On the occasions that he'd had liaisons since he'd lost her, they had been with independent, wealthy and aristocratic widows, who were neither vulnerable nor wishing to remarry. There was of course no possibility whatsoever of his beginning to feel anything approaching love for Cecily, or any other woman, but he didn't want to feel any inappropriate *temptation*, either.

It was probably because they'd just taken luncheon together; that was not something he'd done alone with another lady of quality other than his female relations since Aurora had died. Naturally, sharing a meal, just the two of them, had bred a certain level of intimacy. Friendly intimacy, though, that was all.

He watched the carriage draw out of the inn's courtyard and then turned to the groom holding his horse to swing himself up into the saddle.

It was certainly a good thing that he would be riding rather than accompanying Cecily in the carriage; he needed a little time apart from her to recover from his moment's insanity.

They stopped very briefly again to change horses, during which time he exchanged only a few words with Cecily, making himself busy instead with conversations with the grooms, and by the time he was back in the saddle and they were approaching London, he was feeling completely back to normal; Cecily was his childhood friend and he had helped her out of a terrible situation, that was all.

He would spend two or three days in his London home, attending to some business while he was there, and he would escort Cecily to some of the sights that she would like to see, and then he would return to Garth, safe in the knowledge that she would be well looked after by his aunt and considerably happier than she had ever been living with her own aunt and uncle.

Perhaps, in fact, he would join her and Lizzie inside the carriage for the last part of the journey, so that he could point out any places of interest that they passed.

'Yes, of course,' Cecily said, when he asked if she would be happy for him to travel inside the carriage.

'I hope you have enjoyed the journey thus far?' he enquired. 'Comfortable and not too bored?'

'Oh, not at all bored,' Cecily said. 'Lizzie and I have continued to derive great enjoyment from looking at the scenery, watching the hills disappear and the landscape become flatter, and wondering what London will be like.'

'Have you visited a large city before?'

'Never,' said Cecily. 'And nor has Lizzie.'

'Well, I do not wish to raise your expectations too high, but I believe that you will be most struck by the sights and sounds of London. Not to mention the smells.'

They were now perhaps ten or twelve miles to the south of the city.

'Are we close to our destination?' Cecily asked.

'We are still some miles distant. This is Kingston-upon-Thames, a market town.'

'It seems remarkably busy, much more so than Lewes.'

'Yes,' Felix agreed, 'but not as busy as London itself.'

'*This*, I fancy, must be close to the heart of the city,' Cecily said some time later as they had left the village of Wimbledon and were travelling through the village of Putney in order to cross the River Thames at its bridge. 'This is *so* exciting.'

Lizzie was fairly bouncing in her seat too.

'We are still a few miles distant.' Felix couldn't help smiling; the majority of people he knew pretended boredom most of the time and few of them were excited by travel, accustomed as they were to much greater journeys than this. He personally nowadays rarely went anywhere particularly new to him. It was indeed refreshing to witness someone seeing the city through new eyes. Charming, in fact.

The remainder of the journey passed very much more quickly than he would have expected as they shared interesting facts and stories, so much so that it was a surprise to see out of the carriage windows that they were already sufficiently close to their destination to be skirting the edge of Devil's Acre, one of London's notorious slum areas.

Soon, they were driving through much more salubrious areas and entering the well-lit roads of Mayfair.

'We are nearing my house,' Felix told Cecily. 'It is in Berkeley Square, which is—as you might surmise from the name—a square of houses around a garden.'

'It all looks very beautiful,' Cecily said. 'It is so extraordinary that this opulence exists almost right next to such extreme poverty.'

Felix nodded. 'It is awful.'

'It is astonishing that the rich don't do more for the poor.'

'Not that astonishing,' he said. He himself did make sizeable donations to the poor of London and was in the process of overseeing the setting up of additional schools in the poorest parts—he would not be able to sleep easy knowing that children of the same age as his own sons were living in such abject poverty while his boys had every material benefit imaginable, through a pure quirk of birth—but he knew that many of his acquaintance made no such efforts to help those less fortunate than themselves. There was no need for him to tell Cecily of his philanthropy; it was not something he should be thanked for or congratulated on. 'A lot of the rich are really not particularly pleasant people.'

Cecily turned and studied him for a moment before

observing mildly, 'Those in need who come within your orbit are fortunate.'

Felix had the strangest sensation that she had just read his thoughts.

'My duty,' he observed equally mildly.

Cecily shook her head. 'But not everyone *does* their duty.' She looked out of the carriage window again. 'It really is quite extraordinarily magnificent here.'

Felix nodded.

'I hope that you will enjoy your stay.' He very much wished to be able to give her some enjoyment; she might not have grown up in a slum, but she had not experienced very much kindness.

'Oh, yes, I will, I am sure. I feel…' She paused as though gathering her thoughts, and then continued, 'I feel that it would be almost rude to those less fortunate not to take advantage of the opportunity I have been given to enjoy this stay and make the very most of it that I can. As though I would almost be throwing away something that they would give anything to experience.'

Out of the corner of his eye, Felix could see Lizzie nodding vigorously.

'Yes,' he said, swallowing, more affected than he would have expected by Cecily's words. 'Tomorrow, then, we can walk around the area and go for a drive in Hyde Park if the weather is clement. You will also of course wish to visit some seamstresses with my aunt and we might also visit the National Gallery or some other such place.'

'It all sounds like the most wonderful treat.' Cecily looked like a little girl who had been given her first ever present. Felix felt yet another stab of dislike for her aunt and uncle.

He chose to laugh, however; there was no point reminding Cecily of past misery. 'You should reserve judgement until after you have stood for hours being poked and prodded for dress measurements and queued in an enormous crush to see the latest portrait and concluded when you got to the front of the queue that it was not the best you've ever seen.'

Cecily laughed too. 'I am sure I will enjoy—or at least appreciate—it all.'

When they entered his house, Felix saw to his surprise that the staff were lined up to welcome him, which was not something they usually did when he came to London; his visits were fairly frequent and he did not have any great love of pomp and ceremony.

'Lady Cecily.' His London butler, Deedes, bowed low. 'Allow me to introduce the more important members of our household to you. May I say that we are all very much looking forward to welcoming you as the new Duchess.'

Of course.

And, oh, God.

Felix had clearly lied to Cecily earlier, insofar as obviously his motive in helping her *had* been duty. He couldn't have done anything *other* than enter into this fake betrothal and then invite her to London to stay with his aunt. However, because it had been a split-second decision—well, two split-second decisions, made entirely out of duty because he couldn't in good conscience leave Cecily to her fate—he hadn't at the time thought about the ramifications, and then throughout the day he'd had a niggling feeling that it wasn't going to work out particularly well for him, but he hadn't allowed himself to spend time exploring what it really meant.

Now, though, his thoughts—worries—were crystallising.

Clearly word had already spread that he was bringing his soon-to-be new Duchess to stay here. There would be a great deal of talk, and instinct told him that he didn't wish for that.

It couldn't be helped, however. He had after all had no choice. And, in fact, it really didn't matter, as long as no one got upset during the course of their charade. And there was really no reason that anyone *would* be. He hoped. As long as he managed things well with his mother-in-law and his sons.

'Felix.' His Aunt Davinia was moving very fast towards him and Cecily, past all the servants. 'I'm exceedingly pleased to see you. And even more pleased to be introduced to Lady Cecily.' She beamed at Cecily. 'I refuse to stand on ceremony with you; you will shortly become my niece after all.' She leaned forward and drew Cecily into a hug.

Cecily was, for the duration of the hug, barely visible—she was a small lady and Felix's aunt was much taller—and when she emerged she looked somewhat as though she had been dragged through a hedge backwards. She was smiling broadly, however, and, if Felix wasn't mistaken, her eyes were glistening a little. And if he again wasn't mistaken, it was almost certainly because it was a long time since she had experienced much affection from family members.

'Mrs Spraggs will show you where your bedchamber is so that you may change and rest a little after your long journey, and then we will get to know each other better over dinner,' his aunt told Cecily.

'Thank you very much,' Cecily said, still smiling.

'I hope you don't mind my aunt's exuberance,' Felix murmured to her as Mrs Spraggs led her towards the stairs and he followed.

'Not at all; it was delightful. I think the last person who hugged me was my mother.'

Felix thought back to his own childhood. His mother—and of course his aunt—had very regularly embraced the children of his generation. His father, too, had certainly slapped him on the back and shaken his hand very vigorously in physical demonstration of regard. How could someone be so cold towards a recently orphaned child?

He would have to stop thinking about the way her aunt and uncle had treated her, or he would find himself in a permanent fury.

Felix made sure that he changed and descended for dinner very quickly so that he would be with his aunt before Cecily. He didn't think that Cecily was particularly shy, but some awkwardness must nonetheless attach to her situation, and there was also the possibility that his aunt would ask probing questions; he knew from sometimes bitter experience that she had no shame whatsoever about asking any question that came to mind.

'She seems delightful,' his aunt said before he was even fully inside the room.

'She is,' he agreed, closing the door behind him and walking over to take a seat next to her.

'When is the wedding?'

'That…is a good question,' he said. A good question and also a very obvious one; he should have thought of an answer to this before now. 'We thought that we would like to get married in the spring.'

His aunt frowned. 'That's a long time to wait.'

'Yes,' he said, 'it is, and we have a good reason for that.'

His aunt raised her eyebrows and said nothing, clearly waiting for him to elaborate. Well, he was not going to elaborate, because, well, he couldn't.

So he smiled and said, 'Cecily needs a new wardrobe. I hope that I can rely on you to take her to the very best dressmakers and buy her whatever she needs and direct all the bills to me.' Obviously his aunt would not be surprised if he covered his fiancée's expenses, and obviously he was not going to tell her—or anyone—that Cecily would soon become a lady of independent means due to her writing; many frowned on ladies publishing novels, which was why Cecily had chosen to publish anonymously.

'Certainly. I shall very much enjoy such a task,' his aunt said, her attention immediately diverted, to Felix's relief. 'I have recently found a new modiste—recommended to me by dear Lady Crossley—and I am sure she will make the time to see the future Duchess of Garth tomorrow. As your fiancée, Lady Cecily will obviously command the utmost attention and respect.'

Felix nodded. As Cecily had pointed out during their journey yesterday, and as he himself had experienced—he had once or twice journeyed to the further reaches of England, to visit some of his minor estates or friends, and had discovered that a travel-stained gentleman on horseback enjoyed considerably worse service than that garnered by a duke travelling under his own crest surrounded by his entourage—people did indeed receive different treatment depending on their station and wealth. The prospect of dressing a future duchess would almost certainly cause a stampede of tradespeople desperate for her business.

His aunt leaned forward and tapped his knee. 'I won't ask *what* your good reasons are for delaying the wedding, but I hope that you are marrying for love, given that you do not need an heir. I feel it my duty to your dear late mother to say so.'

Felix looked at her and considered for a moment and then decided to turn their conversation into a joke.

'Damn,' he said. 'I thought I had successfully changed the subject.'

His aunt looked right back at him, her eyes slightly narrowed, visibly deciding how to react. After a long second, she chose to laugh.

'As long as you are happy,' she said mildly. 'Now let me tell you the latest *on dits*.'

She had a *lot* of quite excellent gossip and—even though Felix did not habitually engage in gossip himself—he couldn't help very much enjoying her conversation, and the minutes flew by until Cecily descended for dinner.

Felix saw his aunt's eyes open just a little wider when she saw the gown Cecily had changed into.

Cecily had clearly noticed the same thing.

'I am afraid that I have not been in the habit of dining in Society,' she said, 'and therefore I do not own any evening dresses.'

'I do not regard it,' his aunt said, patently untruthfully. 'And it is easily remedied; we will choose new gowns for you tomorrow. I'm sure we can have some made up very quickly indeed. May I ask if this is your *best* gown?'

'Sadly, yes,' Cecily said, impressively uncowed by his aunt.

'Then we must visit Madame Chardon before we do anything else.' His aunt looked at Cecily's brown robe with a pained expression. 'While much might be excused in a duke's fiancée, eyebrows will still be raised if you present yourself like that in public. And, being truthful, I have no great desire to chaperone a young lady who will immediately be stigmatised as an eccentric.'

'Of course,' said Cecily. 'I am extremely grateful to you and will do whatever you think best.'

'Lady Cecily's aunt, with whom she has resided for many years, did not consider it necessary for her niece to be dressed in the high kick of fashion,' explained Felix, knowing that his aunt, while possessing a heart of true gold, was also a stickler for convention, with little experience of people less fortunate than herself.

'Indeed.' His aunt nodded. 'I see. A selfish aunt.

Lady Milton?' She nodded in answer to her own question, as though that explained much. 'Indeed. Yes. Well. We should soon remedy the situation.'

'Perhaps—' Felix was quite sure that Cecily would like to explore London a little on the morrow '—if we were to go somewhere not particularly fashionable, and outside—so that Cecily could be cloaked—that might be acceptable?'

'Certainly not, from what I saw of Lady Cecily's cloak,' said his aunt. 'However,' she addressed Cecily, 'I am sure that I can lend you a pelisse of mine. You are a little more voluptuous of figure than I, but much shorter, and therefore I think that if we can but shorten one quickly, which I'm sure Madame Chardon will be able to do, it will do just for tomorrow until we have your new ones delivered.'

'New ones?' asked Cecily. 'I'm not sure that I will need more than one?'

'New ones,' his aunt said firmly. 'You will certainly need several.'

'Oh, I…'

'Cecily has of course been reared in a frugal environment,' Felix said. She was clearly worrying about the cost. He would speak to her later and ask her if she would—as a favour to him so that he wouldn't be concerned about her—allow him to make her a present of her new wardrobe. He couldn't say that in front of his aunt, though, and he needed to allay

Cecily's worries now. 'But I believe you told me earlier that your dressmaker was particularly cheap?' he said. She was almost certainly extremely expensive.

'Yes, she is,' said his aunt, reacting admirably quickly to his hint and barely blinking. 'Very much so.'

They were interrupted by the arrival of Felix's two great-aunts and elderly cousin who also lived in the house, and some time was spent introducing Cecily to them—quite a difficult task due to deafness on the part of the cousin and one of the great-aunts.

'Now that we are all assembled,' Felix's aunt commanded when the introductions were eventually concluded, 'I think we should eat dinner. I am of an age where I can freely admit to hunger.'

Felix had asked that dinner be laid for them in the smaller of the two formal dining rooms, so that they would not have to shout to each other around the grand silverware that adorned the table in the larger dining room. The table in this room was hardly small, but family tradition allowed them to dispense with real formalities when in here, and all sit round one end of the table so that they might converse more easily.

Catching his aunt's eagle eye on him and his fake-betrothed, and remembering her frowns about their supposed wedding not taking place immediately, he was careful to be at his most solicitous with Cecily.

'You will find, I trust,' he told her as they entered the room together, her hand through his arm, 'that my chef here is particularly talented.' It had been extremely endearing how very delighted Cecily had been with their luncheon in the inn; the food there had been good, hearty fare, but certainly not exceptional.

'I look forward to finding out,' she said, smiling at him, 'although I have already been spoilt today at the inn.'

'Garth at the head of the table and Lady Cecily to his right, of course,' his aunt instructed, before arranging herself on his left and directing their other relatives to be seated further along.

'I knew your mother,' she wasted no time in saying to Cecily as soon as they were seated and the first dishes had been placed in front of them. 'She was a wonderful woman.'

'Oh, did you really? Do you…?' Cecily hesitated and then continued, 'Did you know her well?'

'Yes, really quite well. She was several years younger than me, but we nonetheless enjoyed many a comfortable cose at various soirées, and I counted her a particular friend of mine. She used to make me laugh very much.'

Cecily bit her lip for a moment, as though uncertain, and then said, 'I would very much like to hear any stories you might have about her. I… I can't really remember her or my father very well any more. I was only seven when they died.'

'I'm so sorry,' Felix's aunt said. 'Of course, my dear. I have many stories about your mother. And indeed some about your father, too.'

And the rest of their dinner was occupied in his aunt reminiscing about Cecily's mother, while Cecily, unsurprisingly, hung on her every word.

Eventually, they all acknowledged themselves to be replete.

'I think that was the most wonderful meal I have ever eaten,' Cecily said. 'Your chef is indeed supremely talented.'

'Your enthusiasm is most refreshing,' his aunt said. 'I believe that we ladies should retire and leave the Duke to his port.'

'I will immediately join you,' Felix said. He didn't think it prudent to leave Cecily with his relatives before he'd had a chance to have a moment alone with her to concoct a background story to their engagement. In hindsight, knowing his aunt in particular, they should have thought of one while they were eating their luncheon. He also, he realised, had no great fancy to sit alone in his dining room; he'd been enjoying his conversation with Cecily and wished to continue it.

'Perhaps we might all play cards?' his Great-Aunt Leonora suggested.

'Certainly.'

The game—Commerce—dragged somewhat. Felix's cousin, Lady Ariadne, was neither a natural card player, nor an enthusiastic one, and Cecily, while enthusiastic, was not entirely conversant with the rules. Felix was not, however, going to retire for the evening before anyone else; ideally he would find an opportunity to speak alone to Cecily this evening to discuss their situation.

Finally, Lady Ariadne placed her cards down on the table, rose and said, 'I must bid you all goodnight.'

Felix could, frankly, have cheered.

Both his great-aunts immediately followed her example.

When they had all left the room, his aunt said, 'I, too, will now retire. I am sure that, as an affianced couple, you will wish to spend some time conversing alone together and I do not subscribe to the old-fashioned view that you should not be alone until you are wed. Goodnight.'

Felix waited until she was safely out of the room and then moved to a chair closer to Cecily's and lowered his voice.

'I think we need to talk,' he said.

'Is it that you wish to put an end to our pretence?' Cecily asked. 'I fully understand and will leave to-morrow. I must thank you for a wonderful journey and a most enjoyable evening. Not to mention the truly delicious dinner.'

'No, no, certainly not,' Felix said. 'I am very happy to continue the pretence.' That wasn't true—he was quite sure now that the complications that might arise as a result of it were even greater than he had originally feared—but he would feel like the biggest cad alive were he to consign Cecily to a return to her previous life with her aunt and uncle, and possible marriage with the Earl if he would still accept her as his bride. In fact, they might none of them take her back; she might now be entirely ruined if he didn't continue with the charade. Good God; he hadn't thought of that before. He would certainly not be abandoning her now. 'I am *extremely* happy to continue,' he reiterated.

Cecily's huge smile of relief lit up her face. Objectively, she was extremely beautiful—even more so than usual—when she smiled like that. Her aunt was very silly not to have given her a Season; she would almost certainly have met more than one man who was both seduced by that smile and her sunny personality and rich enough not to mind about her lack of dowry.

'Thank you,' she said simply.

Felix shook his head. 'We've already discussed this,' he said mock-sternly. 'The only onerous thing about this entire charade is your thanking me.'

Cecily laughed. 'I apologise for my temporary forgetfulness and will now revert to accepting all your many kindnesses without a word of gratitude.'

'Finally,' he said, laughing.

'I *would* like to thank your chef, however. I think that was the most delicious meal I've ever eaten in my whole life. My aunt's cook is excellent, but I think does not have the wherewithal, or perhaps the knowledge, to produce dishes of that nature.'

Felix, to his shame, could barely remember what they'd had to eat. It had certainly been good—excellent, in fact—but he *expected* that of his staff. In return he remunerated them very highly and treated them very well, and he liked to think that everyone was happy with that arrangement. It *hadn't* been the best meal he'd ever had, though; it was just one of many very good dinners.

It seemed that he should really stop taking so many things for granted and he should also do his best to make sure that while she was here Cecily had as many enjoyable experiences as possible.

'What was your favourite dish this evening?' he asked.

Cecily considered very seriously for a moment. 'The mackerel with fennel and mint was wonderful. And of course both the venison and the turtle. I had never tasted either before and very much enjoyed them both.'

'I'm very pleased that you liked them.' Felix made a mental note to request that they be served to Cecily again in a few days' time. First, though, she would have the opportunity to sample whatever other delights his chef thought fit to grace their table with. 'I hope that my chef's work will continue to please you.'

If it weren't for his sons, he'd be tempted to stay a day or two longer than he had at first planned; he would very much enjoy seeing Cecily experience new culinary delights.

'I'm sure it will.'

He smiled at her and then said, 'I think we need to discuss our situation a little.'

'Of course.' Cecily folded her hands in her lap and sat and waited, her head tilted a little to one side.

'Firstly, my aunt was asking me why we're planning not to marry for a while. What good reason could there be for that?'

'What reason did you give?'

'Well, none. I was mysterious.'

'Mysterious?' Cecily smirked.

'Why is that amusing?' Felix enquired.

'Just… I don't think you're a particularly mysterious person.'

'What? I can be mysterious.'

'Do you *want* to be mysterious?' Cecily was giggling properly now.

'It isn't a question of *wanting* to be, it's just that I *can* be, should I so choose.'

'Why would you so choose?'

'Many reasons.' Felix had a strong sense that this conversation was ridiculous, but he couldn't quite work out exactly why.

'Give me one of those reasons.'

'I…' He frowned. 'I am *really* bad at thinking of reasons. This is what happened when Aunt Davinia asked me why we aren't getting married for three months.'

'Why did you want to set off immediately this morning on our journey?' Cecily asked.

'Um.' A strange change of topic, but he supposed he should humour her. 'Because if we hadn't done we probably wouldn't have reached London before nightfall.'

'*Indeed*,' she said, looking remarkably smug.

'Indeed what?'

'You *can* think of reasons for things, *when they're true*. You couldn't think of a reason for us not to get married for three months, because none of it is true. And you can't think of a reason that you might want to be mysterious because you *can't* be mysterious.'

'I certainly can be mysterious.' He had no idea why the conversation had gone in this direction and even less idea why it was genuinely somewhat annoying that she doubted his mysteriousness.

She opened her eyes wide and said, 'Can you be mysterious now?'

'Yes, of course.'

Cecily just sat and waited, eyes still wide open, brows raised too.

Felix looked at her and frowned. 'This is ridiculous. No one ever commands someone to be mysterious.'

'Yes, they do,' Cecily said triumphantly. 'An actor might be commanded to be mysterious. As might a spy who is trying to double bluff someone.' She shook her head. 'Unfortunately, it seems as though you would not be able to be either an actor or a spy.'

Felix shook his own head. 'You are completely wrong. I…' He frowned a little, and looked over Cecily's shoulder towards the other end of the room.

'Are you…being mysterious?' she asked a few moments later.

He refocused his gaze on her face. Her *laughing* face.

'Well… I thought I was. But…'

Cecily was laughing so much now that she was almost gasping. 'So very *un*mysterious,' she said between hiccups of laughter.

Felix began to laugh too. It was, frankly, *bizarre* that he'd suddenly been quite so anxious to prove to her that he could be mysterious. He had no idea what had come over him. And her laughter was extremely infectious.

They laughed for a long time.

Eventually, both holding their sides and wiping under their eyes, they stopped.

'Do you think…?' Cecily asked, 'Do you think we might have been a little hysterical with shock due to the very peculiar day that we've had?'

'Perhaps.' That would explain a lot, actually. It would explain the strange…*warmth* he'd been feeling towards Cecily this evening. They'd had an extremely surprising day. If he'd been asked this morning what he would be doing this evening, he would have predicted that he would be at home in Sussex, perhaps having supped with one of his neighbours.

He looked at Cecily. Yes, he still had a point to prove.

He waggled his eyebrows and tapped the side of his nose.

'Oh my goodness!' she cried. '*Mystery* personified!'

He grinned at her. 'Thank you. Finally. I *knew* that you would eventually admit my talent.'

As she laughed, that warm feeling spread through him again.

# *Chapter Five*

*Cecily*

Felix was…ridiculous. He was also extremely handsome and extremely amusing and extremely…wonderful.

It was so very enjoyable funning with him like this.

Cecily couldn't remember when she had spent a more pleasant evening.

He'd asked a serious question, though.

'You wanted to discuss what we should say to Lady Bradstock if she asks again why we plan to wait to get married,' she said.

Felix blinked. 'Oh, yes, I did. Yes. Why *don't* we want to get married for at least three months?'

'We must be able to think of a lot of good reasons.' The most obvious one was that he wished to introduce her properly—as their new step-mother-to-be—to his sons first, but apparently he hadn't thought of that, or didn't wish to say it to anyone, perhaps because it would make him feel sad in regard to his late wife. Cecily certainly wasn't going to mention it if he didn't.

She thought for a moment, before saying, 'Firstly, clothes. It is clear that Lady Bradstock was somewhat astonished—horrified—by my gown. If I were truly to become a duchess I would need a very large new wardrobe, which might take some time to assemble.'

Felix nodded approvingly. 'That is a good start. And on that subject, I think, to allay suspicions, you *do* need a large new wardrobe and I think that it might be very expensive, perhaps uncomfortably so for you. You will not, I presume, wish what you spend in London adversely to affect your future. I should therefore like to make you a present of your new wardrobe.'

'Oh, no, I couldn't,' was Cecily's immediate reaction.

Felix shook his head. 'I *knew* that that would be your response. But consider: you have observed yourself that I am very rich, through no ability of my own beyond birth; you are my very good friend; you have not been particularly well-treated by your aunt and uncle; I would derive huge enjoyment myself in giving you such a gift. You would be denying me that enjoyment.'

Cecily could feel herself *almost* persuaded.

'I couldn't, though,' she said, but very weakly.

'But, also, you *could.* Just think about my aunt's confusion if you have to curtail your expenditure. And think how much *she*, as well as you, will enjoy your shopping expeditions. And how very happy it will make me. A good gift is of as much benefit to the donor as to the recipient. And I would have liked to have made you presents of any number of things over the course of our friendship but clearly could not do so.'

'You are very persuasive.'

'Is that a yes?' Felix grinned at her and her heart did a little flip at how handsome he looked.

'Maybe.'

'Maybe definitely yes?'

'I…' She suddenly made her mind up. His arguments *were* persuasive. She was going to have to buy a full new wardrobe of his aunt's recommendation, or it would be very suspicious, and she didn't have enough money to do that *and* buy her cottage and continue to support herself and Holly modestly. And if he would *enjoy* giving her the gift it couldn't be that bad. 'Thank you. It's extremely kind of you. I will spend as little as possible.'

'I don't wish you to spend as little as possible. I would like you to spend exactly what you would like to spend on this one occasion. That would make me happy.'

'Thank you. You are a very kind man.' Cecily wanted to hug him.

'Nonsense. Now, where were we? We—you—were thinking of reasons to delay our marriage.'

'Oh, yes, of course. Well.' Cecily enjoyed this kind of challenge. 'I have always wished to travel to the Lake District and Scotland and that is where we plan to go after we are married, and we can't travel there during the winter.'

'Oh, yes—an excellent reason. And I would like our tour of the north to be perfect for you and for us to undertake it immediately we marry, to make the occasion particularly meaningful for both of us, so, rather than marry now and then not set off for three months, we prefer to wait for the wedding.'

'Yes, that is perfect. Also, as I have been living in near seclusion in the country, you are quite desirous of my making the acquaintance of some of your wider family and friends before the wedding.'

Felix shook his head. 'Why, though? Why not make their acquaintance as the new Duchess rather than as the Duke's fiancée?'

'That is a good question.' Cecily thought for a moment and then said triumphantly, 'I wish to emulate royalty and have a particularly large wedding, but I have always thought that it would be rather odd not to be well acquainted with all the guests at one's own wedding.'

'An excellent answer.' Felix's headshake had turned into nods. 'You're very good at this. I begin to wonder if you have led a life of secret crime as well as secret novel-writing.'

Cecily laughed. 'I *haven't* to date undertaken any criminal activities, but perhaps I should.'

'I imagine that all successful miscreants would claim never to have done anything nefarious—how am I to believe that you're telling the truth?'

Cecily was enjoying herself hugely. 'You have no way of knowing. You will just have to trust me.'

'Indeed.' He waggled his eyebrows at her, which made her laugh. 'I hope that you are more trustworthy than I am mysterious.'

'You might never know.'

'*That*,' Felix said, 'was genuinely mysterious.'

'Clearly you could learn from me.'

'Indeed.'

They smiled at each other and then Felix said, 'Well. I think we have enough reasons for the late date of the wedding. I feel that we should spend a few moments considering whether there are any other difficult questions that might be asked of us.'

'I'm sure there are quite a lot of difficult questions,' Cecily said, suddenly serious. She really could not bear to be returned to her previous life, which would, almost certainly, be even worse than it had used to be, so she did not wish there to be any possibility of their bluff being called.

'I agree. And we should do our best to think of them so that we can then counter them.'

'What we need to do—' Cecily was thinking hard '—is put ourselves in your aunt's position. If we were her, what would we think if you suddenly turned up with me as your fiancée?'

'That is a very good point. We would perhaps be surprised by the suddenness of it, given that I do not need to marry for an heir, as I have my boys. It could of course be explained away by a story of our having very suddenly fallen in love, except we have known each other forever, so why would we suddenly be struck by a *coup de foudre*?'

'Why indeed?' said Cecily as lightly as she could, to disguise the fact that she suddenly felt a little sad. Why indeed would Felix ever suddenly be struck by any kind of romantic feelings for her? 'I'm sure we can concoct a story about it, however.'

'Really?' The look of scepticism on Felix's face was not flattering. It seemed that he really did not think it remotely plausible that he and Cecily might ever fall in love. As though she were not someone who a man like he—perhaps any man—might ever love.

Which should not be at all upsetting, because she already knew it to be the case. If her own aunt and uncle hadn't found anything in her to love when she had arrived with them as an orphaned seven-year-old desperate for comfort and affection, why would anyone else love her? And since it *shouldn't* be upsetting, she was very silly to feel any kind of hurt now and she was going to do her best to banish such feelings.

And of course this conversation was not about that. It was a light-hearted but serious discussion about how they might hoodwink Felix's aunt into believing that they were indeed a mutually besotted affianced couple who would wed in three months' time.

She took a deep internal breath and spoke firmly. 'Really. Of course we can convince people that we have recently fallen in love.'

'All right,' Felix said. '*When* did we fall in love?'

'I think it was *very* recently,' Cecily said, pushing away the pang of longing that had just washed over her and taking great care to focus all her thoughts on considering their fake falling-in-love story. It might be very important to get it just right. 'Lady Bradstock seems from her conversation to have many friends, and when someone as eligible as the Duke of Garth, who also happens to be her nephew, begins to show a strong interest in a lady, she would expect there to be rumours, which she would hear through one or other of her wide circle of acquaintances and friends. So it must have happened very recently indeed and that is why she hadn't heard anything about it before today.'

'Very true. Society certainly does gossip, and, yes, she would have heard about it. So the falling-in-love happened very recently. Where did it happen and how?'

'I think that if one is going to lie it must always be easier to adhere as closely as possible to the facts so that one is less prone to forgetting one's story.'

'As always, you are very wise.' Felix smiled at her and then raised an eyebrow. 'Listening to you, one might suppose that you were already practised in the art of lying?'

Cecily laughed. 'Only a little, and only really in regard to treats given to me by my aunt's cook, of which my aunt would certainly not have approved.'

'Did you ever get found out?'

'Never. I don't *like* to lie, but I positively adore baked treats, so I had no option on occasion but to engage in falsehood, and I have to admit that I was extremely good at it.'

'I'm very pleased to hear it,' said Felix. 'We might have need of your skill tomorrow if my aunt chooses to quiz us.'

'My skill is entirely at your disposal.'

'Good.' His smile was quite heart-stoppingly delightful. Probably due to his very nice, strong teeth and the way the smile started small and then gradually widened, and was just the tiniest bit lopsided. She wished that she could paint a faithful picture of his face in this moment and keep it forever. 'So tell me exactly how we met?'

'How we…?' She'd fallen out of a tree and he'd helped her, many moons ago. *Oh*, but her attention had wandered while she meditated on what it was that made his smile quite the best she'd ever seen. They were talking about their *fictitious* recent first meeting, not their real one.

'Well.' She considered for a moment. 'Since we have agreed that we wish to adhere as closely to the facts as possible, and since my aunt knows perfectly well that I did not usually meet others socially, I think we must have met and conversed while out walking.'

'Of course.' Felix nodded. 'Perhaps we discovered a mutual love of botany and from there we discovered a mutual love of…each other.'

Cecily pushed aside hurt at the way he spoke as though such an occurrence could only ever be fictitious and laughed. 'Felix, you clearly have a missed vocation as a poet.'

'Yes, I impressed even myself with that phrasing.'

'Do you have an interest in botany?'

He screwed his face up, which made Cecily laugh more.

'Moderately,' he said.

'By *moderately*, do you mean that you like pleasant scenery or that you single-handedly grow a particularly unusual variety of pineapple in your greenhouses and are so careful of its prowess that you will not allow even your most trusted gardener to touch it? Or perhaps somewhere in between?'

Felix laughed too. 'I have to admit that my deep love for botany currently extends no further than a deep liking for pleasant scenery.'

'My own love of botany is exactly the same.'

'Perhaps, therefore, we just discovered a mutual love of…pleasant scenery?'

Cecily tilted her head to one side and pretended to think before permitting herself to reply with sarcasm. 'Certainly, it is *very* rare for two people both to have a fondness for pleasant scenery, so it could hardly be surprising that they should immediately tumble into irrevocable love on discovering their mutual unusual taste.' She allowed herself to roll her eyes just a little as she finished.

'Minx,' Felix said, appreciatively, which was gratifying, because no one in her aunt and uncle's household had ever appreciated any sarcasm she had used. 'What then do you suggest?'

'Perhaps…' Cecily reflected for a moment on how one might fall in love with Felix if one hardly knew him. It wouldn't be difficult; really, one would merely have to see him and speak to him a few times. He was, surely, most maidens' idea of the perfect husband-to-be. 'Perhaps we should aim for simplicity. We met once by chance and enjoyed a walk—drawn together initially by a mutual appreciation of the beautiful weather and scenery—and then we met again, and then we fell into the way of meeting, and we very quickly realised that we loved each other.'

'You're right. That *is* how it happened. How could it have been otherwise?' Felix smiled at her and Cecily suddenly felt her heart beat very much faster, as though for one moment she had begun to believe her own story.

It wasn't, of course, true. For the simple reason that, if she *had* ever fallen in love with Felix—which she hadn't, well, not entirely, because he was her best friend and that was all, and one should not be in love with one's best friend—it would have been long ago, after their friendship flourished as that between two adults after his wife died, not just this week.

And she *wasn't* in love with him, not really. She held him in extremely high regard, that was what it was.

'Do we think there are any other questions that Aunt Davinia might ask us?' he said.

'Let us again put ourselves in her position,' Cecily suggested.

'Good idea. We should bear in mind that—purely in a very kind manner, of course—my aunt does allow herself to ask questions that others perhaps would not. So we must try to imagine anything that might cross her mind.'

Cecily nodded, a little alarmed. Their ploy *couldn't* fail; it would be too awful. 'That is a good point. I imagine that she might, while making small talk, ask why you brought me to London, how long you propose to leave me with her and what you plan for the next three months for me. It is easy, I think, to say that I am come to London to purchase clothing that I am lacking. But how long should she expect me to stay here? She might want to know if I will, for example, be returning to my own aunt and uncle before the wedding?'

'I think,' said Felix slowly, 'that it can do no harm for us to be somewhat honest with Aunt Davinia, insofar as I have already intimated that your aunt and uncle did not indulge you and I can tell her more in confidence. We can then say that your reason for coming to London was to purchase clothes, which will not surprise her, and for me to introduce you to her, of course, and to other relatives and close friends, and that you will remain here until just before Christmas. You will then, I think, of course be spending Christmas at Garth, with her, I trust, as chaperone in addition to my mother-in-law.

'In fact, I will, I realise, be inviting a large number of people to stay for a Christmas house party, to introduce you to as many family and friends as possible. And after Christmas, you will return to London to stay with her to continue your acquaintance with Society, while I move backwards and forwards between London and Sussex so that I might see my boys very regularly.'

'Excellent,' Cecily approved. 'I am most impressed. You are in a fair way to becoming as accomplished a liar as I.'

'Thank you.' He bowed slightly. 'I can think of no higher compliment. I am tempted to suggest that we now retire for the night, before I can say anything that re-lowers me in your estimation and causes me to fall victim to your sarcasm again, but feel that we should first discuss quickly what our plans are for the morrow.'

'I will undertake not to be sarcastic at all during such a discussion, however low you fall in my estimation,' said Cecily, laughing.

'That is extremely kind of you.' Felix smiled at her, before leaning back against his sofa and spreading his arms along the back of it, which gave her an excellent view of the width of his very rock-like chest, which almost made her gulp out loud. 'My aunt intends to take you shopping before you do anything else. I would like to make it very clear that I think that the gowns that I have seen you wear are quite unexceptionable and Society is quite ridiculous, but I do agree that—because many of the *ton* are sadly judgemental, and brown and grey are not precisely the most fashionable hues this year, and the cut of your gowns doesn't remind me of the cut of other ladies' gowns—it might be wise to do so before you attend any indoor events, just so that you will be as comfortable as possible.'

Cecily couldn't help laughing again, at the expression of near-anguish on Felix's face as he grappled with the challenge of trying to tell her politely that her gowns were not wearable in polite society.

'Thank you very much,' she said, 'for trying to spare my feelings. There is no need, however, to beat about the bush in this instance; I know very well that my gowns are neither fashionably cut nor fashionably hued, and they were also not made from expensive fabric. They are very different from the gowns purchased by my aunt for her own daughters and of course for herself.

'I am very much looking forward to buying some modish robes for myself and am very grateful to your aunt for suggesting that she lend me a pelisse until I have a fashionable one of my own. And very grateful to you for making me a present of some of my wardrobe.'

'Of the entirety of your expenditure during this stay, I hope, and, as before, you must not thank me. I'm pleased that you're looking forward to it and am certain that you will be in very good hands with my aunt. I am not a great connoisseur of female fashion, but I am aware that my aunt very much enjoys to shop, and remember my mother—who herself had a very extensive wardrobe—commenting on how very many gowns my aunt owned.'

'I am very much looking forward to being in her hands.' Cecily couldn't help smiling at the thought.

Felix laughed. 'I am pleased to see how much the idea causes you to smile. I hope also to make you smile by taking you for a drive in Hyde Park tomorrow afternoon, where you will see the park itself and of course many of Society's notables. I am not able to stay for very many days in London, as I don't like to leave my boys for too long, but will undertake to escort you to as many places of interest as possible over the next two or three days before I leave.'

'That would be wonderful. I feel very spoilt! I trust that you aren't putting yourself out too much on my behalf and not taking you away from your boys for longer than you feel comfortable.'

Felix shook his head, his features suddenly grave. 'Not at all. We are friends, are we not, and one likes to do one's best for one's friends. As I have already stated, any enjoyment you derive from your stay in London will in turn cause me enjoyment. And I will return to the boys soon. They are very happy with their nurse and their grandmother, who is returning home today.'

Cecily hesitated for a moment and then said, 'I'm sorry, but I'm just going to have to do it one more time: thank you, thank you, thank you.' She smiled at him as he shook his head at her, and continued, 'And now, before I can thank you any further, should we perhaps both retire to bed so that we are not too tired to enjoy what tomorrow has to offer?'

'Wise as always; we should indeed.'

They stood up together and as they did so Cecily couldn't help noticing the breadth and solidity of Felix's thighs and, for some reason, in that moment completely forgot how to balance herself and wobbled quite alarmingly on her feet.

Felix shot his arm out and put it round her waist for a moment to steady her.

'Are you quite all right?' he asked. 'Are you feeling faint?'

'Not at all,' Cecily lied. She was feeling fainter by the second, from where his arm was supporting her; she couldn't think about anything other than how—even through the coarse fabric of her dress—it was as though his touch was almost *searing* her. Truly, she was losing her wits. 'I'm…' What *was* she…? What had she been about to say? She closed her eyes for a moment to gather herself. Unfortunately, that was a bad idea, because now she couldn't see anything to distract her from where she could feel Felix's strong arm still holding her.

She opened her eyes again, found that she was looking directly into Felix's concerned eyes, and quickly moved her head so that she could see something less disturbing to her senses.

The mantelpiece. It really was very fine; it was sculpted marble.

'I like your mantelpiece,' she said.

'Why…thank you?'

She risked looking back at Felix to see that the corner of his mouth was quirking upwards in a most alluring manner. Her own lips widened in response.

This would not do.

Her heart should not be beating so fast. She should not be thinking about Felix like this, observing every little thing about him so very closely.

'Yes,' she said with as much dignity as she could muster, because she couldn't have Felix realising in what direction her thoughts were going. 'The mantelpiece is particularly fine.' With great reluctance, she moved away from his arm and over to the fireplace so that she could examine it in greater detail. 'Such intricate sculpting. It is very impressive.'

'Are you a particular connoisseur of mantelpieces?'

'Yes…and no. That is to say, I have no particular great knowledge of them, but I do enjoy a fine one when I see it.'

'I must hope that my other mantelpieces meet with your approval.' Felix was definitely laughing at her. There was a very strong hint of a—very attractive—laugh in his voice.

'Yes,' she said, 'I shall be extremely disappointed if they aren't impressive. And on that note, I will retire, and of course inspect the one in my chamber very thoroughly.'

'I will be extremely interested to hear your thoughts on it in the morning,' Felix said as they made their way towards the door of the room.

As he opened the door for her, Cecily couldn't help delighting in his nearness to her. It felt for a moment as though she was surrounded by him; she could breathe in his enthrallingly masculine scent, see his profile very close, almost touch him again.

And then the door opened and she looked straight into the face of Deedes, the butler, only two or three feet from her, and had to bite back a yelp of shock.

'Deedes,' came Felix's deep voice from behind her. 'There was no need to…wait up for us.'

'It is a pleasure to see you, Your Grace, when you come to London, and as such I am most happy to wait until you retire, to see to the candles for you.'

'Thank you; very kind,' murmured Felix.

They walked up the wide stairs side by side, not speaking, while Deedes busied himself in the hall below snuffing candles.

When they rounded the banister Felix leaned towards Cecily and spoke into her ear. 'I would wager a large sum of money that Deedes will have a great battle tomorrow morning between his desire to remain haughty and not be seen to chatter with the remainder of the household staff and his urge to impart all that he has gleaned about you this evening.'

'I know,' said Cecily. 'He was standing *very* close to the door when we left the room.'

'And that is why I sat close to you and spoke in a low voice throughout,' said Felix, in an extremely self-congratulatory manner.

His manner made Cecily smile, but his words, if she were being truthful, made her a little sad, because she might, perhaps, have enjoyed the closeness and low voice a little too much, and she might, perhaps, because she was very silly, have wondered for a few moments whether Felix was enjoying it too. But of course he wasn't; it had all been entirely to discuss practicalities and to ensure that they were not overheard in so doing.

'Well done,' she said, aiming for a manner as light-hearted as his.

'Thank you. Now, I trust you know the way to your chamber?'

Cecily nodded. 'At the end of this corridor.'

'Splendid. Goodnight, then.' He moved very slightly closer to her and Cecily held her breath—for what, she really didn't know—and then he…did nothing else.

They just stood there, together for a moment, almost hovering, and then Cecily took a deep breath and said, 'Goodnight.'

And then she performed a quite amazing feat and walked away from him, along the corridor, without looking back.

She very much wanted, she realised, to be alone in her chamber to have the time to reflect on a truly extraordinary day.

Except…where *was* her chamber? Was this it? She stared at the door that she'd reached. And then at the one next to it. They looked very similar to each other. Was either of them *her* door?

Perhaps she should retrace her steps back to the top of the stairs and try again to find her way.

When she rounded the corner, she saw in the dim light that Felix was still standing at the top of the stairs.

'I was waiting to hear the click of your door to know that you were safely inside your chamber,' he told her in a whisper. 'Do you need anything?'

Did she want to tell him her problem? Not really. It suddenly felt too *much* to talk to him any more this evening. She did, however, very, very much wish to go to bed now. And she had no way of doing that unless she knew where her bed *was*.

'Unfortunately,' she replied, also whispering, 'I am afraid that I have forgotten where my chamber is.'

'Oh, dear.' Felix gave a whispered snort of laughter.

'It *is* amusing,' Cecily said, 'but, also, it is not. Because I do wish to sleep tonight.' Perhaps she could manage to sleep in one of the oak chairs she had just passed in an alcove. She *couldn't* just knock on doors and enter, and how else would she find which was her room?

'This is where we need Deedes,' Felix said. 'I fancy that he still won't have finished for the night. I think it might be best if you wait here for a moment, while I go to look for him.'

Cecily nodded as he ran lightly back down the staircase.

Soon he was returning, accompanied by Deedes.

'It is indeed a large house, my lady,' Deedes said, his lips definitely twitching a little. 'Let me show you to your chamber.'

'I will accompany you both,' Felix said.

And the three of them traipsed along a different corridor from the one that Cecily had ventured down.

'I don't think I'd ever have found my way myself,' she told Deedes. 'Thank you very much.'

'It is my pleasure, my lady.' Deedes looked between Cecily and Felix, who was apparently waiting for him to leave, and then nodded his head and said, 'Goodnight.'

When he had rounded the end of the corridor, Felix said, 'Are you quite all right now? Do you have everything you need?'

Her eyes suddenly moist, Cecily just nodded, not sure whether or not her voice would sound normal if she tried to use it. The last person who had been this solicitous in regard to her welfare had been her mother, a very long time ago.

'Are you sure?' Felix was looking at her very closely.

His air of concern threatened to overset her; suddenly Cecily found herself saying, 'Yes, indeed, I am. It is merely that this has been the most momentous day in my life since…'

'Since the loss of your parents,' Felix supplied after a long moment.

'Yes. In fact, it is as though my life has hitherto been divided into two parts, before and after. And today I have entered a third part, away from my aunt and uncle, and it is quite wonderful and quite overwhelming.'

'That is very understandable. You deserve—' Felix took both her hands in his '—you deserve some good fortune.'

'I had great good fortune today. If we had not chanced upon each other on our walks I would now still be entering the third part of my life, but as the Earl's new wife.'

'Good God, that is very true.' Felix was still holding her hands. Cecily could not have removed them from his grasp if she had been paid to do so. He smiled down at her. 'I…' And then he looked deeply into her eyes, and his smile dropped a little and his expression grew more serious. 'I…'

And then suddenly he dropped her hands, said, 'Goodnight,' and strode down the landing away from her far more quickly than anyone would ever normally walk in a house.

Cecily remained, statue-like, staring after him for a long moment, before entering her chamber and discovering that Lizzie had been waiting up for her.

'You should go to bed now, Lizzie,' she told her. 'I can very easily prepare myself for bed.'

'Oh, no, my lady. I'm your maid and I am here to help.'

Cecily stood blinking. Four-and-twenty hours ago she had been alone in her freezing cold, top-floor chamber in her aunt and uncle's house.

And now she was in the most luxurious chamber she had ever seen, with velvet and brocade furnishings, a large four-poster bed and, wonder to end all wonders, a fire burning in the hearth, with a maid of her own brandishing a hairbrush and about to *look after her.*

Truly, this third part of her life had begun very well. If it also included some very confusing thoughts about Felix, that was probably to be expected. The entire day had been, well, unbelievable. Of course she was thinking odd things.

# *Chapter Six*

*Felix*

'The first of your many breakfasts together.' Felix's aunt smiled at him and Cecily as she scraped the thinnest coating imaginable of butter onto a slice of toast.

This was exactly why Felix had been extremely tempted to take himself off for a hard gallop down Rotten Row rather than break his fast with the ladies.

Well, not just this. He also hadn't entirely wanted to see Cecily this morning after the strange moment that had passed between them last night. He had struggled to sleep afterwards for thinking of the betrayal of Aurora, not to mention his sons, if he allowed himself to feel attraction of that nature towards another lady.

And when he hadn't been torturing himself with those thoughts, he'd been wondering what on earth his mother-in-law, Aurora's mother—and of course the boys—would think when they heard that Cecily was his fiancée and she then joined them for the Christmas season. He'd wondered in the early hours whether it might even be possible not to mention that she was—currently—his fiancée, but had come to the sad conclusion that, no, of course it would not be possible; his mother-in-law would almost certainly already have heard about his engagement from one source or other.

He should of course tell her the news himself and had spent some considerable length of time lying awake trying to determine in his mind how he would word his explanation. He wanted to confide the truth to her, but not in writing, in case the letter somehow fell into other hands.

Equally not possible would be to convince Cecily somehow that her publisher had advanced her funds early and lend them to her, so that she could purchase a house immediately and they could immediately end their engagement. Firstly, it would just not be possible to arrange it before Christmas was fully upon them, and secondly, and more importantly, there was no hoodwinking her in these matters, and he would not wish to do so; it would be to insult her intelligence.

He had no choice, therefore, but to continue with the charade, because he could not consign Cecily to the alternative, which might be even worse than marriage to the Earl would have been; it was entirely possible that her aunt and uncle would indeed cast her out.

And, therefore, he had a part to play.

'Indeed,' he said, cutting into his steak. 'We have much to look forward to.'

'I am afraid, however,' his aunt continued, 'that I will certainly have to tear Lady Cecily away from you this morning. She cannot possibly be seen in company dressed like this.' She waved a hand in the direction of Cecily and the brown, somewhat shapeless gown that she was wearing. Felix stared at the gown for a moment, wondering whether it was the same as yesterday's; it really was impossible to tell.

'Lady Cecily is, I believe, very much looking forward to visiting the modiste with you, and I would not wish to stand in the way of her happiness.' He stuck his fork into the piece of steak he had just cut and placed it in his mouth. If he spent enough time chewing, he could avoid conversation with his aunt for a while.

'Indeed I am,' Cecily agreed. 'I am very grateful to you, dear Lady Bradstock, for agreeing to take me.'

'The pleasure is all mine, Lady Cecily. I enjoy shopping and count myself quite an expert in fashion. In addition, I believe that underneath your—frankly—dire robe we will find that you have a neat figure and will look very well in the current fashions. I don't scruple to tell you that your aunt should have done a great deal better by you than to dress you like that.'

Cecily—thankfully—laughed in the face of Felix's aunt's extreme rudeness, and said, 'Thank you very much.' She looked at Felix and then back at his aunt, before saying, 'I am ready to leave whenever you would like to go, Lady Bradstock.'

Felix swallowed his mouthful and said, 'Please don't consider me; I am very happy to peruse the newspapers by myself.'

'In that case—' his aunt rose to her feet '—let us leave immediately so that we have as much time as possible.'

Cecily directed a half-laughing smile at Felix as she left the room, which he somehow felt right in his stomach.

He didn't want to think about that, so he buried himself very firmly in the newspapers until he'd finished eating.

A morning sparring with Gentleman Jackson followed by a meeting with his lawyers to discuss some pressing business allowed him respite from thinking about Cecily and the situation in which they now found themselves, and by the time they were due to meet for luncheon, Felix was feeling quite restored to his usual self. He was always polite, of course, but when going about in Society he did not show any preference for any one lady over another, and he did not allow himself to feel anything for any particular lady; and, now that he had become accustomed to the oddness of this interlude with Cecily, it would be the same with her.

As he waited for the ladies to join him, he reflected that his reaction to Cecily had not really been a reaction to *her*; it had rather been a reaction to their fake engagement. Obviously. She was his old childhood friend and yesterday had been an odd day. He obviously didn't *really* have any kind of feelings other than platonic friendship for her.

'Garth.' His aunt bustled into the room followed by...well, followed by...a vision, frankly.

Cecily, clearly. But not a Cecily that he'd ever seen before.

The Cecily that he'd previously known had a very nice smile. Beyond that, he might, if pressed, have said he thought her hair was brown, and probably curly. He would have had no idea of the colour of her eyes, or anything else about the way she looked. She'd always been dressed in somewhat shapeless gowns in dull colours, and, other than when she smiled, she'd always looked a little drab, frankly.

*This* Cecily was wearing a pale-blue dress, which became her considerably better than the browns and greys she'd always before worn in his presence. Against it, her hair, which fell in delightful loose ringlets, didn't just look *brown*, it looked darkly rich and lustrous. Her eyes were blue, a much darker blue than the dress, which he'd never noticed before. Like the colour of a lake on a clear winter's day, he thought.

'Felix?' Cecily asked, a little hesitantly.

And, good God, he'd been staring like an awkward young sprig in his first Season.

'That is a very nice gown,' he said, stating the obvious. 'I collect it is a new purchase?'

'Madame Chardon did her best.' His aunt waved her hand dismissively in the general direction of Cecily's body. 'It doesn't fit perfectly, of course, in the time that we had, but it will do.'

Didn't fit perfectly? Really? It fitted her much more closely than did her old gowns, showing that she had a much more attractive figure than anyone might previously have supposed.

'I think it fits very well,' he said, before immediately realising that he really shouldn't have phrased his words that way. 'That is to say, I'm sure no one would think that it was not made exactly to measure.' No. No better. 'What I wish to say,' he finished lamely, 'is that it looks perfectly nice.'

'Why, thank you.' Cecily was laughing, her hesitance gone.

His aunt shook her head at him, but was smiling approvingly, very much as though…well, as though he had just demonstrated warm feelings towards his fiancée, so, actually, it was a good thing that he had momentarily become somewhat unable to string together an acceptable sentence. He didn't have warm feelings, obviously; he'd just got a shock, as would anyone who'd seen Cecily before and after she got her first new gown.

'It will do for walking or driving in the park, worn with a pelisse,' his aunt said, 'while we wait for some of her other gowns to arrive. We have much more still to purchase, of course.'

'We do?' Cecily asked.

'Certainly. More robes, as well as gloves, reticules, stockings, which I do not scruple to mention in front of your betrothed. Shoes. Boots. Ribbons. Bonnets. We will be shopping for days.'

Felix looked at Cecily, hoping that she wouldn't be disappointed that her time would be filled with such mundane matters rather than visiting as many of the historic sights of London as possible, and saw that she was in fact smiling very widely.

'Thank you very much for spending so much time helping me,' she said. 'I count myself very fortunate in having your advice on which to rely.'

'The pleasure is all mine,' his aunt said. 'It is rare that one has both the opportunity to form an entire new wardrobe from head to toe for someone and for that person to be so beautiful. I could hardly have asked for a more enjoyable task. Now, what I would like from you, Lady Cecily, is your company at the opera this evening. Madame Chardon has undertaken to have an evening dress delivered for you by eight o'clock this evening—the simple light-green silk that required very little alteration—and you will be able to wear it with the white gloves and the navy velvet pelisse.'

'Oh, that would be wonderful,' breathed Cecily.

'You will of course accompany us,' Felix's aunt instructed him.

'Of course,' he agreed.

Luncheon was a light-hearted affair, with some laughter as the ladies discussed the further purchases that Felix's aunt deemed it necessary for Cecily to make, and Felix—who had very little interest in ladies' apparel and less knowledge—did his best to participate somewhat in the conversation out of politeness.

He felt, as the meal drew to a close, that he would remember both yesterday's and today's meals for a long time. He ate in the company of his older relatives at times, and also in that of friends of course, but the conversation of a female friend of his own generation was a nice thing, which he had been missing since he'd lost Aurora, and it was enjoyable conversing with Cecily, both alone and with his relatives.

The meal drew to a close as quickly as his aunt

could reasonably manage; she was an energetic woman at the best of times and now that she had a mission to perform she was positively brimming with vigour, and had Cecily on her feet and out of the room on her way back to the shops almost before she'd swallowed the final mouthful of her lemon cheesecake.

Felix had other business to attend to while Cecily and his aunt were shopping, but nonetheless found himself wondering during the afternoon how they were getting on and whether Cecily was still enjoying herself. When she and his aunt arrived back at the house shortly after he did, just before the time they'd agreed they would go out to drive in the park, he found himself genuinely looking forward to hearing about her afternoon.

'Go and enjoy your drive,' said his aunt, shooing them towards the front door once Felix had called for his curricle to be brought round and she had Cecily satisfactorily attired in a new pelisse, gloves, a fur muff and a particularly fetching bonnet. 'My bones are older than yours, Lady Cecily, and I need a rest now before we venture out this evening, but you will I am sure enjoy seeing Hyde Park.'

'Are you sure you are not also tired and would perhaps like a rest?' Felix asked as they descended the steps from the house.

'Certainly not. I mean to make the most of my time in London in case I do not have the occasion to visit again in the future. Unless—' she turned her face up to his '—you yourself are tired or do not now wish to drive in the park?'

'Not at all; I am looking forward to our drive.' He wondered whether she was aware how remarkably becoming her bonnet was in the way it framed her heart-shaped face. 'Let me hand you up.' He held his arm out and—after a moment's hesitation, perhaps because no one had ever before treated her as the lady she was—she leaned on it lightly to climb up to the curricle's seat.

'My goodness—this is very high.' She looked down at the ground as Felix sprang up to seat himself next to her. 'So much higher than a gig.'

'I must confide—' Felix took the reins in his hands and the horses began to move '—that my first driving experience was with a gig, which I found reasonably easy, so I was quite certain that I could drive any carriage of any type very well, and I did get a shock the first time I attempted to drive a curricle and found myself much less of a nonpareil than I had imagined.'

Cecily laughed. 'I would like to imagine you failing to drive to perfection, but must confess it is difficult.' For a moment he recognised something similar to the hero worship with which she had used to regard him when they were children; he had known that he could do no wrong in her eyes and somehow it had made him a better person, even during the most selfish years of his youth. The look wasn't exactly childish hero worship any longer, though; it was now more…adult, and it made him swallow, hard, especially when he saw her gaze travel very briefly down to his shoulders and chest before returning to his face.

He blinked, as Cecily asked, 'How long did it take you to learn to drive well?'

'Well, without wishing to sound boastful…not very long,' he said, laughing, and then enjoying the fact that she laughed in response.

'That immediately, of course, makes me wish very slightly for you to have an embarrassing incident right now,' Cecily told him. 'Obviously not one that would cause any injury to anyone or anything other than to your pride.'

'Oh dear,' he said, grateful that the strange look was no longer passing between them. 'I am probably now more likely to have an accident than I have been at any time these fifteen or so years.'

'I must apologise. Any such accident would of course be entirely my fault.'

'It would indeed.' Felix slowed the horses to join the queue into the park and grinned at her.

'Should you not be looking ahead?' Cecily enquired. 'For safety?'

Felix laughed. 'Thank you for the advice.'

They were interrupted by a wave from a purple-turbanned lady in a stately chaise bearing down towards them from their right.

'Your Grace.' The lady—Viscountess Dart—looked with open interest at Cecily. 'And…?'

'Lady Cecily Carlow.' Oh, God. Felix looked between Cecily, who was sitting very upright with her head tilted just a touch to one side and a small smile on her lips, and the Viscountess. It would look suspiciously odd if he didn't own up now to the betrothal, so he would obviously have to do so. And by the end of this evening, when they had been seen together at the opera, the whole of the *ton* would know that he was engaged.

Which was no more than he should have expected, but it did *feel* a lot.

Because it felt, again, like a betrayal of Aurora. As though he was signalling, very publicly, that enough time had now elapsed since he had lost her that he was now able to contemplate a life with another lady.

He needed to write to his mother-in-law immediately upon their return to Berkeley Square to tell her before she heard the news from some other source. Or, in the not unlikely event that she'd already heard it, to ensure that his letter arrived without an unseemly delay. It was beyond the pale that he'd been putting the writing of it off for the entire day. And it was obvious what he should do; he would tell her now that he was engaged and ask her to allow him to tell the boys himself, and then when he arrived home in a couple of days' time he would explain to her the true nature of their betrothal.

Right now, however, he needed to make his announcement.

'My fiancée,' he said, far too loudly, so that his words rang out like the crack of gunfire.

'Oh!' The Viscountess opened her eyes very wide and then bowed very slightly in Cecily's direction. 'I must felicitate you, Lady Cecily.' She paused for just a moment too long, and then continued, 'And you, of course, Your Grace.'

'The felicitations are all mine,' Felix said, suddenly coldly furious at the implication that Cecily had achieved more highly than he had in becoming engaged to him. Yes, many in Society might believe that to be the case, given the difference in their stations and wealth, but she was a very beautiful young lady and, more importantly, excellent company and very kind, and he was sure she might look to the highest levels of Society for a husband, should she so wish, as long as she had a sponsor and the man who fell in love with her was rich enough not to have any need for her to have a dowry.

The Viscountess looked more closely at Cecily and then said, 'How long do you stay in London, Lady

Cecily? If you are able, you must join me for a select literary soirée I intend to hold in the coming days.'

'I should be delighted, if I am able,' Cecily said, the musical tone of her voice contrasting most favourably with the more strident one of the Viscountess.

'I believe that we must move on, or risk creating a long queue. Good afternoon.' Felix nodded at the Viscountess before urging his horses a little forward, to catch up with the dashing phaeton in front of them.

'I must apologise,' he said to Cecily in a low voice.

'In the same way that you wish me not to thank you too regularly, I would prefer you not to apologise too often; I can't help but suspect that if I go about in Society with you or your aunt I will receive any number of near-snubs and envious comments. Even though I have never before been to London, or attended many local events in Sussex, I know enough about life to be aware that when an unmarried, still-young duke announces his engagement, many noses will be put out of joint.'

Felix grimaced. 'Very true, I suppose.'

'Really—' Cecily smiled around her at the occupants of nearby carriages, many of whom were openly staring at them '—we should not care at all, and you should take it as an opportunity to determine which of your acquaintances are kind people who are happy for you and which are jealous and not particularly kind.'

'Those are wise words.' Felix turned to look at her for a moment. She really did have a most enchanting profile when it was visible, which it was much more now that she had her hair done so becomingly. 'When did you become so grown-up?'

'I am four-and-twenty years old. I haven't been a scrubby little schoolgirl who falls out of trees for a long time.'

Felix nodded. 'Yes.' Apparently he hadn't entirely noticed until now. Or perhaps he *had* noticed somewhat, but he hadn't thought clearly about it.

Cecily looked around. 'I'm very pleased to see Hyde Park. I have of course heard about it, and there is nowhere like this in Sussex.'

Felix looked around him at the trees, the paths, the bushes, with fresh eyes.

He opened his mouth to tell her about the sheep that grazed at the other end of the park but was interrupted by a strident *Hallo* from a carriage passing in the opposite direction.

'My godmother,' he told Cecily in an undertone. 'Lady Fortescue.'

'I presume that *this*—' his godmother pointed her parasol at Cecily's face '—is your fiancée. I was surprised not to have been apprised of your betrothal by you personally.' Good heavens—word certainly did travel fast.

'I was intending to call on you tomorrow,' Felix

lied. 'We arrived in London only last night and my aunt deemed it imperative that she take Lady Cecily shopping this morning.'

'I will look forward to receiving you *both*.' His godmother jabbed the parasol in the direction of Felix's face before jabbing again in Cecily's direction.

'We will look forward to it too.' Felix bowed.

'Indeed; thank you very much,' Cecily agreed, with a smile, before Felix moved his reins a little and the horses drew them forward and out of the line of fire.

The frequency with which they were greeted by interested parties in other carriages left them no time for conversation beyond the very banal. In some ways that was fortunate, because Felix needed to try to cope somehow with the self-disgust that filled him at the fact that he hadn't yet had the discipline to write his uncomfortable note to his mother-in-law, when it was now evident that there was every chance that she would already have heard that news from at least one gossipy friend or acquaintance.

'Felix, are you all right?' Cecily asked after they had had yet another conversation with an over-curious lady—a very close friend of his late mother's, who had also intimated that she might have liked to have heard the news first-hand—and he'd entirely lost track of what they were saying.

'Yes,' he asserted. 'Yes, I am.' If he said it forcefully enough, it would be true. And then something—maybe the concern in Cecily's eyes—she obviously didn't believe him—prompted him to begin to explain, 'It's merely that…'

'You don't like the fact that our—fake—engagement is being talked about so widely?' she supplied after his pause had grown too long.

'I… Yes.'

'Of course,' Cecily said very quickly. 'I'm sorry.' Her eyes were hidden from him because she was looking down at her gloved hands, so he couldn't determine the expression in them, but her rigid shoulders and small smile told him that she was trying to hide hurt.

He had to give her the real explanation—what if she thought he was embarrassed by her?

'The reason is that, as you probably know, my mother-in-law, Aurora's mother, resides with me and the boys in the country, and I feel that it is likely that at least one lady—if not many—will have immediately written to her on the subject of our engagement, and, since she *will* have to find out—which, being honest, I would not have chosen—I would have preferred to have told her myself.

'That is to say, I *should* have told her myself, immediately, by letter. When I do tell her I will ask her not to tell the boys until I am home and able to tell them somehow myself. I don't think that she would tell them on my behalf and hope that no one else would either, but I cannot be certain.'

'I'm so sorry.' The eyes Cecily now raised to his were suddenly brimming with tears. 'I've been so selfish. I have been thinking only of myself, but your situation is so much more complicated than mine. We should put an end to this silly charade immediately. You should just go home now to your boys and never have to tell them anything. If you tell them, it will be very confusing for them when I then disappear.'

'No,' he said, so loudly that heads in other carriages turned to stare. He directed a wide smile and a nod at all the curious eyes on them, before repeating, much more quietly, 'No. I don't want to let you down. I will think of a way of telling the boys that doesn't upset them either now or in the future.'

'Felix…'

'No, I… Oh, good God. Another one.'

Another lady was gesturing to them from a passing carriage.

And then they had to spend another few minutes smiling and receiving insincere felicitations.

Eventually, they were able to move on. As soon as he judged their recent interrogators out of earshot, Felix said, 'I would count myself the shabbiest creature alive to abandon you to the fate of returning to your aunt and uncle. I will always wish to do everything in my power to avoid that happening to you. In addition, we *are* now engaged in the eyes of the world, and in many ways it would, I think, seem much less odd if our engagement lasted a little longer.

'I have never…courted…another lady since I lost Aurora, so this will of course seem significant.' He paused and then continued, 'Well, of course it will seem significant; it is a betrothal, which in the normal course of things would lead to marriage.'

He could see Cecily biting her lip and her eyes still looking suspiciously moist and had to fight an urge to put his arm around her to hug her against him to provide comfort.

'Cecily,' he said very gently. 'Whatever the views of my mother-in-law and my sons on our purported engagement, I have no regrets whatsoever; my only regret is that in the great rush to depart and make our way here I have not yet written to my mother-in-law to apprise her of the news. I should have written to her yesterday evening or earlier today, but I was cowardly and I did not have the words. I will write to her before we leave for the opera and then there is no more to be done until I reach home and am able to discuss it with her.'

'I…' Cecily gulped and then gave a large sniff.

Felix couldn't help himself reaching to wipe away the large tear that was rolling down her cheek. Another one followed the first and then one on the other cheek.

He found himself reining his horses in and then cupping her chin with both his palms and wiping her tears carefully with his thumbs until they ceased to fall and he was just holding her lovely face, so familiar, but also now strangely different, as though he was seeing her in an entirely new light. He stroked her cheeks again, very gently, even though she was no longer crying, instead just gazing into his eyes.

His own gaze was drawn to where she was now, perhaps unconsciously—surely unconsciously; Cecily could never have been taught the art of flirtation—moistening her lips and… *Damn.* All of a sudden he wanted to kiss her. A sense of physical longing was uncomfortably flooding his entire body. He moved his hands backwards, very carefully, so that he couldn't possibly hurt her, so that they were in her hair, one hand cupping her neck, the other holding her head. She parted her lips a little, and he heard himself groan, and leaned forward.

And then…

He remembered.

Only a few minutes ago he'd been talking to Cecily about Aurora, and Aurora's mother, and how the news of their engagement would shock her. And *now*, he was planning to kiss Cecily. And if he kissed her, especially in such a public place…well. Maybe he would *have* to marry her, go through with the engagement. And, also, he had never kissed a lady in such a way since the loss of Aurora. When he'd had relations, he hadn't kissed anyone on the mouth. It would feel like an immense betrayal. He…couldn't.

He summoned as much self-control as he could and did his best fond smile, released Cecily and drew back, and said, 'We should…enjoy looking at the park.'

'Yes, of course,' Cecily said, very, very brightly.

Felix took a deep breath and nudged his horses to move forward.

This was terrible. He felt like the greatest cur alive.

# *Chapter Seven*

*Cecily*

Feeling as though her own body barely belonged to her any more, Cecily turned her head slowly away from Felix to hide her face from him, blinking to try to dispel the new tears she felt forming.

The touch of his fingers on her cheeks, when he'd put his hands into her hair and held her head so gently but firmly…the tenderness and yet the strength she'd felt in his hands…it had been intoxicating, delicious, tantalising… She wasn't sure now whether she was more deeply disappointed that he hadn't kissed her, or deeply embarrassed in case he had realised how very much she had wanted him to do so. The way he'd been looking at her had led her to believe…

She was both deeply disappointed *and* deeply embarrassed, she realised, as she stared blindly out of the curricle.

She couldn't do anything about the disappointment, but surely she could do something about the embarrassment.

'The park is beautiful.' There. She'd managed to speak entirely naturally, she was certain. 'The bushes. And the trees. Quite lovely. The way the road weaves through is most taking.'

'I agree; we are very fortunate to be able to drive in the park whilst in town. Walking along the paths is also very pleasant.'

'I imagine that it is and hope perhaps to have the opportunity to walk here during my stay.' Cecily was extremely impressed with her own ability to sound so *normal* at this moment. Oh, but perhaps she had implied that she wished to walk with *Felix*. 'With Lady Bradstock, perhaps. I know that she told me that she very much enjoys taking as much exercise as possible and likes to walk daily.'

'Walking daily is an admirable thing to do—most healthy.'

'Indeed.'

Cecily and Felix had never before been unable to find things to talk about. This was excruciating.

'Do you enjoy walking while you're in London?' she asked.

'I do walk, and also ride in the park—one can gallop along Rotten Row, to the south of the park. I also box.'

'Oh, I didn't know that.'

'Yes. I find it most enjoyable.'

'I'm so pleased,' Cecily said, with extreme politeness.

'Thank you.'

Neither of them twitched at the thanking, despite the jokes they'd shared yesterday on the subject; it was as though Felix wiping Cecily's tears had destroyed their comfortable friendship in one fell swoop.

Cecily sniffed hard, as her eyes began to feel damp *again.*

'Cecily…' Felix's deep voice had emerged as a croak.

'Yes?' She sniffed again but her stupid tears wouldn't stop. 'I'm sorry. I must be very tired, I think. And of course this pretend engagement has come as a great shock to both of us.'

Felix turned the horses so that they began to take them down one of the side paths. 'Let us try to avoid having to converse with anyone else. It is entirely natural, one would imagine, that both of us would feel a little surprised at the situation in which we very suddenly find ourselves. I should not like… I should not like the easy friendship that we have always enjoyed to be changed. I hope that you feel the same way.'

Cecily tried to say that she did, but her tears had

turned to ridiculous gulps and it really wasn't possible to talk through them.

Felix gave a muttered exclamation—possibly using quite strong language, which Cecily was aware she would usually—in a most unladylike manner—find amusing but which had no effect of any kind on her now—and reined his horses in under a tall, bare-branched oak.

Cecily was dimly aware through her waterfall of tears that he'd turned to face her, and moved her head to the side, vaguely disappointed to discover that even when sobbing like this she couldn't help thinking about how she wouldn't like Felix to see her face red and blotchy from tears.

She felt him reach for her hands.

'Cecily?'

'Mmm?' It was very difficult not to reply to someone when they were speaking to you, especially when they were holding your hands so gently and the very tone of their voice seemed to reverberate through you.

'I'm so very sorry that you're so upset,' he said gently. 'I think that, for both of us, in our different ways, this has been a huge event. We've discussed me. I just need to write my letter and then explain things to my mother-in-law when I return home, and similarly with the boys, who I hope will not have been told anything and are in any event very young and do not comprehend adult matters, and of course this is only temporary anyway, so really I have nothing to worry about at all.

'You, however… You have been threatened with an awful marriage. You have then been rescued from that, but the rescue involved leaving your home of many years. I hope that you will be treated very well in my household, but it is nonetheless a great upheaval for you. It is entirely natural that you would feel a little tearful.'

Cecily nodded, sniffed, and sniffed again, before finding her voice. 'That was a very kind thing to say.' And true, surely. Surely that *was* why she'd been weeping. Surely it hadn't been because she felt so very sad about Felix.

No, if she was being truthful, *all* her tears were because she felt sad about Felix. Sad for him that he was so sad about Aurora still. Sad for him that he was so worried about his mother-in-law and sons and how they would be affected by this news, albeit only for a few weeks.

But also…sad for herself that he was never going to kiss her even though it had seemed for that long breathtaking moment as though he would.

And sad for herself because…well, perhaps because for a few moments she had enjoyed the experience of being Felix's bride-to-be. There was no denying that *really* marrying Felix, rather than just pretending like this, would be very pleasant.

She was being silly. Marrying *any* rich and powerful man would be pleasant, as long as he was also kind—and handsome and very good company. There were no doubt any number of men to whom a lady would be lucky to be married.

And Cecily was almost certainly not one of the ladies who would ever marry one of those men, and she should remember it. She was probably not someone that anyone whom one would like to marry would ever fall in love with. Well, perhaps they might briefly, but they wouldn't necessarily *stay* in love with her.

And men of the type to whom one would like to be married usually had the luxury of only having to marry if they fell in love. And, of course, even if someone *did* fall in love with her, would she ever love them back? Quite possibly not, because she would almost certainly not enjoy with anyone else the wonderful friendship that she'd always enjoyed with Felix, and that friendship in itself was part of the love one would wish to feel for a husband.

She sniffed again.

'We had a long journey yesterday, too.' There was a note of desperation in Felix's voice, as though he was clutching at any straw he could think of to try to cheer Cecily up, which did make her smile a little.

'Was that a smile?' He squeezed her hands again and said, 'We *did* have a long journey. *And* you've had a very busy day today. Shopping can be quite a tiring experience.'

Cecily smiled a bit more. Felix's attempts to cheer her were very endearing. And, also, if he genuinely thought that her tears were due to tiredness, well, good. They weren't, of course, but she'd rather be thought an easily-tired goose than a lady pining to be kissed by him.

'So this is all because you've had a very big surprise and have had a particularly tiring two days.' The slightly odd firmness with which he spoke made her look closely at him between her lashes. It was as though he was *telling* her that that was why it was; as though he was trying to convince her and perhaps himself too. Presumably because, like her, he also didn't wish her to be crying in response to that strange moment they had shared.

'Yes, it is,' she replied equally firmly. 'Are we able to walk for a few minutes? I would like to explore the park, and feel that I would benefit from a little exercise, so that I sleep more soundly tonight.'

'Of course.' Felix paused and then asked, 'Presuming that you do not find yourself too tired?'

Cecily had better make sure that she never cried again in front of him. It really was quite tiresome being presumed an easily-fatigued person.

'Walking is not tiring,' she said.

'Splendid.'

'Then…' She tugged her hands very gently out of his; as she did so he looked down as though surprised that he was still holding hers and then very suddenly let them go as though they were scalding hot.

'Splendid,' Felix repeated after the slightly awkward pause that ensued.

Cecily was very careful as he handed her down from the curricle to hold on to his arm for as short a time as possible so that she wouldn't find herself thinking about kissing him again and then embarrass herself again.

And it really was easy to become—almost entirely—engrossed in the park around them. As she had already remarked, the trees, the bushes, the way the paths wove, it was all quite lovely.

They came to a lake after a few minutes and stood and watched some very graceful swans.

'Did you know that there are sheep in Hyde Park?' Felix asked suddenly, just after Cecily had commented on the prettiness of some moorhens. 'One might imagine oneself quite in the countryside there. It is very different from the hustle and bustle of the city.'

'Yes, you mentioned them earlier, I believe. And, yes, the noise is quite fantastic,' Cecily said, 'if you have never been used to living anywhere other than in the depths of the country.'

'I hope you weren't too much disturbed during the night.'

'Oh, no, it's quite wonderful; I will cherish it all as part of my experience of visiting the city. Even the fog and the smells add very much to the novelty, which I am greatly enjoying.'

Felix laughed. 'I hope we can find some even better experiences than fog and city odours. Is there anywhere particular that you might like to visit tomorrow?'

They beguiled the next few minutes in discussing various possibilities like art galleries and the Tower of London, both of them addressing each suggestion extremely earnestly, and eventually it began to feel to Cecily as though they might really be entirely comfortable in each other's company again.

Felix was right; they *had* both had quite a shock and it *had* been a somewhat tiring experience. That moment had been silly and had meant nothing to either of them, actually; of course they could return to their delightful old friendship. She had *always* had a very fond regard for Felix; this was no more than a natural extension of that, given their current position.

'I wonder whether we should return,' she eventually said, regretfully, 'so that you might have ample time for composing the letter to your mother-in-law.'

'Oh, yes, indeed; thank you for reminding me. Yes, if you're quite sure you have seen enough for today,

I think we probably should indeed return. It will in any case be quite dark soon.'

The return journey in the curricle passed uneventfully, with fewer conversations with acquaintances now that night was falling. Felix and Cecily conversed amicably but still sadly with some constraint and hardly any joking, which had the effect of making Cecily fail to see the humour in anything, which meant that she made fewer jokes than usual, which… Yes, it was a circle. A circle of misery, because her friendship with Felix had changed for the worse.

'You seem tired again,' Felix ventured as they drew up in Berkeley Square.

'Not at all,' Cecily said. 'Merely…well, yes, perhaps a little fatigued.' Better to say she was tired than miserable, especially since she had no reason in the world to be unhappy; things had changed immeasurably for the better for her since yesterday morning. 'I shall be much better after a short rest.'

'My lady, your evening gown has arrived,' Lizzie interrupted Cecily's dream an hour later. Her beam was so wide it looked as though her face might split. 'It's so very beautiful. And will look even more beautiful on.' She moved closer to the bed and peered at Cecily's face. 'Are you quite all right, my lady? Your cheeks are very flushed.'

'I'm very well, thank you.'

Anyone's cheeks would be flushed if they'd been woken while having a dream as *warm* as *that* about their fake—very fake, she must remember that—fiancé.

What had Lizzie been saying? Oh! Her gown!

'Oh, how exciting,' she said, trying very hard to push Felix and the kiss she'd just imagined in her dream out of her mind. She sat up and looked properly at the gown. 'Oh my goodness,' she breathed. 'That really *is* beautiful.'

'It will look even more beautiful when you're wearing it,' Lizzie told her.

'Not necessarily,' Cecily said.

'We'll see.'

An hour later, Cecily was dressed in the gown, which was quite the most delicate and beautifully coloured robe she had almost ever seen, let alone owned, and Lizzie had been working on her hair for what felt like an appreciable length of time.

'Nearly ready, my lady,' Lizzie said, her mouth full of hairpins. 'With hair as lovely as yours, it doesn't take long at all.'

'Doesn't take long?' Cecily questioned. How long had Lizzie *expected* it to take?

'That's right.' Lizzie clearly wasn't really paying

attention to their conversation; she was too focused on Cecily's hair to have time for anything else.

She placed another pin in her hair, before saying, 'I'm happy. Now come and see yourself in the looking glass.'

Cecily allowed herself to be led across the room to the full-length glass on the opposite side, and then stood in front of it with Lizzie next to her.

'Oh,' she said.

'I know.' Lizzie looked almost tearful. 'I knew you were beautiful, my lady, but this is wonderful. It was a crime to dress you in those horrible, old, *baggy* brown dresses. I'm so proud.'

Cecily turned and looked at her.

'I'm so proud of *you*, my lady.' Lizzie's eyes were definitely filling.

'Oh, Lizzie, thank you very, very much.' Cecily's own eyes were filling too, yet again; today she had turned into a veritable watering pot. It was a very long time since anyone had told her they were proud of her, though. She suddenly had a memory of herself as a little girl, her mother holding her in her arms and telling her she was proud of her after she had fallen over and grazed her knee but managed not to cry.

'My lady?' asked Lizzie, sounding concerned now.

'Oh, Lizzie. Thank you for being such a wonderful lady's maid. And for being proud of me.' Cecily smiled at her through her own tears and reached for her to hug her.

'No,' shrieked Lizzie, darting away. 'Your dress! And your hair! Don't ruin them! And don't cry!'

Cecily laughed and sniffed. 'Thank you.'

'I'm very happy to help you. His Grace's eyes are going to pop out of his head when he sees you.'

'Lizzie! How very vulgar,' said Cecily, laughing again, and trying not to feel any misery about the fact that Felix's eyes would almost certainly remain very firmly un-popped when he saw her.

But when she descended the stairs in as stately a fashion as she could manage a few minutes later, Felix did stare when he saw her. The ladies were standing behind him, but his was the only face Cecily was looking at, so she saw every gratifying change in his expression, which began with vague interest, travelled through eyes-wide-open staring and finished with what looked very much like admiration.

'Good God,' he said after a few moments. 'Cecily. You look…magnificent. Beautiful.'

Annoyingly, because Cecily was very much enjoying seeing what, yes, really did look like admiration on Felix's face, Lady Bradstock bustled past him as Cecily reached the bottom of the staircase.

'Lady Cecily,' she said. 'A triumph for your first venture into Society. Madame Chardon is indeed a genius. Although little genius was needed with a figure, skin, hair and face like yours. She is a genius with speed, however; I had feared that it would not be ready on time or that it would not fit you quite perfectly. But I should not have doubted her.' She stood back and regarded Cecily critically before reaching forward to give her skirts a tweak. 'Perfection. I shall take some of the credit myself; we have done an excellent job. With excellent materials—you—with which to work, of course.'

'Lady Bradstock,' Cecily replied, laughing. 'You will cause me to blush.'

'I make no apology,' Lady Bradstock said. 'Now, should we go in to dinner?' She looked over her shoulder at Felix, who immediately sprang forward and held his arm out to Cecily.

No one had ever deemed it necessary to teach Cecily how to go on in Society, but she had had the opportunity to observe her cousins and the lessons they'd learnt, and Holly had been very careful to include Cecily whenever she could. Which was fortunate now, she realised, or she could easily and quite unwittingly give high sticklers such as Lady Bradstock a disgust of her by not knowing things as simple as how to take a gentleman's arm.

'You look beautiful,' Felix said in her ear, just for her, which gave her a thrill that went right from the tips of her toes to the top of her head. 'I might be repeating myself, but I think it bore being said twice. I hope you're enjoying wearing your first evening gown.'

'Very much so.'

'I hope you will also enjoy both my chef's offerings this evening and the opera.'

'I'm sure I will.' She couldn't really imagine a greater treat than this—well, other than, perhaps, Felix suddenly deciding that he really would like to kiss her, but that wasn't going to happen. This *was* going to happen.

Felix turned to his relatives. 'I was so taken with Lady Cecily's appearance in her gown that I nearly forgot that I have a small present for her. You will forgive us if we join you in a few moments' time?'

He waited for them to enter the dining room, before leading an almost painfully agog Cecily into a small parlour and closing the door behind them.

'It suddenly occurred to me earlier today that, as a duke's betrothed, you do of course need some jewellery to go with your newly fine wardrobe, and I wished to buy you something to felicitate you on your freedom from your aunt and uncle and on this next stage of your life, something that you can remember it by forever. So I purchased a small present for you.' He took two boxes from a drawer in a side table and placed the smaller in Cecily's hands.

'Oh, Felix, thank you.' She just stood there, almost holding the box, almost overcome.

'You are very welcome to open it,' he said, laughing.

'Thank you.' She lifted the lid and saw, lying on blue velvet, a beautiful pair of pearl drop earrings. 'Oh, Felix, no, this is too much.'

'Not too much at all. We are friends, and friends buy each other presents at times. I *wanted* to buy these for you, and I shall take great pleasure in seeing you wear them. Allow me.' He placed the larger box on the table and took the small box from her, Cecily nearly squeaking as their fingers brushed.

He took one of the earrings out and began to fumble in the direction of her right earlobe. The sensation of his fingers brushing over and over again against her neck and her ear and the side of her face was almost too exquisite to bear; Cecily wondered whether she might faint from the shivers that were beginning to run through her.

And then, as he said, 'Damn it,' for the fourth or fifth time, she began to laugh, possibly a little more hysterically than she would have done if the gentle touch of his fingers hadn't been making her feel quite so much as though she had extremely active butterflies in her stomach.

'Not funny,' he grunted, which made her giggle more.

'This is ridiculous.' He sounded a little breathless,

as though he were in the middle of some extremely arduous physical task, akin to sawing logs or tossing hay bundles.

'Shall I do it myself?' asked Cecily, still laughing.

'Certainly not; I would feel as though I had failed abjectly.'

Cecily had no wish to dissuade him from continuing such an enjoyable pastime, and so they remained there, with his fingers on her skin, while she enjoyed his touch, watched the wonderfully endearing concentration on his face, felt his breath against her cheek, and continued to laugh at his incompetence.

Eventually, he said, 'My aunt is going to wonder where we are. I think—and I would like to impress upon you the extreme unusualness of such an eventuality—that I must admit to failure and suggest that you do them yourself.'

'Failure, your Grace?' Cecily raised both eyebrows at him. 'I am shocked.'

'Minx,' he said.

'It's an extremely easy task. Look.' Without needing to check in the looking glass, she slipped each earring in.

'Good God. It's almost witchery. How did you do that?'

'I'm obviously just marvellously talented.'

'You certainly are.' He shook his head, while she laughed, before taking her hand and drawing her towards the looking glass about the fireplace. 'Even though you had no need of visual assistance when placing them in your ears, I do think that you should look at yourself now. While I might have failed when I attempted to put them in your ears, I believe that you will agree that my purchase of them was a marked success.'

Standing before the looking glass, Cecily almost felt faint at the picture before her. It wasn't just the—certainly beautiful and most becoming—earrings that she wore that took her breath away though; it was the sight of Felix standing behind her, his height and breadth of shoulder dwarfing her, his handsome blondness contrasting with her dark hair, that made her quite so breathless.

Their gazes caught in the glass and they stood and just *looked* at each other for a long moment, before Cecily saw Felix's hands rise as though they were about to clasp her shoulders, before falling again.

She swallowed, hard, before hearing him say, in a particularly hoarse voice, 'The earrings become you very well.'

She made herself turn and laugh, and say, 'As you yourself pointed out, you are apparently very talented when it comes to purchasing earrings.'

He shook his head, his features suddenly very serious. 'No. No talent was needed; you would make any pair of earrings look like the most magnificent jewellery.'

'I…' Cecily swallowed again. 'Thank you. That is one of the prettiest things anyone has ever said to me.'

He shook his head, and then said, 'The other box.' He moved away from her and took the larger box from the table before placing it in her hands.

Opening it, Cecily saw that inside lay a necklace to match the earrings.

'Oh, Felix. This is so very lovely. I don't know how to thank you.'

'Aside from the fact that we agreed there was to be only moderate thanking, I have a very easy way in which you can thank me: allow me to place it round your neck and demonstrate that I do have *some* skill in fastening jewellery.'

Cecily laughed. 'Of course.'

He lifted her hair very gently, before successfully snapping closed the necklace's clasp.

'First time,' Cecily said, trying hard to ignore how very much she was enjoying his proximity. 'Truly, a genius.'

'Certainly a genius.' He grinned at her for a moment, before saying, 'Come; you should look at yourself again.'

And then they were together again in front of the looking glass, Felix just behind Cecily, so close that, as when he'd been trying to help with her earring, she could feel his breath whispering across her cheek.

'Either I am indeed a genius, or you are extremely beautiful,' Felix said eventually, his voice sounding a little odd.

'You must be a genius!' Cecily said lightly, suddenly extremely uncomfortable. She'd been in danger of almost forgetting that the entirety of their situation was make-believe, and he'd just reminded her of it with his weak joke; a loving fiancé would of course have told his betrothed simply that she was very beautiful, with no joking accompaniment. 'We should join the others for dinner. There will be consternation in the kitchen at our tardiness; your chef will be wondering what to do to prevent his dishes going cold.'

'You are right, of course,' Felix said.

And off they went. It seemed to Cecily as though they each kept a careful distance from the other as they left the room, but perhaps it was only from her side.

Dinner was as delicious as it had been the evening before, and the conversation perfectly satisfactory, with Lady Bradstock asking no further difficult questions and Felix and Cecily eventually making each other laugh several times in a way that indicated to her that they could retain their friendship despite these odd awkwardnesses that were occurring between them; as Felix had said, they were probably quite natural given the strange situation in which they found themselves.

The carriage journey from Berkeley Square to the Theatre Royal on Drury Lane was enjoyable for its own sake: the enjoyment of venturing out clad in the most divine of gowns topped with the most beautiful of pelisses and of course Felix's earrings and necklace; the opportunity to drive through the London streets at night, past the magnificent sconce-lit mansions; the hedonism of remaining in the carriage until the last possible moment because a lady could apparently not walk even the smallest distance to arrive at her destination. And of course…sitting opposite Felix in the carriage, basking in his attention and smiles.

When they finally descended from the carriage and entered the theatre, Cecily's senses were immediately assaulted from all directions. She had never seen so many people all together in such a small space before. The noise, the heat, the smell, the sights of so many dressed in their finery—and quite a number of considerably less fine and much more bawdy people too. If it hadn't been for Felix's reassuring light touch on her back, she might for a moment have felt almost overwhelmed.

He spoke into her ear. 'Quite a change from the country?'

'Indeed.' She smiled up at him and delighted in the way he smiled back at her; it felt as though it was a smile entirely for her, one that signalled a mutual understanding of their homes in Sussex and the differences between there and here, and also a mutual friendship and understanding of each other's qualities.

Somehow, Felix had them through the incredible crush inside the theatre and into his box—a separate seating area that effectively belonged to him, Lady Bradstock had explained—before Cecily had time to wonder whether she should actually be scared at the extraordinary number of people jostling in the foyer and outside the box.

The thing was, though, with Felix at one's side, one would never be scared.

It was very hard not to feel a little wistful about that, but that was silly. What she should do was enjoy this delightful evening in the company of this wonderful man and just be grateful that she had this at all.

So when he asked her in a murmur whether she was quite comfortable, she flashed him her best smile and said, 'Yes, of course. It's all quite perfect.' She gestured at the velvet-furnished opulence of the box and the painted ceiling and gilt decorations. 'I love everything about it. The skill and endeavour involved in all the decorations. One cannot help but marvel at it. I apologise, but you will have to allow me to thank you at least once for this treat.'

He looked around the theatre and then at Cecily—first at her eyes, then at her smiling lips, then back at her eyes—and then swallowed for some reason, before saying, 'I should rather thank *you*. It's a long time since I really *looked* at this theatre, or indeed at many of my surroundings. You are opening my eyes to things to which I have been accustomed for far too long, and I am enjoying them anew as a result. You're right. This *is* a marvellous place.'

He smiled at her as their gazes held for a long moment and Cecily felt her heart swell inside her chest.

This was one of the very best moments she'd ever experienced.

# *Chapter Eight*

*Felix*

Felix couldn't take his eyes from Cecily. She had of course always been beautiful, he realised; but he'd never *thought* of her beauty before. He just hadn't really noticed it; she'd always been his neighbour, his childhood friend, several years younger than him, someone to enjoy walks, laughter, conversation with, but not someone who would take his breath away like this.

He didn't know what had happened. But at some point in the past day or two he had begun to be uncomfortably aware of her as a *woman*. A very, very beautiful, desirable, alluring woman. A woman who made him laugh, who made him look differently at familiar things. A woman who, if things carried on like this, could almost make him cry.

He didn't want to think about her like this any

more, but he wasn't really sure how to stop. And, even though he *wanted* to stop, he also *didn't* want to stop. Which, frankly, was enough to give a man a headache, the confusion of it.

Currently they were just staring at each other. He didn't know why Cecily was looking at him but he knew why he was looking at her. It was because he couldn't not.

'Lady Cecily, are you a fan of Mozart?' His aunt's voice cut across his thoughts.

Cecily blinked, looking dazed, and then said, 'I have had little opportunity until now to listen to his music, but I do very much like all kinds of music and I'm sure that I will enjoy it.'

'So this is your very first time at the opera?' his aunt enquired.

'Yes, it is, and I am very pleased to be here.'

'In that case, we must explain the story of *The Magic Flute* to you.' His aunt immediately launched into a description of the story.

Her description was somewhat convoluted, but Cecily didn't seem to have any difficulty in following, asking pertinent questions quite regularly during the discourse. Felix found himself becoming engrossed too in what his aunt was saying. He'd seen this opera before, but had never really thought about it. There was a lot about which he didn't usually think, it seemed.

'And so it does have a happy ending?' asked Cecily.

'Indeed it does, together with a more serious message,' his aunt said. 'With the thrill of the final arias and the conclusion of the story, we are left with a feeling of deep satisfaction. And, look—' she pointed the monocle she'd brought in the direction of the stage '—I believe that it is about to start.'

'I will enjoy it all the more because of your description of the story.' Cecily smiled with what looked like real fondness at his aunt. 'Thank you!'

'My pleasure. I will very much enjoy having a niece-in-law who is kind enough to listen to me when I wish to impart my knowledge.'

Felix couldn't help wincing, again, at the deception they were practising.

Hopefully Cecily and his aunt could remain friends, however.

Oh, God. That would be another hurdle to clear. They would have to orchestrate Cecily's jilting of him in such a way that it didn't give any of his family or acquaintance with whom she had struck up a friendship a disgust of her.

This was a remarkably complicated situation.

He glanced down at Cecily and saw that she was clearly not worrying about anything complicated at this moment; she appeared to have abandoned herself entirely to enjoyment of the opera. She was leaning forward, her mouth formed into a small 'o', her hands clasped together, her chest heaving as the—very impressive—soprano on the stage began an ascending run of notes in a crescendo.

Felix found himself smiling and relaxing at the mere sight of Cecily's enjoyment.

Watching the opera through the eyes of someone who had never before had the experience dramatically enhanced his own enjoyment of it. He didn't wish to think about how much his enjoyment was also enhanced by the way Cecily naturally clutched his arm at moments of high tension and by the way her delicious softness and delightfully heaving bosom were pressed quite closely against him.

Unlike his aunt, he was not a natural opera-lover. When he attended, it was usually only to see friends and he rarely arrived before the interval. He had been wrong, he perceived now; there was much to be said for watching the thing from start to finish. Especially with Cecily at one's side.

When the interval came, she stared at the stage for a few moments after the curtain came down, her whole body almost shuddering with the emotion that she clearly felt.

Felix wasn't looking at the stage; he was looking at Cecily and he found his treacherous mind wondering how it would feel to make her shudder like that himself.

She turned towards him, with an enquiring look on her face, and he wondered for a horrified moment whether he had somehow moaned out loud at where his thoughts had taken him, before realising that he must have involuntarily given his own shudder—for a quite different reason from Cecily's pure, opera-loving one—and she had felt it from where her hand still rested on his arm.

'I see that you enjoyed the first half,' he said as blandly as he was able.

'Indeed,' she agreed, laughing. 'As must anyone, I am sure, when it is their first time seeing such a spectacle. I am very much looking forward to the second half. Such beautiful sounds that they made. And their acting! One would almost believe oneself to be transported to ancient Egypt.'

'Yes, I—' Felix was interrupted by the arrival in their box of a large number of his particular friends, approximately half of whom were apparently extremely interested to discover the identity of the beautiful young lady he had brought to the opera, while the other half had already heard that he was betrothed and wished to confirm the rumours and meet his fiancée.

How very, very stupid of him to have attended this evening with Cecily. Why had he not had the common sense to have realised that of course this would happen and suggest that she came with his aunt after he left for the country?

To what he realised was his vague surprise, Cecily instantly charmed all his friends. She distributed her smiles evenly amongst them, she laughed at any mild jokes, she regurgitated just the right amount of the knowledge she had gleaned from his aunt about the play, and she accepted the felicitations on their engagement very prettily.

He hadn't ever seen her in this kind of social situation before—indeed, she probably hadn't ever had such an experience before—but it was as though she'd been born to the role of soon-to-be duchess.

As they passed him on their way out of the box as the second half began, his friends—none of them men who gave compliments lightly—all had words to drop in his ear:

'Very nice young lady.'

'Charming.'

'Like her very much.'

'Congratulations, Garth; very pleased for you.'

And so on.

They were all correct, of course. She would make another man a wonderful wife. He had a mad moment of feeling real envy of whoever that man might be, followed by another of chiding himself and reminding himself that he wanted only the best for his friend and wondering whether he could somehow orchestrate some kind of Season for her, before realising that, no, that could never happen for her, because, in the eyes of the *ton*, she would forever be the lady who had jilted him.

Only a very rich heiress would be able to marry someone else after that. Unless she met another man quite naturally and fell in love with him and he with her. Someone in the country near her new home, perhaps. And that might of course happen. Because who, on getting to know her better, *wouldn't* enjoy her company and be attracted to her beauty?

He frowned. How many men might there be who were genuinely good enough for her?

Ridiculously, he found himself edging a little closer to her, as though to protect her from unsuitable suitors.

When the tension in the music mounted, Cecily clutched his arm again. And then, at some point, he couldn't have said when, their hands somehow found each other, and some time later he realised that he was clinging on to her hand quite as much as she was clinging on to his.

Her hand felt right in his. Small—but not too small—soft—but not too soft—and exactly the right size for his hand to fit right around. Holding it felt… right.

No one else in their box would be able to see their hands in the darkness. And if they did spy them holding hands like this, well, who wouldn't excuse a recently betrothed couple the liberty? It wasn't fashionable for members of the *ton* to be besotted by their spouses, but much would be excused in a duke.

He *wasn't* besotted, of course, and Cecily wasn't *actually* his betrothed.

A moment of drama on the stage caused her to squeeze his hand a little harder and he found himself squeezing hers back. And then, almost absent-mindedly, he began to stroke her thumb a little, moving his own thumb in circles. She moved her hand in response and entwined his fingers with hers. The feel of their skin touching felt surprisingly intimate given that it was limited to their hands. He very much liked it, he had to admit.

When she shuddered—he wasn't sure whether it was due to the tension building on stage, or the tension building between the two of them as they held hands in the dark—it seemed entirely natural to slide his hand up her arm to cup her elbow, before slipping it round her waist, and gathering both her hands in his other hand. He was sure that no one else could see them in the darkness, and it was as though he just couldn't help himself.

Cecily certainly seemed happy with the arrangement; she leant into him in the most delightful way, and, just as her hand had seemed so perfect to be held by his, she fitted very well inside his arm, wriggling just a little so that she was positioned exactly right against him.

He continued to hold Cecily as the opera continued, and it was as though they were enjoying it as one, their bodies almost melted together. Felix was enjoying this more than he'd ever imagined he would enjoy an opera.

It ended far earlier than he had expected. Too early, in fact: he could very happily have sat here with Cecily gathered in his arms for the rest of the evening. In fact, he didn't want to let her go. He should release her, however, for the sake of propriety.

As he did so, Cecily blinked at him with unfocused eyes.

'That was…wonderful,' she told him. He really wasn't certain whether she was referring to the opera or to being in his arms. In his own opinion, the former had been perfectly acceptable and the latter had been extremely enjoyable.

What, though?

What had he been doing?

He'd been *cuddling* her. Why? How had it actually happened? Why had he done that?

He didn't want to cuddle her.

There should be no more holding of hands or cuddling or anything else.

Clearly the emotion of the past two days had affected him very strangely.

'Felix?' Her clear gaze was on his face now and he couldn't remember what they'd been talking about.

'Oh!' said Cecily, looking over his shoulder.

Felix turned round to see what had surprised her and saw that the box was markedly emptier than it had been earlier; none of his aunts were there.

A footman standing at the door to the box stepped forward and cleared his throat.

'Lady Bradstock asked me to apprise you that she and the other ladies left shortly after the interval because—' he cleared his throat '—the music was so loud.'

Cecily giggled. 'Oh dear.'

'They've probably seen it several times.' Felix didn't want her enjoyment of it to be spoilt by the thought that others had not liked it so much.

'Yes,' she agreed. 'And also I understand that, when one has an earpiece for hearing, loud noises can echo most unpleasantly.'

'Oh, yes, of course. Yes, I'm sure that was the reason for their departure.'

Cecily giggled again. 'That, or *they* are philistines, or *I* have a most unusual liking for Mozart.'

Felix laughed too, relieved that Cecily was amused.

The footman cleared his throat again. 'I understand that Lady Bradstock instructed the coachman to return here to collect you in the chaise after taking them to Berkeley Square.'

'Splendid,' Felix said. 'Thank you.'

The throng outside the box, on the stairs, in the foyer, was immense. Felix couldn't help feeling that it must be quite intimidating for someone unused to it, although Cecily, he was beginning to realise, was not easily intimidated; so far she had taken the fake betrothal, her first long journey, her arrival in London, meeting his aunt, getting a new wardrobe and this outing to the opera almost entirely in her stride.

Nonetheless, he couldn't help himself placing a protective hand against her back and using his height to shield her from the crowd. A number of men looked appreciatively at her and seemed on the brink of making the mistake of speaking to or about Cecily until they saw the pugnacious scowl that Felix knew he was now wearing.

He had her out of there and into the carriage so fast that he impressed even himself.

When they got into the carriage together, they sat down as one, and somehow, the protective arm that Felix had had around Cecily stayed there, so that he had her hugged against his side.

'Did you enjoy your evening?' he asked.

She turned a beaming face up to him. 'Oh, yes. It was truly wonderful. Thank you.'

The way her lips were parted, just a little, the way

her eyes sparkled…it was all too much for Felix's sanity…suddenly, he found himself—as though drawn by an invisible and very strong cord—leaning his head down towards Cecily's until he could brush her lips with his.

The momentary contact wasn't enough; he groaned and pulled her closer into his hug and with his other hand reached to cup her cheek, before kissing her harder, deeply.

He heard her give a little sigh before she opened her lips further and began to return the kiss.

It was blissful. It felt almost like…coming home, as though this was what he *should* be doing. She tasted sweet, desirable, *perfect.* It felt as though she belonged in his arms. And from her response it seemed as though she was enjoying it as much as he was.

For a while—he couldn't tell how long—all thought disappeared and they just kissed and kissed. It was as though nothing in the world existed except them and the kiss. It was exploratory, but it also felt as though, somehow, they had some pre-existing knowledge of each other. At first Felix was aware of thought, the fact that this was the first time he'd kissed another woman since Aurora, but then he gave himself up entirely to the beauty of this moment with Cecily, unable to think any more, entirely focused on her and their kiss.

And then—after he didn't know how long—Cecily

wriggled a little to extricate her arm and wind it around his neck, which had the delightful effect of pushing her chest up against his. She pushed her hand into his hair, and, as she did so, he found himself sliding his hand further around her body, so that it was resting against the underside of her breast.

She gave a little gasp and drew back a little, studying his face.

'You're beautiful,' he said hoarsely, before taking a finger and tracing down her cheek, and then along her jawline.

She smiled at him and bit her lower lip, looking into his eyes the whole time.

His fingers, almost of their own volition, reached for the fastenings of her pelisse. He paused for a moment to confirm that she was happy for him to loosen them, and she gave a great sigh and leaned to make it easier for him. He tugged at them so that her pelisse came open, and then he continued to trace along her skin, down the side of her delicate neck and down the silken skin of her chest to the low neckline of her dress.

As he bent his head to drop kisses along the line that he'd traced, Cecily pulled his head hard against her and reached her other hand to explore his back. When he pulled her dress aside, and he explored her beautiful, perfectly-shaped breasts with his hand, she gave a juddering gasp, before digging her nails into his back. And when he followed where his hands had been with his lips, and began to nip gently with his teeth, she almost screamed, before moving her hands to explore more of his body.

He couldn't have said how long they spent there, becoming gradually more dishevelled, their pleasure building and building, until Cecily—who was now somehow entirely on his lap—wriggled and nearly fell onto the floor.

As he caught her, he realised that the carriage was entirely stationary, and had probably been so for some time.

'We are here,' he whispered.

'Here?' Cecily's previously immaculate coiffure—her mass of curls had at the beginning of the evening been tamed and turned into a very sophisticated, almost smooth roll at the back of her head, with delightful ringlets at the front—was in complete disarray, and her dress pulled right down her chest in the most wanton manner, and he couldn't imagine a more enticing sight.

'Here, in Berkeley Square, at the house,' he clarified.

'Oh.' She just blinked at him, her gaze not entirely focused.

'And so I wonder whether we should perhaps go inside,' he said.

His hands and mouth weren't obeying him, however; he was already pulling her back securely on his lap, and *dammit*, she felt good as she moved against his hardness. He anchored her against him with one arm and ran his hand up her leg under her skirts. He stroked her soft inner thigh, before finding her most intimate parts with his finger.

'Felix.' Her voice was almost a scream. 'Ohhhhh, Felix.' She was clinging on to him, her head thrown back, and, God, he wanted her, every part of her.

He could take her now, here, in the carriage. His groom would know better than to disturb them; Cecily was—without perhaps even understanding what she was doing—urging him on, exploring him with her hands, driving him almost to the point of madness.

But it would be wrong. What if she became with child? Then he would have to marry her and neither of them wanted that.

They should stop.

They *should*.

'We should stop,' he said, his voice sounding ragged to his own ears.

'I…' Cecily began, before stopping and then saying, 'Yes, of course.' She looked at him and then down at herself, and gasped. 'Oh my goodness.' She pulled ineffectually at her open dress, which had the effect of making her naked breasts move in a way that sorely tested Felix's resolve.

'Allow me,' he said, trying to remember that he was a gentleman. He gently pulled her dress up, doing his best not to notice the way she jumped as his fingers skimmed her breasts despite his best efforts. He then helped her pull her pelisse securely around herself and tried to help her pat her hair back into place, before shaking his head. 'I'm not sure that we can do very much about your hair,' he said. 'It's…' It was glorious. But not at all how it had been at the beginning of the evening.

'Thank you,' she said in a small voice.

'Cecily, I…' he said as he adjusted his own clothing.

'Yes?'

He didn't know what he wanted to say. He was beginning to feel very…well, a great mix of things, most of them extremely uncomfortable.

He opened his mouth to apologise and then closed it again. An apology might not sound good to her ears.

Perhaps he should thank her; no, certainly not.

Perhaps he should…

What he *wanted* was for her not to be upset in any way. And to understand that that had been an insane aberration that wouldn't be happening again. And he wasn't sure that he had adequate—and unhurtful—words to accomplish his aim.

After a particularly long and uncomfortable pause,

during which Cecily alternated between looking at him with a small smile and staring at the wall of the carriage, and Felix tried desperately to work out an appropriate thing to say, she said, 'I believe that you thought we should go inside now?'

'Yes, yes, I did. I do. That is exactly it.'

'Let us go then?'

'Certainly. Yes.' He really hoped that Lizzie wouldn't have waited up for Cecily, but rather thought she might have done; during the journey to London she had seemed most enthusiastic about her new role.

When he had handed Cecily down and could see her in the light of the lamps at his front door, he was quite sure that an eagle-eyed maid—unless particularly innocent—would know immediately that her mistress had been engaging in rather indecorous activities. Well, there was nothing to be done about it; it would be too excruciating to say anything to advise Cecily to try to avoid Lizzie. What they had just done was obviously scandalous, but Lizzie was, he thought, very loyal, and it would at least give further credence to their betrothal.

He *really* hoped Lizzie was indeed loyal; if not, and she told others and was believed, he would have to marry Cecily or she would be ruined far more than by jilting him, and might not be *able* to marry a nice man she met in the future in the country.

*How* could he have been so stupid?

They'd reached the point on the landing where they were to go their separate ways to their own chambers.

'Goodnight,' he said to Cecily in a low voice.

'Goodnight.' Oh. Her voice sounded entirely as normal, as though nothing out of the ordinary had happened.

'Goodnight,' he repeated, and then turned to go to his chamber.

He told his valet that he had no need of his services this evening; he had a very strong sense that he needed to think. His thoughts were muddled, however. It had been a long time since he'd been with a woman; Cecily was remarkably attractive but she'd never affected him like this before. That was obviously because they'd been thrown together so much, in new circumstances, due to their fake engagement. Was it just a feeling of warmth towards a very close friend, or was it something more? And was it acceptable for him to feel like this, or was he betraying Aurora and by extension their boys? He didn't know.

He did know that what had happened this evening couldn't happen again.

The only course of action he could sensibly take, therefore, was to leave London tomorrow, so that he wouldn't be tempted to do anything so stupid again. As agreed, he would invite Cecily to Garth for Christmas, but he would avoid spending time alone with her. Although he would miss her greatly, he realised, if they didn't see each other at all. And he wanted to make sure that she had a wonderful Christmas; he knew that she had never received gifts from her aunt or uncle and had been included in their family celebrations to no greater extent than had the family governess, and he wished her to experience inclusion, warmth and enjoyment. So he would certainly choose to spend *some* time with her. Just not so much that they might fall victim to temptation again.

He was out of bed and galloping down Rotten Row to clear his head almost before daybreak, before returning to the house to break his fast before he set off.

When he entered the dining room, there was—most unfortunately—a single, slim-shouldered occupant. Cecily had her back to him and was peeling a peach very slowly.

He still had no words for her, beyond the note he had penned late last night telling her that he had to leave, so, despising himself even as he did it, he turned silently and left the room. He could stop for a meal at one of the first staging inns he passed on the road.

When he arrived home, intent on speaking to his mother-in-law as soon as possible, he found her in the nursery with the boys.

When he had scooped his sons up into his arms, swung them round, obliged them with a brief play-fight and then ruffled their hair and told them that he very much hoped they had behaved well while he was away, he asked his mother-in-law if they might converse alone for a few moments.

'Of course.' She gave the boys' nurse a few suggestions, before following Felix out of the room.

Neither of them spoke until they had reached the sanctuary of Felix's library, which made him quite sure that she had already heard the news.

She confirmed that with the words, 'I understand that congratulations are in order,' accompanied by a sweet smile. The sincerity of the smile almost made his heart crack; he knew that it had broken her heart when she had lost her daughter and now he was reminding her of her loss. 'I am very pleased to see you happy,' she continued.

He shook his head. 'What I am about to tell you I say in confidence,' he said. 'It could do great damage if you were to tell anyone else; I know that you won't.'

His mother-in-law lifted one eyebrow and said, 'Of course not.'

'Lady Cecily is an old friend of mine, perhaps a closer friend than many realise; we were in the way of walking together quite regularly on my land from when we were quite young.'

His mother-in-law nodded but didn't interrupt.

'Lord and Lady Milton have not treated her like another daughter, as one would say they should have done; they have treated her as an unwanted distant cousin. I bumped into her earlier in the week—' it seemed inconceivable that it had only been three days ago that the fake betrothal had occurred '—and discovered that the Earl of Steed had proposed to her and her aunt and uncle proposed to marry her to him as soon as possible. One thing led to another, and she and I entered into a fake betrothal to save her from the Earl. Our plan is for Cecily to jilt me in three months' time and retire to a house in the country with a companion.'

'Ohhhh. I see.' His mother-in-law stared at him for a long time, before continuing, 'That was very kind of you.'

'Not at all. No one would stand by and watch a friend forced into an awful marriage, if they were able to help.'

She nodded. 'I will of course say nothing to anyone and will do all I can to help with your subterfuge. Poor Lady Cecily. The boys know nothing; I said nothing to them myself and would not expect any of the servants to do so either. I judged it best to wait for you to tell them whatever you like.'

'Thank you. That's a great relief.' He smiled at her, and then remembered that he had a trifling—or enormous—housekeeping matter to mention to her.

'I have invited Lady Cecily for Christmas, of course, and would like to hold a large house party for the Christmas period. I should be very grateful if you would like to decide on whom to invite.'

'Certainly.' She was always comfortingly unflappable.

And, just like that, everything felt—*almost*—normal again.

What had happened over the past few days had been a strange interlude, that was all. There would certainly be no more kissing or anything else of that nature between him and Cecily.

# *Chapter Nine*

*Cecily*

'How delightful,' repeated Lady Bradstock for perhaps the twentieth time. She was very verbosely excited at the prospect of a two-week festive house party in Felix's castle.

The repetitions were not helping Cecily's steadily increasing headache.

'Indeed,' she murmured.

'You will be very pleased to be reunited with your betrothed, I make no doubt,' Felix's Great-Aunt Leonora said, very loudly, as was her wont—she was very deaf.

'Certainly,' Cecily said.

'It was a shame that he had to depart so precipitately this morning,' Lady Leonora persisted, still at very high volume.

'He is a devoted father,' said Lady Bradstock. 'He will always return to his boys if they need him.'

'Indeed.' Cecily was quite sure that his precipitate departure had not been because of his sons. He would obviously always be pleased to see them, and he had mentioned that he always missed them when he was away from them, but the *particularly* early departure had clearly been because of her.

Because of their kissing and…other things…last night.

When they had stopped kissing in the carriage, he had suddenly seemed extremely distant and quite desperate to get away from her.

She had summoned all her strength and behaved entirely normally when saying goodnight to him, of which she was very proud, but she had been on the verge of tears by the time she got into her chamber and had not been pleased to find Lizzie waiting up for her and very eager to dissect the evening. When Lizzie had expressed astonishment at the state of her hair, she had said that it was windy outside and had pulled her pelisse more closely around herself, and had then told Lizzie that she had the headache and thought that just this once she would be better putting herself to bed.

Her lie about the headache had very rapidly become true, and after a miserable night she had woken early, unrefreshed.

She had wondered whether Felix's chef's breakfast dishes might help her feel a little better, so had descended early, only to discover firstly that she had no appetite, and secondly that Felix, on entering the room and seeing her, had obviously decided to leave immediately—possibly genuinely believing that she wouldn't have noticed. All she had seen of him had been his departing back, and her headache had increased tenfold.

She had finished her breakfast and had then gone to the drawing room to await Lady Bradstock for the shopping trip they had planned for the morning. There, Deedes had passed her a note from Felix. The note was written as though to a mere acquaintance, stating very briefly that he was returning to the country to see his sons, that he hoped that she would enjoy the remainder of her stay in London and that he looked forward to seeing her over Christmas at the house party he was hosting, and he hoped that she wouldn't mind if he instructed Lady Bradstock to make all the necessary travel arrangements on behalf of all the ladies in his London house.

And that was it.

The rest of the day had passed in a blur of misery. Even the purchases of such desirable and wholly necessary—according to Lady Bradstock—but in reality wholly unnecessary items such as long silk gloves, additional silk stockings and evening reticules had only lifted her heart a very little.

Which was quite ridiculous, she scolded herself, as Felix's aunts continued to discuss the upcoming Christmas festivities.

She was extremely lucky to have been rescued from marriage to the Earl and to be experiencing this taste of London life, the opera and the entertainments that Lady Bradstock had told her they would be attending this week.

And—really—she was privileged to have been kissed, just once, because that was an experience that a lot of people—most people, probably—had, and it had been much more enjoyable—truly wonderful in fact—than she had imagined it would be.

It was, of course, a dreadfully lowering thought that kissing her had caused Felix immediately to flee to the country, and she was sure that she would be very embarrassed when she saw him. But she must try to overcome that feeling and think about it rationally. He should be as embarrassed as she, especially since he was the one who had started it.

She hoped that she *would* be able to overcome the embarrassment.

Worse was the fact that…well, for a moment she had had the most stupid hope…

No, she must not even think that. Life—her aunt and uncle—had demonstrated that she was not lovable, and clearly someone like Felix would never entertain anything other than perhaps a rare—blatantly immediately regretted—momentary wish to kiss her, nothing more.

'Of course,' she said, as her thoughts were interrupted by a request from Lady Bradstock to help her untangle her embroidery silks.

This was a much more enjoyable chore (and companionable, accompanied as it was by all manner of gossip) than any she had been tasked with when living with her aunt and uncle, and she should be very grateful about the change in her circumstances.

The next few days passed in a whirl of still more shopping, writing in any spare moments she had (which diverted her thoughts most satisfactorily from her own problems), soirées, drums, ridottos, balls, all attended by an air of anticipation of Christmas fast approaching.

Cecily discovered that the fiancée of the Duke of Garth was very popular with both young—and not so young—men and the women who wished to enjoy her friendship and patronage once she was wed, and if it felt as though there was—ridiculously—a Felix-shaped hole in all her evenings, she was able to beguile her time by chatting to other charming men and interesting women. It was really only during the nights that she *particularly* spent too long thinking about him.

And then it was time to prepare to leave for the trip to Sussex.

Felix—ever thoughtful, which was more than he had to be, so Cecily should actually count herself lucky rather than hate the impersonal tone of his letters—had written more than once to set out arrangements for her future. She would spend the next fortnight in Sussex at his Christmas house party and then she would return to London with his aunts to remain here until such time as she received her monies from the publisher and Felix was able to help her purchase her house in the country. And then she would 'jilt' him and break their fake engagement.

They had discussed how they should end it and Felix had insisted that she should be the one to jilt him. If he jilted her, it would make other men think of her as less desirable a marriage prospect, and those with suspicious minds might wonder whether he had discovered some scandal about her.

If she jilted him, especially after she had 'inherited a sum sizeable enough to allow her independence'—as they had agreed they would describe her publishing money—she might well just be viewed as eccentric, especially if Felix and his family had nothing bad to say about her. Felix had suggested that she visit his aunt in London again, to demonstrate that to the world.

After the jilting…well, then she would probably

rarely, if indeed ever, see him again. If he continued acting as her agent, which he had intimated he would like to do, they could easily correspond entirely by letter. As an unmarried lady she would not be able to travel to visit him; she would only ever see him if he happened to travel to wherever she lived. Which might very well be never.

And that thought should not be so dreadfully depressing. Yes, he was one of the few close friends she had ever had, but, free of her aunt and uncle and able to attend social events with Lady Bradstock, she was already making friends here in London, and she would be able to make friends near her new home too. And then she was *sure* that she wouldn't feel Felix's absence so keenly. She hoped.

They left London early in the morning amidst a flurry of snowflakes. Lady Bradstock had contemplated for a moment waiting until there was no threat of snow, but then had declared, on behalf of all of them, that they were more than capable of withstanding a little snow, and, if they didn't leave now, what if they were unable to leave for another few days and missed a large proportion of the party.

Cecily hadn't been sure whether she would rather go or stay. She was, on the one hand, quite desperate to see Felix, but, on the other, quite desperate *not* to see him. It might be dreadfully embarrassing, since he had so clearly regretted their kiss, or indeed it might be very painful receiving no particular special attention from him.

It was irrelevant, of course, what anyone else wanted; Lady Bradstock decided that they would set off and so that was that; they were on their way to Sussex.

The journey was perfectly pleasant—when Cecily was able to put worries about seeing Felix out of her head. She and his aunts played a number of parlour games that had them all laughing quite uproariously. The snow continued to fall in only a very mild way, and, after a pleasant luncheon at a staging inn en route, they were passing through the village of Garth Castle by late afternoon, just as dusk was falling.

'I understand that this is your childhood home?' Lady Bradstock enquired as they entered the village.

'Indeed.' Cecily could barely speak for the emotions flooding through her. It felt as though an enormous length of time had passed since she was last here.

It was a great relief when, instead of taking the road that led towards her aunt and uncle's house, they drove towards the castle.

'I will be pleased to make the acquaintance of Lord and Lady Milton this week,' said Lady Bradstock, clearly entirely ignorant of Cecily's situation.

'Indeed,' Cecily repeated. And then she bent her attention to their arrival.

She had never driven up to the front of the castle before, she realised. In fact, she hadn't ever really seen it properly, only the back, and that only from a distance.

It was a very impressive building: it was stone-built, the main body of it very ancient, with more modern wings, but very sympathetically added. There were several towers and a great courtyard in front of it. One might almost imagine oneself in a fairy tale.

As they drew up outside, Felix came out of the wide oak front door and walked over to their travelling chaise and opened the door.

When she saw his handsome and broad shoulders appear in the aperture, Cecily felt her heart give a most uncomfortable leap.

'Good afternoon,' he greeted them, smiling generally into the interior, rather than directing his smile specifically at Cecily as she had become accustomed to him doing. 'I hope that your journey hasn't been too arduous.'

'A journey can never be too arduous in a chaise as comfortable as this,' Lady Bradstock said, 'and we amused each other very well with games involving plays on words and dice. You must be very pleased to see your fiancée.'

'Indeed I am.' Felix looked directly at Cecily for the first time and gave her a wide smile that did not reach his eyes at all.

Cecily dutifully smiled back. When she was worrying that Felix would accord her only the minimum of attention, she had of course not taken into account that for appearance's sake he would *have* to spend at least a certain amount of time with her. It would be a *good* thing to spend time together; they could get over their awkwardness and, she very much hoped, return to their old friendship. And then her heart would stop turning over uncomfortably every time she saw him, she was sure.

The ladies descended from the carriage one by one, Cecily waiting until last, out of deference to their greater age.

When she finally went down the chaise steps, she couldn't help staring at Felix's arm for far longer than was usual before realising that of course she had to take it. She leaned on it for the shortest time possible, before reaching the ground and letting go. The strength in his forearm had reminded her of that forearm holding her only last week, and she didn't wish to be reminded of that.

'Mrs Jarvis will show you to your rooms,' Felix told them all, before bestowing another fake wide smile on Cecily and ushering her, with the other ladies, into the care of his housekeeper, a woman of a certain age with a commanding manner and jolly laugh.

Mrs Jarvis assigned a maid and a footman to each of Felix's aunts, before herself taking Cecily up the grand staircase ahead of them.

'We're all very pleased to have the honour of meeting you, my lady,' she told Cecily as they walked. 'It's time His Grace was happy again. It's all very well him being a devoted father and son-in-law, but he's still a young man, in his prime. He deserves happiness. And that's all I will say on the subject.' She pushed open the door to a bedchamber. 'Of course we do hope that you *will* make him happy. He certainly hasn't seemed himself since he got back from London. Pining for you, we think. That is to say, *I* think. I wouldn't lower myself to gossip with the servants.'

'Of course not,' Cecily murmured, desperate for her to stop talking and leave the room.

'He hasn't been himself at all since he got back from London,' Mrs Jarvis continued. 'Polite and kind as always, the best of masters, but you can see in his eyes, he isn't himself. Not that I'm one to pry.'

'Of course not.'

'Someone suggested—I couldn't say who it was, because I don't engage in gossip—that he wasn't himself because he was regretting his engagement, and there are some who say it was very sudden. And that it's quite odd that you haven't got engaged before now being as how you used to live so close. I told them not to gossip and enter into unnecessary suppositions. I'm sure it's because the time wasn't right until now.'

She stopped and peered at Cecily. Cecily couldn't now believe that she'd thought that her smile was jolly; the woman seemed pure malice at this moment.

'So.' Mrs Jarvis smiled, much like a fox or wolf might straight before they killed an unsuspecting little creature. 'Of course you'll make His Grace happy, won't you? I wouldn't let anyone say otherwise. There's no gossip in this house.'

Cecily narrowed her eyes. She didn't have to accept this. She was no longer at the mercy of anyone, not her aunt, nor this woman.

'As the new Duchess,' she said, enunciating her words very clearly, 'I will remember your very warm welcome. Thank you so much. Please send Lizzie up to me.'

'I didn't mean…' Mrs Jarvis began.

'Of course you didn't. Thank you.' Cecily nodded at the door and Mrs Jarvis pressed her lips together before turning to leave.

When Mrs Jarvis had closed the door—extremely firmly—behind her, Cecily walked over to the window to look at the view. It was very charming: formal gardens falling away to grass, a lake, and then the rolling pastureland that she knew well from her walks.

She should be pleased for Felix that his staff cared so much about him. He'd suffered a terrible misfortune in losing his wife so early, and it was wonderful that his staff were so very eager that he be happy. Hopefully Mrs Jarvis would not repeat her insolence.

She was proud of herself, she realised, for having made it clear that she wouldn't accept such rudeness. Only a short time ago, when still at her aunt and uncle's, she had almost *expected* people to speak to her like that and would certainly not have summoned the steel to reply in the way that she had today.

Her thoughts were interrupted by a tap on the door, followed by the handle turning and Lizzie's face peering around it.

'Can I help you get ready for dinner, my lady?' she asked.

'Yes, please.'

An hour later, she went downstairs to join the assembled company in the castle's great hall.

Felix was already there, conversing with his aunts.

'My dear,' he said, walking over to her and taking her hand and raising it to his lips. 'That is a ravishing dress; I am most impressed with all your new purchases.' Clearly he had decided that he must do his very best to be as convincing as possible with their charade.

Cecily swallowed, her skin still almost *tingling* from where he had kissed it.

'Thank you,' she managed to say.

Lady Bradstock, from behind Felix, laughed. 'Lady Cecily appears quite overcome to see you,' she observed. 'How very refreshing to see a young couple genuinely in love with each other.'

'Indeed,' said Felix, his smile again failing to reach his eyes. He addressed Cecily. 'Some of our other guests arrived a little after you did; they were shown to their chambers and we expect them to join us shortly, after which we will have dinner. This evening I have little to offer you all beyond some card games and informal music; we expect the party to begin in earnest tomorrow, and you will be pleased, I am sure, to hear that I intend to hold a number of larger parties over Christmas.'

'That all sounds wonderful,' Cecily said. It did, in fact sound delightful. Or it would have done if it didn't feel so heartbreaking to be standing next to a Felix who was acting like a very polite and attentive stranger. Perhaps—hopefully—the activities over the next two weeks would break down this barrier that had sprung up between them.

'Ah.' Felix looked over to the door in a somewhat exaggerated fashion, as though overjoyed at any excuse to talk to someone else. 'Here they are.'

Soon he was performing introductions and Cecily was accepting felicitations and doing her best to remember the names of those to whom she was introduced.

It was *very* difficult not to look out of the corner of her eye at Felix when she was talking to others, which was obviously pathetic but at least, she supposed, if anyone noticed they would be convinced by the engagement.

She didn't want *Felix* to notice, however, so she did her very best to become very busy speaking to the people surrounding her, several of whom were indeed excellent company. She was soon laughing and—almost—enjoying herself.

When everyone who had arrived that day was finally assembled, dinner was called. Felix, from the other side of the room, where he was talking to some ladies—at least two of whom, to Cecily's eye, were far too forward in their behaviour; indeed if one were feeling uncharitable, one might call them unbecomingly flirtatious—nodded at his companions and then began to make his way across the room.

Knowing as she did that their engagement was fake, she really shouldn't have felt the thrill that she did at the knowledge that he was walking towards her.

He held out his arm and said, 'I believe we should lead the way.'

As she took his arm, doing her best not to feel at all conscious of the fact that they were standing so close together, she smiled up at him, to signal to all those who might be watching—it felt as though a *lot* of eyes were on them—that they were indeed the genuinely betrothed couple everyone imagined them to be.

'I trust that you will approve of my chef,' Felix said with what felt like quite awful politeness as they moved forward in stately fashion towards the hall and then the dining room.

'I'm sure I will,' Cecily responded equally politely.

Once they were seated, Felix at the head of the table and Cecily to his side, he said, 'I trust that you are happy with your bedchamber?'

'Yes, thank you. It's even more beautiful and luxurious than the one I had in Berkeley Square.'

'I'm so pleased. Please do let me or Mrs Jarvis know if there is anything else you need.'

'That's very kind; I'm sure there won't be.'

And so it went on. Polite inanity after polite inanity.

The only good thing about the meal was the food—which was extraordinarily good; their stilted and dreadfully polite conversation continued throughout. Cecily felt quite despairing about how dreadful it was. What if this was it? The end of her friendship with Felix? Their friendship had been one of the best things in her life for as long as she could remember and the thought of losing it was almost too much to bear.

She looked at his strong, straight profile as he joked—very mildly— with the jolly Countess on his right about the snow that his head gardener had told him he believed was on the way.

He was *so* handsome. And so kind. And she enjoyed his company so much when he wasn't being this polite.

She wanted that friendship to return.

Maybe she should *fight* for it. Talk to him in the way they used to talk.

'I love snow,' she said.

The Countess laughed and said, 'So do I, although I believe it to be deeply unfashionable to do so.'

Felix said, 'I am ambivalent about snow.'

'Snowballs and snowmen are a great deal of fun,' Cecily said, slightly desperately.

'Snow can be perilous for livestock and poor people,' Felix said repressively.

Cecily tried not to sigh audibly.

'I'm sure that it is not particularly perilous for *your* livestock and tenants,' the Countess said. 'A good landlord, such as you, and my husband, must mitigate such peril to a great extent.'

'Also—' Cecily wasn't giving up on this conversation yet '—any kind of extreme weather is difficult for some people and livestock, I imagine. Excessively hot days must also be difficult for many, but that does not mean that one should not try to find enjoyment in them.'

'That is very true.' The Countess pointed her knife at Felix. 'Do not tell me that you have not enjoyed rowing on a lake on a beautiful summer's day. And do not tell me that you do not enjoy snowballs and snowmen.'

Felix nodded. 'You have me there. I *do* enjoy both a warm summer's day *and* snow activities.'

'We must agree now that if it does indeed snow over the next few days we will wrap up warmly and go outside and enjoy it,' said the Countess.

'Of course,' said Felix, directing bland smiles at both the ladies.

And then the three of them—mainly the Countess—spoke about snow until the next course was brought in.

After which Cecily gave up on trying to re-establish friendly relations with Felix and had a lengthy conversation about growing oranges in a glasshouse with the Countess's elderly husband, who was seated on her other side and very interested in exotic fruits.

Eventually, the end of the meal was reached, and Felix's mother-in-law, Viscountess Beaulieu, told the company that she believed it was time for the ladies to withdraw and leave the gentlemen to their port.

Cecily had very little wish to speak to the Viscountess; one could only feel awkward as the fiancée of a widower when speaking to his late wife's mother, irrespective of whether one's engagement were fake or real.

The Viscountess, unfortunately, did not seem to reciprocate Cecily's feelings. Within a very small number of seconds of Cecily's seating herself on a sofa in the long drawing room to which they had retired, she sat down right next to her, in such a way that it would be impossible for anyone else to join them. It was clear that the Viscountess wished to engage her in private conversation.

Perhaps Cecily could direct the conversation in a non-contentious direction.

'I very much like this room,' she said. 'The pale-blue velvet and the gilt marry beautifully together.' Oh. How annoying. *Why* had she decided to use the word *marry*? It was as though she had a guilty conscience…

'Yes, they do; I like this room too.' The Viscountess did not take her eyes from Cecily's face. 'I am very pleased to have the opportunity to speak to you alone.'

'Oh.' Cecily tried not to gulp out loud. After her unpleasant conversation with Mrs Jarvis earlier in the day she had very little appetite for a second one, with a lady who had even more cause than the housekeeper to be displeased about the marriage, and to whom Cecily could not reasonably speak firmly. 'Indeed.'

The Viscountess laughed. 'You look most uncomfortable. You do not, however, have anything about which to be concerned in my regard. The Duke and I enjoy an excellent relationship and, out of consideration for my feelings, he told me—' she pressed Cecily's hand speakingly and swivelled her eyes to both sides as though checking that no one could overhear their conversation, before continuing '—the exact circumstances under which your betrothal took place. I have every sympathy for you and fully support his course of action.' She raised her voice a little and said, 'I wish you both very happy.'

'Thank you,' Cecily said, hugely relieved. This was much easier than it had been listening to Mrs Jarvis. She supposed that both the Viscountess and Mrs Jarvis had the same aim—Felix's happiness—and it was just that the Viscountess knew the truth and Mrs Jarvis did not. Probably everyone who cared about Felix would feel the same way as did Mrs Jarvis if they thought the engagement real.

'Not at all.' The Viscountess lowered her voice again. 'I am very pleased that he was able to help and pledged to him, and now to you, to do everything in my power to help you too.'

Cecily swallowed, a lump forming in her throat. It

was *very* nice for another person to be so very kind to her.

'I would also say that, before Felix spoke to me, I was pleased for him when I heard the news. It is now six years since we lost my daughter, and, while we will always mourn her memory, I would not expect my son-in-law to remain alone forever unless he wishes to do so. I desire the best for him and would be very happy to see him in a second felicitous marriage.'

'It is wonderful to see how mutually respectful your relationship with the Duke is,' Cecily said, thinking with envy of the young lady with whom Felix might eventually fall in love. 'I agree that—' she stopped for a moment because for some reason it felt as though her voice was in danger of failing '—one would hope that he could find happiness again.'

The Viscountess smiled at her and then said, 'So tell me more about yourself. I understand that life was quite difficult for you with Lord and Lady Milton. I make no bones about the fact that I am shocked that this is the first time I have met you when you have never, I understand, journeyed away since you arrived here aged seven, and I have met your aunt and uncle, and their daughters, on any number of occasions. What are your favourite pastimes?'

Cecily surprised herself by being almost tempted

to tell her about her writing, about the plans she had for further books following the publisher asking Felix if she would provide them with more. Felix and Holly were the only two people she had ever told, and she hadn't ever imagined that she'd tell anyone else.

'I enjoy walking,' she settled on.

'Oh, yes; I understand that it was during walks that you met the Duke?'

'Indeed. In fact, the very first time we met, many years ago, shortly after I arrived in Sussex at the age of seven, I fell out of a tree and he rescued me from the bush in which I had landed.'

The Viscountess laughed. 'Did you regularly get into scrapes as a child? Tell me more.'

The time passed very quickly as they exchanged anecdotes of their own childhoods and that of Felix's late wife, and some of the scrapes into which the Viscountess's grandsons, Felix's boys, often found themselves.

'They sound like delightful boys,' Cecily said.

'Indeed they are,' came a deep voice from behind her, causing her to jump in her seat.

'Felix,' she said, a little faintly.

'Cecily,' he said, sounding amused.

'Come and join us,' the Viscountess said, waving her hand in the direction of the nearest chair, which happened to be vacant.

'Thank you; I'd be delighted.' Felix sat himself

down in the chair, which had seemed a perfectly normal size before his arrival but now suddenly seemed tiny.

Cecily studied him for a moment. Why, having evinced no desire whatsoever to speak to her during dinner, and having then spent a very long time with the men before joining them here, had he decided to join her and his mother-in-law? To maintain appearances perhaps, or because he was nervous about what they'd been talking about. Definitely not for the pleasure of her company.

'I feel that we should have some music.' The Viscountess stood up. 'Do excuse me for a moment while I organise it. Garth, perhaps you might sit here next to your betrothed for a few moments until I return.'

And off she went, looking very much like a woman who did not plan to return at all.

Cecily looked sideways at Felix.

His thigh was so *solid* in his evening breeches.

His shoulder was so *big*.

His profile was so *alluring*. Also, it was a little grumpy looking; he clearly had not been planning this when he came over to speak to her and the Viscountess.

'Do you like music?' she asked.

'It depends.'

'On what does it depend?' Cecily persevered.

'On whether it is good or not,' Felix said, as though

she was very, very stupid, which for some reason made Cecily giggle.

'That is funny…because?' Felix enquired.

'I don't know,' she said, still laughing. 'I think because you sound so utterly bored and despairing.' And suddenly, even though Felix was still looking unusually forbidding, Cecily felt much better, because she'd finally felt able to speak freely to him as she'd been used to do.

'I am of course in no way bored or despairing,' he said, cocking an eyebrow at her, 'but I'm pleased to hear that if I *were* in such a mood it would amuse you.'

Cecily giggled more. 'I will look forward to discovering whether or not you find the music acceptably good.'

'I won't,' Felix said out of the corner of his mouth, as his mother-in-law announced to the assembled company that one of the young ladies of the party would be singing a delightful Christmas minuet for them.

And Cecily—now that she and Felix were suddenly back on their old friendly terms—felt as though her whole being were lighter and happier.

# *Chapter Ten*

*Felix*

Well, Felix had not expected that.

He had not expected his mother-in-law purposely to leave him alone with his 'betrothed', given that she knew that they were *not* in fact genuinely engaged.

And he had not expected that, if she *had* left them alone, Cecily would have managed to disarm him like that.

Since their…since the…he didn't even want to think about it. But since they—he—had been stupid in the carriage, he'd very much wanted to avoid Cecily. Because what they'd done, the way they'd behaved, had been wrong, very wrong. He'd *felt* things, and he didn't want to feel things.

It had shocked him that his mother-in-law had been so ready to accept that he might have fallen in love with and wish to marry someone else. It felt like an incredible betrayal of Aurora. It wanted only his sons to begin to call someone else their mother and the betrayal would be complete.

None of this was Cecily's fault, however.

And she and he had been friends for a very long time. Close friends.

He didn't want to lose her friendship; he wanted *this* from her, what was happening right now between them, what they'd always had: laughter and mutual understanding.

And he didn't want her to be upset just because they had mutually stumbled into this preposterous position.

So he smiled at her chuckling away at his grumpiness about the music and said, 'Minx.'

She halted her chuckling for a moment to direct a particularly delightful—and, quite clearly purposely, minxy—smile up at him, which did something very odd and particularly disconcerting to his heart.

Which was confusing. It made him just want to grin right back at Cecily, but it also made him feel very guilty, despite what Laura, his mother-in-law, had said about him marrying again.

There was only one thing for it: he was going to have to listen to the music.

The devoted mama of the young lady singing quite clearly had her eye on Felix's friend Jim, better known in Society as the outstandingly rich and eligible Mr Beaufort, as a suitable candidate for her daughter's hand; she suggested very forcefully that Jim stand up and turn the pages for her daughter, and, if Felix wasn't mistaken, she actually arranged the two of them so that he would have a direct view down the young lady's dress.

This was the first house party of this nature that Felix had hosted since the loss of Aurora. If he weren't supposedly engaged, he would, he realised, himself be the target of a great number of match-making mothers. He should be grateful to Cecily for the reprieve. Although, of course, he wouldn't have hosted a house party such as this if it hadn't been for the situation in which they found themselves.

The young lady at the pianoforte looked quite pained as she sang. Her voice was tuneful but quiet, perhaps due to shyness; it would have been well-suited to singing in the ensemble at the opera but not to a solo, for example. Jim, keeping his eyes trained resolutely away from the young lady's cleavage and only turning the pages when there was an over-long pause in the playing, looked equally pained.

When her mother stated, at much higher volume than that at which her daughter had been singing, that she would of course bow to audience demand and perform an encore, her daughter looked as though she would like to cry.

'This is terrible,' whispered Cecily. 'We should rescue her.'

Felix nodded.

'Your singing and playing are very beautiful, Miss Lindgrove,' his mother-in-law was saying. 'We must not, however, presume upon your generosity for too long. I trust that one of the other young ladies present will relieve you and take their turn in performing.'

None of the other young ladies looked particularly enthusiastic.

Miss Lindgrove began to look a little tearful.

'Perhaps,' Cecily said, projecting her voice quite impressively, so that she was entirely audible and yet in no way strident, 'we might all sing some Christmas carols together. If no one else wishes to play, I would be happy to accompany the singing. I am not at all expert, however, so must encourage anyone—*anyone*—else to play in my stead.'

'Very kind of you,' Felix told her in a low tone, when it turned out that no one was showing any signs whatsoever of either volunteering themselves or volunteering someone else to do the carol-singing accompaniment. 'Do you—' there was no polite way to put it '—are you in fact able to play?'

'Not at all,' said Cecily sunnily as she rose to walk towards the instrument. 'But how difficult can it be?' she added over her shoulder.

Good God. Felix stood to walk with her and stand

next to her. He was the possessor of a loud, if not particularly accurate, baritone, which he would attempt to employ to drown out any particularly defective playing on Cecily's part. It wasn't surprising that she couldn't play; her aunt and uncle would hardly have paid for lessons for her.

Where the Duke and his intended led, the entire company followed. Very quickly, they were all arranged around the pianoforte, Cecily at the keyboard, Felix behind her ready to turn the music sheets—should she actually attempt to play from them—and sing loudly, the others around them.

'Does anyone have a preference as to what we sing first?' Cecily asked.

Over the ensuing babble, Felix said, 'I think that you should choose, my, ah, dearest. And if you do not have a preference, perhaps it might be my privilege to choose, as your betrothed.' He bent low and whispered in Cecily's ear, 'Is there a particular song that you are able to play?' From the way she was sitting, with her hands in her lap rather than arranged over the keys in the practised way that he had seen with other ladies, it was clear that she did indeed not play, but perhaps she had learnt some very basic notes.

'What is your favourite Christmas song?' she asked him, not whispering at all. 'Do you have a book including words so that everyone might join in?'

'Yes, I think we do.' His mother-in-law stepped

forward and, after a short rummage in a cabinet to the side, produced such a book with triumph.

Felix took the book and, after a short flick through it, realised that the music meant absolutely nothing to him. Choosing one that didn't seem to have many notes for the pianist to play, he said, '"The First Noel".'

'Oh, that's one of my favourites too,' said Cecily.

And then she placed her hands above the keys and Felix braced himself, almost wincing on her behalf. Although she didn't *seem* particularly concerned; perhaps she really didn't care what people thought.

Oddly, the first few notes sounded surprisingly *right*, and in time.

And then quite quickly he realised that her playing was…competent.

As she and those gathered around the piano began to sing, he realised that Cecily's playing was *more* than competent.

It was…musical, it was lovely.

And Cecily's voice, on the high parts, rose above everyone else's in the most delightful way, so that the skin on Felix's arms and at the back of his neck prickled.

As she continued to play and he watched, he couldn't have looked away from her if he'd tried. The curve of her cheek, the delicate line of her neck, the light touch of her fingers rippling across the keys, the view he had of her cleavage—which to his shame he was struggling not to look down, in contrast to Jim with Miss Lindgrove…

And then, during a moment of pause for the singers, as she continued to play, for the merest of seconds Cecily directed a raised-eyebrow smile up at him, as though she'd known all along that he thought she couldn't play. And if Felix's skin had tingled before, he now felt the smile through his whole body.

He felt somehow as though he shouldn't be enjoying this singalong as much as he was. He hadn't *expected* to enjoy it; it really wasn't the kind of thing he would ever have chosen to do. From the smiles on their faces, the enthusiasm with which they were joining in—even the somewhat nose-out-of-joint mother of the previous pianist—and their clamours for more when each song finished, it was clear that the others were all enjoying it too. It was lovely that they could all enjoy such a simple pleasure together, but it did feel odd to Felix. Maybe because he'd found Christmas a difficult time since he'd lost Aurora.

Eventually, after many songs, he noticed Cecily roll her shoulders and neck, just a little, as though they were aching but she didn't wish anyone to know that.

'I think we have imposed on Lady Cecily quite sufficiently,' he said when the song that they were singing, 'Good Christian Men Rejoice', came to an end.

He held his arm out to her so that she might stand up from the stool. 'Perhaps some of us might like to play cards instead?'

Cecily took his arm and they began to walk back across the room towards the sofa on which they had previously been sitting.

'When did you learn to play?' he asked. 'I had not expected Lady Milton to have provided you with lessons.'

'She didn't. Holly is an excellent musician, and she taught me. I can only play simple pieces as I didn't have the opportunity to spend hours on end practising, but I am reasonably competent as you see to accompany singing. And I enjoy singing myself, and no one can hear one or stop one when one is at a distance from the house.'

'You have a beautiful voice,' Felix told her.

'Thank you; that is very kind.'

'Not kind; just true.'

As they sat back down together, his mother-in-law, Laura, joined them.

'I think cards are an excellent idea,' she said. 'Lady Cecily, do you have a preference?'

'I am not a very experienced card player, unfortunately,' Cecily said. 'I will watch so that I do not ruin the game for those of you who are more experienced.'

'Have you played at all?' Felix asked her as Laura turned to organise the moving of some occasional tables so that others might play. 'Other than Commerce when I was in London, with which I think you were not particularly familiar?'

'Only games for children, really. Holly and I did play a few games for two people during evenings where the family were all occupied and we were left to our own devices—truly some very enjoyable evenings I might add—' as always she clearly did not wish for his pity '—but I don't know how to play conventional adult card games.'

'Why don't I teach you?' Felix suggested. 'Now. And then tomorrow evening you will be able to join in, if you wish, without feeling that you are continually having to ascertain the rules.'

'If you're quite sure that you don't mind, that would be wonderful.' Cecily's beam was delightful.

'Of course I don't mind. I will enjoy it.' It was certainly true that one could gain a lot of happiness from helping others; Felix could feel his heart swelling just from how much he could see Cecily was enjoying herself this evening.

As the others arranged themselves into groups for their games, Felix and Cecily moved to a corner to begin Felix's lessons. It was very refreshing, he reflected, to be able to spend time in an environment such as this conversing with a young lady whose company one enjoyed without giving rise to gossip and conjecture about his intentions, because his intentions were already—falsely—known.

'Let us begin with whist,' he suggested.

'I'd be delighted.'

Cecily began to giggle when he'd got perhaps halfway through the rules.

'The rules are perhaps amusing?' he asked.

'No, *you* are amusing,' she said.

'Thank you for the compliment,' he said, knowing that it certainly was *not* complimentary.

'It is merely that I can't remember anything you said because you're going so fast,' she explained. 'I feel that perhaps if you teach someone something you need to go a little more slowly. Or have a considerably more capable student than I.'

'I hadn't thought I was going particularly fast.'

'Well, either you were going very fast, or I am *not* gifted at understanding the rules of card games.'

'As a gentleman—' he bowed his head very slightly '—I can only take full responsibility for the problem and can certainly not suggest that you might have any problems in comprehension.'

'I am very pleased that you are taking full responsibility.' Cecily grinned at him.

'Minx.'

'Would you care to begin again? Much more slowly this time?'

'Certainly. Being a gentleman, I will not, obviously, suggest that you should pay more attention this time.'

'I am very pleased to hear it,' she said, twinkling at him.

A few minutes later, she stared at him, brow furrowed, and then said, 'Trump?'

'Trump,' he confirmed, nodding.

'Um. What?'

He looked at her, one eyebrow raised.

'Hmm,' she said. 'As a lady, I should perhaps acknowledge that there is a small possibility that I have been struggling to concentrate on your explanations and that they might have been perfectly good explanations.'

Felix laughed. 'As a gentleman I must continue to take full responsibility for the fact that you are apparently still almost entirely in the dark as to the rules of this usually very-easily-understood game.'

'That is very kind of you. Are you usually able to explain things well?' Cecily looked directly into his eyes, her own eyes limpid, a bland smile on her lips.

'I am—' he swallowed, unable to take his eyes off hers, and suddenly not quite sure what they'd been talking about '—I am…'

'You are?' She raised an eyebrow, still gazing at him.

'Yes, I am,' he said firmly.

Cecily's smile grew.

'You are what?'

He had no idea what she was talking about. He had no idea what he'd been talking about either. All he could think about was the way her smile displayed her perfect teeth and a dimple formed at each side of her mouth when she smiled like this.

'I just am,' he said, giving up trying to remember and just grinning at her.

Cecily laughed and then bit her lip, and, damn, he wanted to kiss her.

'Would you like to visit my library?' he asked, very sure that he'd like to be alone with her at this moment.

'I would like that very much,' she said. 'I like… books.'

'More than you like card playing?' he asked, catching sight of the cards on the table between them as he stood up and finally remembering how their conversation had begun.

'It is not,' she said, as they began to move across the room, 'that I do not like cards. It is that some people's rules are very confusing.'

'I see.' Felix nodded at his mother-in-law, and said, 'I am just taking Lady Cecily to visit the library so that she might choose a book to read this evening.'

'What a good idea,' she said, smiling at Cecily. 'The library here is excellent; I am sure you will find something you like. What is your favourite reading?'

'I must confess to a very unerudite love of modern fiction,' Cecily said.

'Wonderful. I have the same taste. Garth will be able to direct you to the books he has acquired on my behalf.'

Once they had left the drawing room, Felix, suddenly felt somewhat awkward. Why had he suggested this? Oh, yes. He'd wanted to be alone with Cecily. Why, though? Why would that be a good thing? Well, it would be good perhaps to discuss again how they should navigate their situation while Cecily was staying at Garth. That was it.

And, of course, it *would* be good for her to find a book to read; everyone benefited from burying themselves in an enjoyable book, and she had had a lot of upset in her life recently.

'The library is along here,' he directed her, and then they walked in silence until they reached the door.

'Ohhhh,' Cecily breathed as she entered the room ahead of him. 'This is *wonderful*.'

Felix closed the door and then looked around, as though seeing his library afresh. It was a large, rectangular room, with a gallery, with both levels lined floor to ceiling with leatherbound books, other than a few alcoves for tables and chairs, as well as his desk, the whole decorated with deep reds and dark greens. Yes, when he thought about it dispassionately, through Cecily's eyes, he had to recognise that it was indeed wonderful.

'Thank you,' he said. 'I count myself very fortunate. It was the third Duke who began it, and each successive Duke has added to it.'

'Which number Duke are you?'

Felix laughed. 'Truly, you have been sent into my life as my fake fiancée to stop me taking things for granted. If I am honest, I had assumed that everyone knew what number Duke I am, because, well, I suppose most of the people I know *care*.'

'I suppose they might worry that you would find it rude if they didn't know.'

'And worry that they would then receive less of my ducal favour. Good *God*,' said Felix, revolted.

'I know.' Cecily shook her head. 'You have many crosses to bear.'

'One of them apparently being you,' said Felix, advancing on her as she giggled. 'No respect whatsoever for my ducal authority apparently.'

'Oh, dear. I'm so sorry.' She giggled some more as he came to a halt in front of her.

He put a finger under her chin and tilted her face up so that he could look at her properly. Her face was just so…*perfect*. Heart-shaped, her smile simultaneously innocent and tempting…

He leaned his head down towards hers. He knew he was going to do it; he had a vague feeling that he was going to regret it if he did, but…no, he couldn't help it. He *was* going to do it.

He watched Cecily's tongue trace along her lips and her eyelids flutter.

And then he leaned even closer until his mouth was almost touching hers and his eyes were looking right into hers.

He took a deep breath, just as Cecily said, 'Felix,' on a long sigh, and reached her hands up to rest on his chest.

'Mmm?' he said, bringing his hands up to cup her face.

And then, very, very deliberately—which, somewhere in the far reaches of his mind, he registered and thought was odd because this was surely the exact opposite of what he should really be doing—he moved forward to bridge the gap between their lips.

He kissed her very gently, slowly, languorously, over and over again, for a long time, Cecily responding most delightfully, their lips and tongues exploring and caressing. Felix's hands remained on Cecily's face, and hers on his chest.

And then, suddenly, the hunger, the lust he'd felt for her during their interminable dinner this evening came to the fore, and he was kissing her with a deep passion, which she immediately met with passion of her own.

He swept her up into his arms and carried her over

to the nearest armchair and sat down with her in his arms. He turned her so that she was facing him, somehow straddling him, and then they were kissing again, with great intensity, Cecily's arms wrapped round Felix's neck and his holding her close, one hand in her hair and the other around her waist.

And then she moved her hands into his hair, before leaning back a little and running them down his chest, feeling, exploring with her fingers. She tugged a little at his shirt, and then harder so that it came out of his breeches, before running her hands up inside it, feeling the planes of his stomach and chest, before lifting the shirt and kissing her way down it to the top of his breeches. And then she lifted her head and smiled at him while she ran her hands further down the outside of his breeches.

Felix closed his eyes as desire rippled through his whole body, before running his own hands lightly down Cecily's sides, before moving to cup her breasts with his hands.

'Felix,' she squeaked.

'Cecily,' he murmured.

And then he stroked her gently with his thumbs and she gave a low moan, and he was lost, tugging urgently at her dress and moving so that she could touch him more.

He stroked, kissed, nipped at her breasts and *loved* the way she kept moaning his name. And then, when she reached inside his breeches, he ran his hand up under her skirts, to the top of her thigh, before beginning to touch her intimately as he had in the carriage.

And then, as she held him, he plunged a finger inside her, and then he could see that she was lost, holding tightly to him and moaning his name as he took her to the heights of pleasure with his fingers, climaxing himself at the same time as she somehow knew how to touch and hold him.

Afterwards, she lay in his arms in her glorious semi-nakedness as he kissed her forehead and cheeks and then just held her.

'Felix,' she said a long time later.

'Mmm?' He couldn't believe they'd just done that. In his *library.* With a house full of people. Any of whom might have come in. It had been nice, though. Well, not *nice*. It had been wonderful. Astonishing.

'I didn't…know about…*that*,' she whispered.

'What…exactly…didn't you know about?' he couldn't help asking.

She reached up and pulled his head down and whispered in his ear, which made him laugh, and which also put his head within kissing distance of her breasts, and then, somehow, they did it all again…

And this time, Cecily had more idea of what *she* was doing to *him*, and it was more calculated, not just a happy accident.

It was good. Very, very good. Better than good.

Eventually, when, again, they were lying in a tangle, the candlelight playing over her skin in the most alluring way, she looked up at him, and laughed, and said, 'I think we came in here for you to lend me a book.'

Felix frowned, trying to think back. 'Did we? Or did we…?' *Oh.* He'd suddenly been overcome with a very single-minded desire to be alone with Cecily because he'd wanted to do something very similar to *that*, although he had perhaps not imagined then that they might do quite so *much*. Searching for a book had been an excuse. As had his idea that they might discuss their situation further. Had he even mentioned that out loud, or had he been pretending to himself about that?

No, he hadn't mentioned any of this out loud to Cecily; he had indeed suggested that they go and find a book for her.

'Yes, we did,' he said. 'Would you like to look for a book now?' He looked at her and swallowed as she sat up, still half-naked.

She looked down at herself and then allowed her eyes to roam down his body, which caused him to reach for her again.

'I think,' she whispered eventually, quite a long time later, her voice ragged against his ear, 'we should find a book and go to bed. It must be very, very late now.'

'It must indeed,' he agreed. 'And, yes, we should.' They really couldn't risk anyone finding them. If they did, he would *actually* have to marry her, and he would have to do it immediately.

And he did not want to marry her. Or anyone.

God. What had he been thinking? They were friends, very good friends. They weren't lovers. They were not genuinely engaged. Friends did not do things like this.

They would have to be incredibly careful that no one found out so that Cecily's reputation remained intact, so that if she did wish to marry one day she could still do so.

'Could I ask a question?' Cecily pulled her dress up so that she was covered, and then smoothed her skirts down. They would have to stay in the shadows on their way to their chambers; if anyone saw her looking the way she was they would be able to hazard an extremely good guess as to what she'd been doing.

'Question? Of course.'

'I think you must know about these things, so I presume that there can be no possibility that I could be…' She pressed her lips together and made a vague gesture with her hands.

'That you could be? Oh! You mean… No, you could not be with child after that. We didn't fully… Yes, no.'

She exhaled hard and then said, 'Good. I didn't think you would, but I just…'

'Of course. God, I'm so sorry. We shouldn't have.'

They really, really shouldn't have. Although…

'It was…nice, though?' Cecily's smile was outrageous, and if he hadn't been absolutely certain that it was entirely the wrong thing to do, he would have been hard pushed not to do it all over again.

'You are a minx,' he said very deliberately.

She turned to walk towards the nearest wall of books, before shooting the most ridiculously suggestive pout over her shoulder, which made him laugh, a lot.

They *really* shouldn't do this again.

They shouldn't.

It *had* been nice, however, remarkably nice; Cecily was very much right about that. And, while friends certainly did not do things like that, they'd already done them, and as long as no one found out and he ensured that she couldn't possibly become with child, would it really matter—given that they'd already done it twice—if they kissed a little again? Just occasionally. Just for the duration of their engagement? If that was what Cecily wanted?

'What book would you recommend?' Cecily asked, trailing a finger along the spines of the books, which caused Felix to feel almost envious of the *books*—was he losing his mind? 'In case I can't get to sleep tonight because I can't help thinking about what a terrible host you are?'

'Let me see.' He stood up and rearranged his clothing so that he was decent, if still somewhat dishevelled, and went over to stand behind her, not touching her, but very close. He leaned to speak into her ear. 'Tell me exactly what it is that you like.'

He allowed himself to trail his finger down her back, all the way to the base of her spine, in the way that she'd touched the books, smiling when he felt her whole body shiver.

She leaned back, just a little, so that she was against him.

'I like...*nice* things,' she said, her voice husky. And then she moved against him, just a little. 'Things that make me...*feel*.'

He slid his hands around her waist and then up her body. 'Like this?' He heard his voice rasp.

'Mmm, maybe. Could you...*explain* a little better?'

He leaned down to kiss her in the nape of her neck, and then nuzzled and licked her there while his hands worked on her body.

And then, somehow, she was naked again, fully naked this time, pressed up against the books, and so was he, and, God, it was illicit and daring and breathtakingly glorious.

It was wrong, though. Cecily had been an extremely willing participant and she couldn't become with child through what they had done, and so as long as no one found out, she couldn't be harmed by it, but she had so much more to lose from it than he did that he had a great responsibility to her, and he must make sure, therefore, that they didn't succumb to temptation again.

# *Chapter Eleven*

*Cecily*

Cecily propped herself up on her elbows and looked at Felix's wonderful, handsome face. His features had been so familiar to her for so long. It was almost as though he was part of her. She couldn't imagine her life without him. Whenever he'd been away, she'd missed him so much until he got back and always been so pleased to see him again. She'd always vaguely thought—hoped—they would be friends forever.

But this…

She'd never imagined…

She was never going to forget this.

This was not something that friends did, she was sure. This was something that lovers did.

Felix didn't love her, though; she knew that. He was just…*enjoying* himself. Maybe he enjoyed himself regularly like this with all sorts of women. It was impossible to know how a gentleman might live.

She really didn't like the thought of him doing such things with anyone but her.

Ever.

Because…because she loved him. So very, very much. Which was not a good thing given that he clearly didn't love her.

Although…did it matter? Hadn't she, really, always loved him, she now realised? And did it mean anything? No, it didn't. He clearly wouldn't love her in the way that she loved him, and, actually, she liked the idea of the life she was going to lead. She had her writing, she would have an income, she would have a close companion in Holly, and she would make friends where she lived. For many women, that would be a far preferable way of life to that of a married woman.

And if she and Felix never progressed beyond where they were now, they would never have a relationship that could be ruined. The main thing was to ensure that they maintained their friendship. What would be truly awful would be never seeing him again.

'We should *really* get that book and go to bed,' he said, smiling wryly at her. 'It must be almost morning.'

'Yes.' Given that she didn't want to lose his friendship, she shouldn't make him feel uncomfortable by betraying how she felt. 'We should. You're right.' She smiled at him in the way that she hoped one might smile at someone with whom one was *not* in love.

'Are you all right?' he asked, frowning.

Oh. Obviously the smile hadn't worked. 'Yes, thank you. Just a little tired.'

'Well, that's understandable. It's very late, or indeed very *early*.'

She laughed politely as they moved towards the door.

'Do you know the way to your chamber?' Felix whispered when they got there.

'Yes.'

'Perhaps we should go separately, then, so that there is no risk of our being seen together?'

'Yes. Goodnight.'

And that was that. After the most extraordinary evening, she skulked off alone along the corridors to her bedchamber, where she found Lizzie asleep in a chair in the boudoir that adjoined her chamber, clearly having waited up for her.

Cecily disrobed very quietly and then, once she was in her nightgown with her hair brushed out, woke Lizzie, thanked her and told her to go straight to bed, before herself crawling into bed and crying—for what reason she knew not—before falling asleep thinking, of course, of Felix.

* * *

Breakfast the next morning was a very strange experience. Felix was there, as were most of the gentlemen of the party and several of the women. When you'd had very little sleep, it was extremely confusing having to pretend simultaneously to be someone's fiancée *and* that you hadn't done *that* with them. Cecily settled for smiling at everyone and saying absolutely nothing to anyone, and doing her very best not to follow Felix with her eyes and wonder what he was saying to his neighbours at the table.

She did feel a little less bleary-eyed once she'd eaten some toast and some fruit, and when Felix's mother-in-law suggested that those who liked snow wrap up warm and accompany her on a walk around the castle grounds, had sufficient energy to exclaim, 'Oh! I didn't realise it had snowed overnight.'

'Yes, indeed; it's quite deep,' the Viscountess told her.

Cecily wondered what else she might not have noticed this morning when immersed in her thoughts.

The Viscountess was very good at organising people; she had the entire party of over twenty people—many of whom had *very* strong ideas about what they should wear and do—dressed for the weather and ready to walk within under an hour of the conclusion of breakfast.

Cecily found herself walking in a little group of ladies, including the Viscountess, and bent her attention as hard as she could to their conversation. These were nice people and this was a lovely house party, and she might never have such an experience again, so she should not allow her feelings about Felix to prevent her from taking as much amusement as she could.

She was engaged in deep conversation with Felix's mother-in-law when Felix's voice at her side made her jump.

'It is a beautiful day, is it not?' he said.

'Yes, indeed it is. Lady Beaulieu and I were just commenting on the beauty of frozen spiders' webs. They make one feel as though one were entering an icy fairy tale.'

'Your betrothed has quite a way with words,' the Viscountess said. 'She was weaving stories for me about fairy queens and other wintry beings; I might almost beg her to entertain us this evening with some of her stories.'

Cecily laughed. 'I'm sure no one would like to listen to my imaginings.'

'On the contrary,' Felix said, 'I'm sure they would. I myself have had the privilege of listening to some of Lady Cecily's stories and they are quite wonderful.'

Cecily glared at him.

'However,' he continued smoothly, 'I fully understand that she would not wish to hold forth at a gathering.'

'Indeed I would not,' Cecily said severely.

The Viscountess laughed. 'I will leave you to walk together to complete your argument.' And she fell behind them and joined the group of ladies who were walking a few paces behind.

'Sorry,' said Felix.

'As you should be,' said Cecily.

He laughed and then held out his arm as they emerged from a wooded area into a more open expanse. 'It might be slippery.'

'Thank you.'

Neither of them spoke for a few seconds. Cecily was waiting to see whether Felix would say anything about last night and Felix was in fact saying nothing.

And, actually, he hadn't said anything after the *first* occasion on which they'd kissed, so perhaps it was customary not to mention these things. Or perhaps it was *Felix's* custom not to mention them, in all events.

'I hope you slept well,' he said eventually, into the silence.

'Yes, thank you. I hope you did too.' Cecily didn't dare look at him as she spoke; it seemed quite peculiar to be referring to how well they'd slept when they both knew that they'd only been in their respective beds for a very short time. Obviously a subject change was required. 'This is the first time that I've walked around this side of the castle; it's very interesting to see the area that I know so well from a different perspective.'

'I can imagine. Have you ever walked as far as the lake we have here?'

'No, although I have come across your river on my walks, and found it very pretty.'

'We must walk to the lake while you are here. I am of course biased, but I believe it to be very pretty also.'

'I'm sure it is.'

They continued again in silence for a few long moments. Cecily couldn't decide whether it was a comfortable silence, of the kind that they used to have occasionally when walking—although most of the time they would chatter—or whether it was awkward again due to last night.

It didn't have to be awkward. She had this fortnight in Felix's company and might then only see him occasionally in the future. She had to enjoy their time together now and ignore the stronger feelings she'd developed for him, and do her best to maintain their easy friendship.

She suddenly had an idea, a way of returning things to how they'd previously been.

'Would you mind if we stopped for a moment so that I can adjust my boot?' she asked.

'Of course.'

She bent down and pretended to touch the boot, while Felix—ridiculously, given quite how much he'd looked at her last night as though his eyes were *feasting* on her nakedness—turned away in gentlemanly fashion. She quickly scooped and rolled as much snow as she could.

When she'd gathered enough, she stood up and took a few quiet steps away from Felix, before throwing the snowball as hard as she could, by complete luck catching him squarely in the head.

'Oof,' he said, spinning on his heel towards her. 'You *wretch*.'

As he bent and began to collect snow of his own, Cecily picked up her skirts and ran and hid amongst some of the other ladies.

'If you think,' said Felix, advancing upon them with a large snowball in his gloved hand, 'that hiding here will save you from retribution, you are quite wrong. I will merely be forced to shower *all* the ladies with snow, and it will be entirely your fault.'

'Felix. You wouldn't.'

'Are you prepared to take that risk?'

Cecily looked at him with narrowed eyes for a moment, before pointing behind him and saying, 'Oh my *goodness*.'

As he turned to look at nothing at all, she ran as fast as she could and hid behind a tree, scooping together snow to form more snowballs as she waited in hiding.

She was congratulating herself on her own extreme cunning—Felix clearly did not know where she was—when she heard a crunch right next to the tree and a large hand placed an even larger snowball right on the back of her neck.

'Eeeek,' she screeched.

'Would you like to know the beautiful irony of how I spotted you there?' Felix enquired.

'I don't think I would.' She shook her head vigorously to get rid of the snow and gasped as some of it trickled down inside her pelisse.

'I'm going to have to tell you anyway, for my own satisfaction. You were very well hidden because that is a very large tree trunk. The one thing that I noticed was your hands reaching out to grab more snow.'

'No!' How unlucky.

'Yes!' He grinned at her. 'Clearly, I am an excellent detective. And have won this snowball match before it's even really started.'

Cecily nodded. 'You *are* the winner. Well done.'

As he smiled at her, she brought her hands from behind her back and squished two snowballs right into his face and under his chin where hopefully some of it would go down his neck, before running away in the direction of the other ladies. This time, if he came after her, she would not leave their sanctuary.

In fact…

Oh!

Two strong arms had caught her much more quickly than she would have imagined; they were still quite some distance from any of the others.

'I think,' Felix said into her ear, 'that a serious punishment is in order.'

'And what might that punishment be?' she enquired, very much enjoying the way he had her pulled tight against him, despite the snow that was now squished between them.

'I'm just imagining how cold you would be if I rubbed snow *all* over your body now,' he murmured. 'Down your back, all the way to your bottom, down your legs, down your neck, over your breasts, down your stomach, up your legs, all the way…'

'*Felix*!'

'Yes?' He was still holding her against him, his arms folded round her, her head under his chin, her back resting against his chest. 'You'd be so cold you would shiver. I'd be forced to warm you up, perhaps by kissing you everywhere the snow had touched you, wrapping myself around you.'

'Felix!'

'Yes?' He kissed her beneath her left ear and she felt her skin tingle with the contact.

'You are a very—' she shivered as he kissed her

again and, somehow, worked his hands under her pelisse '—improperly behaved person.'

'I'm so sorry,' he said, doing some very improper things with his hands that caused her to squeak.

'Did you just undo my buttons?'

'I think I might have done.'

'People might *see*.'

'You're right.' He pulled her into the shade of a little group of trees. 'Now we're completely hidden from view.'

'This is *extremely* improper,' Cecily said with as much severity as she could summon as he began to rain kisses on her forehead, her nose, her cheeks.

'I'm just trying to warm you up.'

'I'm not sure I was cold.'

'Really?' He took some snow from a branch next to them and very deliberately pushed it inside the neckline of her dress, under the pelisse which he had somehow undone without her even noticing.

'Felix! Outrageous!'

'Should I…warm you up?' He was already kissing down her chest.

'That's the least you can do.' Cecily reached for some snow, suspecting that any moment she would lose all ability to be cunning, and then in one *extremely* cunning move managed to reach inside his coat, pull his shirt out of his breeches and stuff the snow down the front of them. 'I think,' she said triumphantly, 'that if anyone has won it is me.'

'That,' said Felix, raising his head to kiss her full on the lips, as he reached quite scandalously inside her dress, 'depends on your definition of winning. I would suggest that you are in all honour going to *have* to warm *me* up now and that *I* am therefore the victor.'

His mouth and hands were so clever and causing her to feel so entirely warmly liquid that Cecily had no words left to argue.

'Probably,' she gasped.

Some minutes later, still shuddering and gasping with pleasure from what Felix had just done to her, and delighted that he too had been gasping quite so much, she said, 'The others might wonder where we are.'

'Hmm.' Felix moved her so that she was at arm's length from him. 'I wonder whether it might be wise to return inside via a different door so that we don't see any of the others. We can send a footman to say that we both became so wet from our particularly competitive snowball fight that we both deemed it best to return inside to get changed. We can then perhaps return to the others and continue our walk before we all return to the house to take a nuncheon.'

'Good idea.' Cecily gasped yet again as he traced

a cold finger down between her breasts. 'You are a very bad influence on me, Your Grace.'

'Oddly,' said Felix, 'I was just thinking the same about you.' He stood up and pulled Cecily's pelisse tightly around her before doing up his own coat. 'Come on. Let us go so that we don't arouse too much suspicion.'

'I won that snowball fight by the way,' Cecily said as they took a path towards a side door of the castle.

'You were certainly better at snowballing strategy than at cards strategy, I'll grant you that,' Felix said. 'And an excellent singer and pianist. I've discovered a lot about you in the past four-and-twenty hours.'

He'd discovered a lot that no one else in the world had known about her, Cecily herself included, she reflected. She wasn't sure what she'd discovered about him; she'd already known him to be kind and interesting and, of course, devastatingly attractive. It was more that she'd discovered—or clarified—something about herself: that she loved him.

'Yes,' she said.

By arrangement, when properly attired again, they each made their own way separately outside, so that they wouldn't arrive together and arouse too much suspicion. Engaged people were of course entitled to spend a certain amount of time together, but Cecily was sure, from the snippets of gossip she'd overheard from her cousins and the servants, that a lady of quality should do no more than kiss a gentleman most decorously before she was actually married to him. And, of course, if anyone knew that she and Felix had engaged in such things, they might *have* to get married; it might ruin Felix's reputation if he didn't marry her after that and it might not be feasible for her to live alone with Holly in a country cottage.

It was *very* nice, though, she thought as they walked outside, and for these next two weeks perhaps she should just enjoy as many of these moments as she could have, and after that she would have to learn to come to terms with just being Felix's friend again if she ever saw him. Her life would still be infinitely better than it would have been had she stayed with her aunt and uncle or married the Earl.

Felix was outside before her, and, from the laughter and enquiries that greeted her, she gleaned that he had told everyone that in her haste to throw a snowball at him she had tumbled full length into a snow drift and had decided to change her clothing, and that in helping her up he also had got quite wet and had also decided to go inside for a few moments.

'I would just like you to know,' she told him when no one else was within earshot, 'that I would certainly not in reality be so pathetic as to fall and ruin my snowball success.'

'I must apologise; I panicked and came up with what was clearly in hindsight a poor excuse.'

'Should there be a next time, it must be you who is described as the incompetent one.'

'I will bear that in mind.' Felix grinned at her and her heart squeezed with love yet again.

Luncheon was pleasant; those of the party who had been strangers to each other when they arrived were now beginning to feel as though they knew each other somewhat, there seemed to be a very strong Christmas spirit in the air, and there was much joking and laughter. Cecily was conscious that her eyes went very regularly to Felix, who was seated at a little distance from her, but since his eyes were often on her when she looked at him, she didn't feel too ridiculous. In fact, it was as though they shared a particularly exciting secret, which she couldn't help very much enjoying.

Afterwards, there were more arrivals. In her guise as the fake soon-to-be Duchess of Garth, Cecily was greeted with much interest by the majority of the guests. Felix's mother-in-law remained at her side for most of the time and was a great help in deflecting some of the more intrusive questions directed at her by some of the more elderly guests—and a few of the younger ones—who made Felix's Aunt Davinia look positively restrained in her interrogations.

Cecily found herself giggling with Felix's mother-in-law at one point, after a very deaf dowager, apparently not realising that others had better hearing, mused to herself that if they weren't bothering to get married immediately by special licence she clearly wasn't suspected of being with child and the Duke could clearly wait to bed her. She didn't dare look anywhere near Felix, because she might have found herself blushing to high heaven at the reality.

The remainder of the afternoon passed in a whirl of greetings, light refreshments for the guests, people coming and going from the drawing room and hall as the latest arrivals were settled in their quarters for their festive stay, and then it was time to get changed for dinner again.

Truly, the rich lived very different lives from everyone else.

Cecily was seated next to Felix again at dinner, like yesterday evening, but this evening it felt very different. Somehow, it felt as though they were friends again, despite what had happened last night and this morning. Or maybe *because* of what had happened: in the past they had, on the very rare occasions that they had seen each other in social situations, exchanged smiles that acknowledged that they and they alone knew of the walks they shared.

This morning, Cecily had got the strong impression from Felix that he had somehow made the decision that if she wished to continue to exchange kisses and…other things, he would be very happy to do so, presumably for the duration of her stay here.

She took a mouthful of buttered turbot and stole a glance at his profile as he chatted politely to his other neighbour.

She hadn't ever imagined falling in love with anyone in quite this way, and she knew that she would without a doubt miss Felix hugely when they terminated their arrangement, but it would be *him*, his companionship, his conversation that she missed the most. The kisses were just a delightful extra and, since there was going to be a very big hole in her life when she no longer saw him regularly, no matter whether they continued to kiss or not, she might as well make the most of it.

She suddenly nearly gasped out loud as, under the table, Felix's knuckles brushed her thigh, just for a moment. It was a very quick and very gentle, but extremely noticeable stroke, and it made her immediately think of some of the things they'd done together.

She waited a few moments, and then found his—delightfully muscly—thigh with her hand and gave it the most deliberate and lingering squeeze before trailing her fingers lightly upwards, and was extremely gratified when she felt his whole body jerk slightly, before he leaned towards her and said, 'Minx,' in a very low voice into her ear.

'I know,' she said, quite loudly and very sunnily.

'Incorrigible,' he said on a choke of laughter.

After what continued to be a very enjoyable dinner, the ladies removed to the drawing room to allow the gentlemen to enjoy their port. A number of the newly arrived ladies flocked to Cecily's side and began to bombard her with—in some cases—particularly probing questions.

'I declare, you will quite fatigue Lady Cecily with your interrogations,' said Felix's mother-in-law, inserting herself very neatly next to Cecily on a sofa that had not previously seemed big enough for an additional person. 'What is the latest news from town? I heard that there was a particularly juicy *on dit* about Miss Barlow?'

As some of the others launched into a description of the unhappy Miss Barlow's indiscretions, Cecily mouthed a *thank you* at the Viscountess, who winked, just once, very discreetly, but very definitely.

When the gentlemen joined them, the Viscountess clapped her hands to attract everyone's attention and said, 'I thought we might play some Christmas parlour games this evening. I mentioned my idea to His Grace earlier and he was polite enough to say that he thought it an excellent idea. So we are going to play

Bullet Pudding and Snap-Dragon. We will set up two tables over there—' she gestured to the other side of the room '—and everyone will take it in turns. For those who don't know the rules, let me explain…'

Soon, she had them organised into groups with everyone quite determined to win and avoid having their faces covered in flour—in the case of Bullet Pudding—or get their fingers burnt—in the case of Snap-Dragon.

Somehow, Cecily and Felix became *extremely* competitive with each other, and, when Cecily ended up covered in flour, Felix said with particularly false-sounding concern, 'I'm so sorry that you lost; I hope that you don't feel like an abject failure.'

As he reached a finger to brush some of the flour away, Cecily waited until he got closer and then very carefully blew some right into his face, before saying, 'Oh, dear, I'm *so* sorry.'

'You,' said Felix, very quietly into her ear, 'are a minx and deserve a most horrible punishment.'

Cecily shivered with the naughtiness of being spoken to like that when surrounded by so many people and then shivered some more when she looked up at him and saw him raising his eyebrows in a *most* suggestive manner.

'I will show you later what your punishment is,' he continued, his voice a low, caressing growl. Cecily could only swallow, and *really* look forward to later.

It seemed as though they might be falling into the way of regular kisses and more, which—while it lasted—was so blissfully enjoyable that Cecily knew that she would do nothing to stop it. It would end with the end of their engagement—or perhaps the end of this house party—but it really couldn't hurt to continue with it for now.

So she pouted at Felix and said, 'I look forward to it,' and derived great satisfaction from the way he smiled in return.

# *Chapter Twelve*

*Felix*

Felix could barely concentrate on the parlour games and conversation going on around him; all he could think of was Cecily. When they were next to each other, all he wanted was to remain there talking to her, enjoying her conversation, her laughter, her smile. And when they weren't next to each other, he found himself seeking her out with his eyes and then wondering what it was that had just made her laugh, or cock her head to one side in interest, or just chat animatedly. In summary, he seemed to have become a little infatuated with her.

Which was hardly surprising, given the night they'd had together.

He knew that they shouldn't repeat what they'd done, but he would very much like a little more time alone with her, just to talk, so that *he* could be the one to make her look as though she was bursting with suppressed giggles, as she was now.

She glanced over at him, as though she felt his gaze on her, and directed the sauciest of looks at him, for just one moment, which made *him* now wish to laugh.

He really would like to spend some more time with her this evening.

Perhaps they could return to the library, given that it didn't seem as though they would be disturbed there. Especially if they locked the door—they really should have done that last night but he hadn't been thinking particularly lucidly; thank God no one had come in. Just to talk. Nothing else—they certainly shouldn't do anything else.

But it really would be nice to talk alone again. And surely it wasn't too scandalous to do so, given that they were currently an affianced couple.

Eventually, the games were finished, and a handful of the most elderly guests had announced that they were retiring for the night. When a move came from some of the gentlemen to play billiards, Felix had a strong sense that it was now or never for the evening.

'I believe that Lady Cecily wishes to return to the library to seek another book,' he said.

'Yes, indeed, I have already finished the last one I read,' she said, with great alacrity. 'I stayed up very late last night reading it. It was excellent.'

'Oh, what book was it?' asked Miss Lindgrove.

Cecily stared at her for a few seconds, before replying, 'You know, I really cannot remember the title or indeed the author. How very silly of me. I should have paid more attention. It was excellent, though. I very much recommend it.'

'Let us go now,' said Felix, laughing. 'And let us take particular note of the title and author this time.'

'Certainly,' said Cecily, very primly.

'I cannot *believe* I said that,' she told him as soon as they were out of earshot of the others. 'I could so easily have said instead that I needed to look for another book because the one I was reading was not to my taste.'

'Clearly you are not practised enough in the art of covering up indiscretions.' He resisted the—very strong—temptation to slide an arm around her waist and pull her against him to enjoy the softness of her body and clasped his hands in front of him instead. 'Here we are.' He opened the library door, suddenly quite desperate to be alone with her, and, as soon as the door was closed behind them, turned the key in the lock, so that their conversation wouldn't be interrupted.

'I very much enjoyed the evening.' Cecily moved over to a bookcase and began to study the books in front of her, running her finger down the spine of one of them, which reminded Felix extremely forcibly of what had happened the last time she did that. 'You have a very nice family and group of friends and the games we played were most amusing.'

'It was indeed most enjoyable,' Felix agreed, allowing himself to walk over and stand next to her—to look at the books with her, obviously—rather than because he just really wanted to be physically close to her. He looked more closely at the shelf in the direction of which her eyes were facing. 'Do you read Ancient Greek in the original?'

'No?'

'But you are looking at Greek books?'

'Am I?' Cecily leaned slightly forwards. 'Oh, so I am. Well, the writing is very pretty. The alphabet. I like it.'

Felix nodded very seriously. 'Yes, that's a good reason to read a book.'

Cecily turned and rolled her eyes at him, and despite all his good intentions he couldn't help kissing her.

He only intended it to be one, not particularly deep, kiss, but Cecily's lips were parted when he brushed them with his, and, somehow, the kiss immediately became quite a passionate one.

'Are you sure we should be doing this?' he found the willpower to ask a few moments later. 'It really isn't proper.'

'That is very true,' said Cecily her hands against

his chest, her head tipped back a little. She lowered her voice. 'But the door is locked, and we've kissed before, and so, really, we aren't doing anything *new*, and no one will ever find out.'

'Would you not—' Felix wound his arms around her waist '—rather discuss Greek literature?'

'Hmm.' Cecily tilted her head to one side, as though considering. 'Perhaps I *would* rather look at books. Not necessarily Greek literature, however.'

'What type of book, then?' asked Felix, moving his hands up her sides from her waist and into her hair.

'Fiction?' Her breath was coming a little harder now.

He kissed her hard and then said, 'That's somewhere over here, I think,' before picking her up in his arms. He carried her to the far end of the room and sat down on a chaise longue—which a previous duchess had had installed in the library against the wishes of her Duke and which Felix had never previously liked but now thought was an excellent addition to the room—and adjusted Cecily on his lap.

'This,' panted Cecily, 'is a most delightful—' she moaned as he ran his hand high up her thigh '—kind of fiction. Oh, *Felix*.'

Several remarkably pleasurable hours later, they were lying limbs entwined on the chaise longue, entirely naked. Felix twirled one of Cecily's ringlets around his forefinger and reflected that, while, strictly speaking, they ought not to have been doing what they *had* been doing, at least he'd had the strength of mind not to do *everything*. So she certainly wouldn't have become with child.

She raised her head from where it had been resting on his chest and said, 'Is it very late? Should we go to bed?'

'Probably.'

And eventually they did.

Over the next few days, they continued in a similar way: spending time with Felix's guests, often the gentlemen going out to indulge in masculine sporting pursuits during the day and the ladies staying inside with their embroidery and other such projects during the daytimes and the entire company coming together in the evenings; and stealing blissful moments together when they were able during the day before managing to make their way to the library in the late evenings.

Cecily told him that she'd recommended Lizzie not to wait up for her at night, and Felix had also told his valet that he was currently keeping very late hours and preferred for the time being to prepare himself for bed.

They had also agreed that they didn't wish any further library visits to be noticed by anyone else and that they should make their own ways there separately. Once there, they had continued to engage in delightful conversation and…other things.

By day, Felix was very busy spending time with his boys and with his hosting activities, which allowed him little time for thought, which was perhaps a good thing; he was sure that logic dictated that having kissed once it really didn't matter how many times they did in total, but he did feel as though he didn't wish to examine that logic too closely.

From the occasional narrowed eye and smiles from his mother-in-law, when he and Cecily had just stolen a kiss, he began to think that she suspected, if not *knew*, what they were doing, and…approved.

Which was food—of some kind—for thought.

On Christmas Eve, everyone came together to decorate the castle with holly, ivy, hawthorn, laurel, bay, rosemary, hellebore and of course mistletoe, under which Felix stole a kiss with Cecily, before Felix held a large party at the castle, as was tradition, for his tenants and their families. His mother-in-law, a little inexplicably, given that she did know the situation between him and Cecily, introduced her widely as his fiancée.

Knowing that Cecily had certainly not been brought up in any way to perform the duties of a lady in relation to visiting tenants or ill villagers—

or anything else—Felix stepped forward to support her, but before he reached her side she was already talking very earnestly, with very sweet smiles, to the most elderly and vulnerable of their visitors.

Felix couldn't help glancing over at her on a number of occasions during the party, and, unlike when they were socialising with their own guests, Cecily was almost never looking at him; she seemed fully engrossed in both conversing and laughing with the visitors.

Felix felt his heart somehow break a little each time he looked at her, at the irony that *this* seemed to be something she had been born to do, but she would soon be shutting herself away in a cottage with only her cousins' old governess for company.

He would have to visit her quite regularly; surely she would otherwise be bored.

But he wouldn't be able to visit her regularly; it would give rise to too much comment. He would only be able to go occasionally.

They wouldn't, of course, be able to engage in any physical intimacy whatsoever if he went to visit her; if they did so it would be disastrous for Cecily if someone saw them.

Which would…

'Your Grace?' Mrs Beasley, an elderly lady who lived with her son in one of the cottages on his estate, was peering at him. Good God. He had no idea what she'd just said. He'd allowed his thoughts about Cecily to cause him almost to ignore her. How ridiculously rude of him.

'I'm so sorry,' he said. 'Age,' he improvised. 'I'm suffering a little from deafness. Could you possibly repeat the question?'

When the party eventually drew to a close, it seemed that every single visitor wished to say goodbye to Cecily. She looked—objectively—extremely beautiful, dressed as she was in one of her new gowns, with her brunette locks teased into a very attractive style and her blue eyes sparkling and a ready smile for all. But, while beauty often attracted people, as did a lovely dress and a delightful figure, Felix didn't think that was what was drawing people to Cecily. It was something else, something to do with the way she had a few individual words for everyone, and each time she was speaking to someone appeared to be entirely focused on them and them alone. That was certainly a characteristic that he'd always liked in her and it was something that many of the grand ladies here did not have; indeed some of them had fully discernible expressions of boredom on their faces at this moment.

Cecily would make an excellent duchess.

She would make an adorable duchess.

She…

'Your Grace?' One of his farmer tenants was looking quizzically at him. Unbelievable. He'd done it again.

'Apologies; I'm quite deaf,' Felix said.

Christmas Day itself was a great day. Felix's boys joined them for church and the festivities that followed, and Cecily was, of course, delightful with them. When Felix saw the way in which she had them doubled up with laughter, all he could do was smile.

For the first time during the house party, Felix's boys joined fully in for the day. Before this, Felix had kept them largely separate. They were only eight and six and it was a mainly adult party. There were however a few other children of a similar age, who had joined them in the nursery, where they had had a marvellous time together under the watchful and doting eyes of their own and their visitors' nurses and maids.

Felix had had a very strong desire not to introduce the boys to Cecily, because he had no wish to confuse them; little benefit could be gained from their getting to know her and either liking or disliking her, when her inclusion in their family was only temporary.

Since they had been enjoying themselves greatly, and most of the pursuits in which the adults had engaged would not have been particularly interesting for the children, and their presence might have curtailed the adults' enjoyment, he hadn't even needed to say anything to explain the fact that they only met the rest of the guests once or twice a day, perhaps once during the morning or afternoon and then in the evening to say goodnight before dinner.

Cecily had mentioned once that she would love to meet them and he had murmured something non-committal and she had immediately stopped talking, clearly having understood his reasoning. She had perhaps been hurt, but he had to put the happiness of his children above his friend's, and getting to know her could *clearly* have been confusing for them.

Today, though, they were here, simultaneously very excited and trying to be on their best behaviour so that they would be allowed their presents.

In Felix's household, unlike others, the family exchanged gifts on Christmas Day itself, due to their commitments to his tenants on Christmas Eve and a party for villagers' children on Boxing Day.

There was a certain amount of pushing and shoving amongst the children and their friends on the way to church. Felix sighed internally and prepared to go and break up any fight that ensued, and then saw that Cecily had gone over to the boys from where she'd been walking with Miss Lindgrove. She bent and whispered in their ears, and they all immediately entirely ceased their fighting. Cecily resumed her place next to Miss Lindgrove, smiling to herself.

Felix couldn't resist moving towards her, so that he could ask, 'What did you say to them?'

'A prize for the child who behaves the best from now to the end of the service.'

'Nicely done.' He looked round at the children. 'It is certainly working. What *is* the prize?'

'Well, that is a good question. I told them that I haven't fully decided but that it's going to be a *good* one.' She arranged her features in a particularly soulful expression and then continued, 'I might have made a suggestion about you, for the greater good, obviously.'

'And what was that suggestion?' asked Felix suspiciously.

'Well.' Cecily swung her parasol as though trying to look unconcerned. 'I might—in the moment, just because it occurred to me that it would be an excellent incentive and benefit all of us—have suggested that the child who behaves the best might be allowed to place three snowballs down your neck.'

'I see. You couldn't think of any other good prizes on the spur of the moment?'

Cecily shook her head. 'Not ones that would appeal to children of that age.'

'And you couldn't suggest one snowball, you had to suggest three?'

Cecily nodded, definitely having to make an effort not to giggle.

'I see,' he said.

'You'll be grateful to me when they all behave like angels throughout the service.'

An hour and a half later, after a service involving an extremely lengthy sermon that had certainly not been composed with children in mind, the children, who had indeed behaved angelically throughout, had certainly—one of them at least—earnt a prize.

'Who was the best?' Felix's older son James asked Cecily immediately they left the church to begin the return walk.

Felix was astonished. James had been a very lively toddler but had become very withdrawn after the loss of his mother, and, while with the love lavished on him by not only his father and grandmother and other relatives but also the entire household of servants, he had settled and grown into a happy-seeming little boy, he remained reserved and shy with people he didn't know well. But now he was jumping up and down and tugging on Cecily's hand.

Had he been another child, a less worryingly reserved one, Felix would almost certainly be telling him off now and recommending that he behave with much greater decorum, but as it was it seemed better to turn a blind eye.

Cecily was laughing and saying, 'I really can't think over such a great racket.'

James and the other children were all laughing too.

Cecily placed a finger to her lips and they all immediately calmed down a little. She seemed to have the most extraordinary knack with them.

'I think I have it,' she said, just quietly enough so that they all had to fall silent to hear her words. 'I think you were *equally* well-behaved.'

'What does that mean?' asked James above murmurs of dissatisfaction.

'Well, *clearly*,' Cecily said, 'you are *all* winners.'

'Does that mean we're *all* allowed to put snowballs down Papa's neck?' squealed Robbie, Felix's younger son.

'I think it does,' Cecily said, looking at Felix with the most ridiculously fake innocent smile on her lips.

Felix shook his head at her, just because he thought he ought to, but he could only laugh and feel very grateful that somehow she had caused James in particular to come out of his shell a little.

They walked with James and Robbie all the way back to the castle, the boys skipping along, both of them talking nineteen to the dozen. Cecily listened with the utmost seriousness to what they had to say and replied to them as though everything they said was extremely important.

'At what point would you like to take your prizes?'

he asked when they were nearing the castle. 'Now, perhaps?'

The screams of pleasure from all the children, especially his own boys, were a great reward for what followed, which wasn't the *most* enjoyment Felix had ever had in the snow—well, obviously it wasn't, because that had been with Cecily, a few days ago.

Once he had received all the snowballs, and made all the children scream and run away inside with Cecily, by telling them very conversationally that he was considering exacting terrible revenge, he went up to his chamber to change. He found himself smiling the whole way, thinking about James's animation. Cecily seemed to have had an excellent effect on him.

When he returned downstairs, fully dry, the first person he saw was Cecily, who sniggered when she saw him.

He shook his head at her, smiling. 'You deserve a terrible retribution for that.'

'Garth, Lady Cecily,' his mother-in-law said, joining them just inside the door of the sitting room. She nudged them both slightly so that they had to take a couple of steps towards the room's mantelpiece. 'Oh, look! You are standing under mistletoe. You will have to exchange kisses.'

Felix really didn't want to think about the fact that his late wife's mother seemed to be *commanding* him to kiss his fake fiancée. It certainly didn't seem that analysing it would make him feel comfortable.

He gave Cecily a peck on the cheek, and then she pecked his cheek in return, and then she smiled her minxy smile and—right in the middle of a group of people including his mother-in-law—he realised that all he wanted to do was take Cecily somewhere quite private and do extremely private things with her.

They ate a luncheon of light delicacies in the drawing room, with the children, all of whom flocked to Cecily, who ended up entertaining them with stories while their parents ate and conversed.

Afterwards, they all went for a walk around the grounds, before returning to the castle to exchange gifts. By the time they got back, Cecily had James and Robbie holding a hand each and hanging on her every word.

'Do you have presents for us, Lady Cecily?' asked James.

Felix felt his heart sink until he saw Cecily nodding.

'Of course I do. You have very kindly allowed me and all these other guests to stay in your home for two weeks and you've been wonderfully well-behaved, so, yes, of *course* I have gifts for you.'

And lo and behold, she had, and when the boys

opened them, it seemed that she had bought them in London and chosen well.

'Papa, look,' shouted James. 'Battledore rackets with handles like *soldiers*.'

'Thank you,' mouthed Felix at Cecily over his head.

She shook hers at him and smiled at the boys.

A few minutes later, he saw that Cecily was in a small group of ladies, from whom he should be able to extract her without leaving any guest alone.

'I hope that you will excuse Lady Cecily,' he said to her companions. 'I would like to give her my gifts.'

'Of course,' they all agreed.

'This time next year you will be a married couple,' one of them said.

'Indeed,' Felix said, not wishing, for some reason, to think about the fact that this time next year Cecily would have been living some distance away in her cottage for several months.

'I bought you several gifts,' he told Cecily, when they were finally alone in the corner of the room.

Knowing that she had rarely if ever received any gifts while living with her aunt and uncle, he had found it difficult to resist the impulse to buy present after present for her.

'Felix, you shouldn't have!' she exclaimed. 'Although, also, I *love* everything and am extremely touched. Thank you so much!'

He had bought her some new writing materials, a number of modern novels that he knew she wished to read, and some trinkets such as new hairbrushes, gloves and a muff that his Aunt Davinia had recommended.

'Can I give you my presents now?' she asked.

'Of course.'

A moment later, he gasped. She had drawn for him, and had framed, incredibly accurate portraits of his boys.

'I couldn't imagine a better gift,' he told her, extremely touched.

Cecily sniffed.

'Are you all right?' he asked, horrified.

'Just happy,' she said. 'I could never have imagined such a wonderful Christmas, or such a lovely exchange of gifts. I love everything that you've bought for me and I'm so very happy that you like the portraits.'

He wished very much that he could gather her into his arms at that moment, and had they been alone in the room would certainly have done so.

He had to content himself with saying, 'I'm so pleased that you are enjoying it,' and the knowledge that he would be able to hug her later in the library.

'I have some other gifts for you,' he murmured, 'but will give them to you this evening.'

* * *

And that evening, in the library, he gave her the simple diamond necklace, with matching bracelet and earrings, that he had bought her. He remembered that when he'd purchased them it had partly been because he felt that his fiancée ought to own such items. Now he knew that the reason for giving them should only ever have been that they would bring her pleasure and because she deserved, was worthy, of special gifts.

He was rewarded by a gasp of gratitude, one of her beautiful smiles, and, some time later, most deliciously, by her modelling the diamonds for him wearing nothing *but* the diamonds.

Boxing Day was also an excellent day, again with Cecily's presence integral to its success and the boys clamouring to be the one allowed to sit closest to her when they all played childish but extremely enjoyable parlour games—at which Cecily excelled.

In accordance with tradition, they held a large party for the village children, at which they gave each child a present, and it seemed as though every child there wished to receive their present from Cecily.

She really would make an excellent duchess.

She ought to marry someone.

With each day that passed, with all the games, theatricals, different pursuits in which they all engaged together or in groups, and the activities in which Felix and Cecily engaged very much *à deux*, in the privacy of the library—and occasionally behind a tree or down by the frozen lake, amongst other locations—he somehow began to feel as though he couldn't imagine Cecily not being with him here forever.

Except…he wasn't sure whether that felt right.

He'd always believed—*known*—he would never marry again. He thought he had, anyway.

He'd always felt that he couldn't betray Aurora's memory. *She* had been his wife, his one true love.

Except, it had begun to feel as though maybe that wasn't true. Maybe one could have two true loves in life, at separate times.

*If* that were true, though, and *if* that were acceptable in regard to Aurora's memory, and the well-being of his boys, could *he* be happy being married to someone he loved? Would it not just mean that he would be putting himself in a position where he could again lose someone with whom he was deeply in love? The pain that he'd experienced after Aurora's death had been so utterly awful, second only to the pain he'd felt in watching his sons become motherless.

Without her, though…his life had been sterile, lacking in certain ways.

He really didn't know.

Maybe he *would* like to marry Cecily…

* * *

To conclude the house party, they held a large ball to welcome in the New Year, inviting guests from many miles around.

Felix refused absolutely to invite Cecily's relatives, Lord and Lady Milton. When one or two of the guests commented on their absence, he explained that they were not particular friends of his because they had not treated Cecily very well when she was in their care, for which Cecily thanked him—in a very seductive manner.

When she descended the stairs dressed in a ball gown that he hadn't seen before, in pale blue and flattering her form most delightfully, and wearing her new diamonds, the sight of her took his breath entirely away.

And when they waltzed together, twice, and then, most unfashionably and almost unacceptably, thrice, because, he reasoned, she was known to everyone here as his fiancée, so why should he not dance with her several times, he barely gained his breath at all.

The majority of the guests left during the course of the next morning—many of them exceptionally bleary-eyed and a number of them having engaged in some particularly indiscreet indiscretions, which they were now pretending had never happened.

Over an informal luncheon for those remaining, dispersed at tables in the long drawing-room, his mother-in-law said to him, 'I presume that you will be escorting Lady Cecily back to London whenever she and Lady Bradstock choose to leave, and that you will then perhaps spend some time with her there? I will of course delight in the opportunity to have my grandsons to myself during that time, so there will be no need whatsoever for you to rush back; you may stay for as long as you like. And perhaps bring Lady Cecily back with you when you return, if you wish?'

He looked at her, wondering what lay behind her seemingly innocent smile.

Had she decided that she would actively like him to marry Cecily?

She placed a hand on his arm. 'I wish only for your happiness, Felix.'

He nodded. 'Thank you.' It seemed as though she was almost…giving him her blessing, almost on behalf of Aurora.

Could he…accept the blessing?

Did he wish to do so? Did he wish to marry Cecily?

Maybe he did…

He *did* wish to escort her back to London, he realised. He'd wished to take her to see so many places of interest when she first arrived and now he had an even greater desire to do so.

His sons would be safe and happy in the care of

their grandmother; she had looked after them many times and she and they shared a strong mutual love. There was no practical reason for him not to go.

'Yes,' he said, suddenly decisive. 'I do intend to escort the ladies back to London.'

# *Chapter Thirteen*

*Cecily*

'I believe that we must leave for London tomorrow,' Lady Bradstock said to Cecily later that afternoon.

'Of course,' Cecily said, horrified by how very uninspired she felt at the thought of spending more time in London with Felix's aunts. She should be pleased. Happy. This had of course been a truly wonderful, magical interlude in her life, but London, living with Felix's aunts, was lovely too. In comparison to her previous life, with her aunt and uncle, it was almost utopia. It was unfortunate that she now had this time with Felix to which to compare, well, the rest of her life.

'I understand that the Duke will escort us,' Lady Bradstock continued.

And now Cecily was horrified by how very much happier she suddenly felt.

One day, in a few weeks' time, she would have to say goodbye to this pretence. It would, she realised, be quite—very—depressing for a while.

She was still, however, extremely lucky to have had this time with Felix, and she would of *course* recover from any misery when it came to an end.

She should just enjoy any time she might have with him in London.

And she should never let him know that her feelings for him ran deeper than mere flirtation, because she did not wish to ruin their friendship.

Cecily's exchange of farewells with Felix's mother-in-law and sons was protracted and extremely fond.

'I look forward to seeing you again,' the Viscountess told her. 'I have very much enjoyed your company.'

Cecily half-shook her head and the Viscountess said in a low voice, 'Whatever the future holds, I should very much like to remain friends,' before folding Cecily into a tight hug.

'Thank you. I should also like that,' was all Cecily could say around the large frog that had grown in her throat.

The boys both also hugged her very hard. Burying her face against their heads as she hugged them back, Cecily tried hard not to think about the fact that it was entirely possible that she would never see them again. She had become very attached to them in the time they had spent together. James in particular had initially seemed quite timid but had then lost his reserve and was now when playing outside as noisy as small boys ought to be in her opinion.

'Please write letters to us while you're in London,' he begged.

'Of *course* I will,' she said. 'On one condition.'

'What is that?'

'That you reply.'

'We both will,' James declared on behalf of himself and his younger brother and then they all shared another hug.

Cecily's eyes were so full of tears when she got into the carriage that it almost felt a good thing when Felix told her that he planned to ride for the first part of the journey.

By the time she'd recovered her equilibrium, she did have to admit to herself that she found it a little flat in the carriage without his company, although she did very much like his aunts and their conversation, and she was—as she must keep reminding herself—very fortunate to be living under their roof rather than with her aunt and uncle.

They all took luncheon together in a staging inn, and, sitting at a dining table next to Felix while they waited to be served, Cecily found herself considerably more animated than she had been in the travelling chaise without him.

'This stew smells quite delicious,' she said happily, as the servers brought dishes to them.

Felix smiled at her. 'I see that you have not yet become inured to good food.'

'I don't think I ever will.' Or to any of the rest of this wonderful new life that she had having left her aunt and uncle. Which *would* be wonderful, with or without Felix in it. It would just require a little adjustment, that was all, when she no longer saw Felix all the time. She would miss him, but then she would get used to his absence. She was very fortunate to have had this time with him. 'I'm sorry for using the *th* word, but thank you so very much for saving me from my old life.'

'No thank yous. Try some of these sweetbreads.'

At the end of their meal, Felix said, 'If you don't mind, I will join you in the chaise for the remainder of the journey.'

'That would be lovely.' Cecily felt as though she was suddenly glowing inside.

The rest of the journey, with Felix's company inside the chaise, was indeed lovely, as was their dinner eaten with Felix's aunts. There was something very nice about their smaller group, as though Cecily had more of Felix than she'd had when it was a larger group.

Afterwards, they all withdrew together to the smaller drawing room, Felix having told the ladies that he saw no need to sit and drink port by himself.

After perhaps twenty minutes of conversation, during which both Felix's great-aunts nodded off in their chairs, Lady Bradstock said, 'I will now retire for the night. I am aware that it is still early, but I find myself quite tired from today's journey.'

An exodus ensued, so that Felix and Cecily were left alone.

'Perhaps you might like to come and see my library here?' Felix suggested.

'I do think that I am need of a good book to read,' Cecily agreed in her primmest tone.

When they reached the library—a smaller room than the magnificent one at Garth, but still impressive—Felix, as had become their custom, locked the door behind him and pulled Cecily into his arms.

'I've been wanting to do this all day,' he murmured in her ear. 'Thank God for locks on doors. That drawing room has far too many doors; anyone might come in at any time.'

Cecily had found it difficult not to spend a large part of the day wondering whether Felix would wish to continue their nocturnal activities, and whether she herself wished to continue them. At some point they would have to stop… And they couldn't afford to be caught…

'Is this wise?' she asked him, putting her hands on his chest and wriggling backwards a little.

He immediately released her and took a step away from her.

'Almost certainly not,' he said after a pause.

'Perhaps we should…not,' she said.

'Of course. You're completely right.'

Cecily couldn't help wishing that she hadn't been so cautious. It was *so* unlikely that anyone would surprise them if they *were* to kiss, given that the door was so firmly locked. This might be her very last night with Felix.

She stepped towards him and reached up and put her hands on either side of his face and kissed him right on the lips.

He returned the kiss for a moment but then drew back and said, 'Are you sure?'

'*Very* sure.' She ran her hands up his chest and then down, and derived great satisfaction from the way he groaned.

'Definitely?'

'Yes.' She stood on tiptoes and kissed him again. He returned her kiss gently for a few moments, and then suddenly they had their arms round each other, and everything was passionate and urgent—driven perhaps by the feeling that this might be their last time ever together—and it felt as though she was the one fully in charge, leading him exactly where she chose to go. It was *extremely* enjoyable.

'That…was…that was… I have no words,' Felix gasped some time later. He hugged Cecily against him tightly and then said, 'I love you.'

It was as though Cecily's world stopped and then restarted at that moment, shifted somehow on its axis.

'I love you, Cecily,' he repeated.

'I love you too,' she said simply.

And then they kissed and kissed, without doing anything else at all, for a very long time, before going to their separate bedchambers.

Cecily awoke in the morning with a strong sense of happiness, but wasn't sure why she felt that way, until she remembered… And then she smiled her way through her toilette, feeling as though she might burst. Felix loved her. She loved him. She'd always loved him. But also, *he* loved *her.*

Maybe… Maybe somehow this could…

No. She couldn't even allow herself to speculate in her own mind as to whether somehow this might go on forever, that they might actually… No. She couldn't think it. If she allowed herself to believe in a happy-forever ending, it would be even harder when it didn't in fact happen. She should just enjoy *now* and hope that Felix might decide to stay for another night or two.

'I think,' said Felix over breakfast, 'that I should stay for at least a few more days, to show you some of the sights of London.'

The next ten days were utterly blissful. They visited all manner of attractions from the Tower of London to Westminster Abbey, to Hatchard's bookshop and Gunter's tea rooms. They also attended a number of evening events and danced together far more than was fashionable. And they kissed. A lot.

Felix told Cecily he loved her every single night and she told him in return that she loved him. They never had any discussion about the future, though, whether it might be different from what they had originally planned; and Cecily never instigated the exchange of I-love-yous.

It felt as though they had reached a new level of intimacy but that there was a ceiling to it, as though they couldn't—for now at least—progress to any higher level. Cecily didn't want to say anything that might cause what they had now to end, and she had a sense that Felix was in some way confused, not sure whether he could or should or would act on the love that he felt for her.

* * *

And then one day, during an excursion to Richmond Park, just the two of them, Felix reached for Cecily's hand as they walked through a grassy clearing, and said, 'I hadn't expected to love someone—to fall in love—like this ever again.'

Swallowing a suddenly enormous lump in her throat, Cecily said, 'Oh.'

He tugged her hand a little so that she was standing facing him and took her other hand.

'I love you very much,' he said. 'I have enjoyed our time together very, very much.'

Cecily held her breath, wondering whether he might say something about the future.

And he…kissed her forehead very tenderly and then drew her into his arms and just stood there, holding her.

Which was of course delightful. Lovely. Wonderful. But Cecily wanted—she realised—*more.* Suddenly she couldn't keep the thoughts buried any longer. She wanted this forever. She wanted everything. She wanted to be with Felix forever. She didn't want to go and live in a cottage with just Holly for company, even though she did adore Holly and would certainly wish always to stay in close contact with her and indeed happily ask her to live with her wherever she lived. Hopefully with Felix.

Even though she *knew* that living with Holly in a

cottage would be infinitely better than living with her aunt and uncle, now that she had experienced *this*, she knew that there was more than that.

She wanted, she realised, Felix to propose to her properly. She wanted him to tell her that he loved her and wanted to marry her and for their engagement to become real.

She wanted that *so much.*

But right now she was standing in the middle of this beautiful park being held in the circle of his strong arms against his broad chest. And it was truly wonderful, it really was. Except it wasn't. In fact, she really wanted to stamp her foot. Because why wouldn't he say more?

*Would* he say more?

And then he drew back a little and said, his voice hoarse, 'I will have more to say on this subject.'

And with that, her hopes soared, and she found herself smiling and smiling.

'Oh,' she said, still smiling.

She smiled for almost entirely the rest of the afternoon, imagining a real proposal, a marriage, a life with Felix, until, on their arrival in Berkeley Square, as they were mounting the steps to the house, the butler opened the front door and pressed a note into Felix's hands before he had even reached the top step.

As Felix read it, remaining where he was just outside the door, he sucked in a deep breath and the colour drained from his usually lightly tanned cheeks.

'I have to go,' he said, staring around him as though he couldn't remember where he was.

'Felix?' Cecily placed her hand on his arm. 'What has happened?'

'It's James. He is ill. Extremely feverish. They fear for his life. He has been asking for me and for his mother. And I am not there, and she can never be there. What have I done? Abandoning my children? I must leave now.'

'Oh, Felix. I'm so sorry. You haven't abandoned them. And James will know that when you immediately hasten to his side.'

She stopped talking and released his arm. It was clear that he wasn't taking in her words and that his entire thoughts were, as they should be, of course, with his son.

He turned, looked at her, blinked as though he had completely forgotten that she was there, and then said, 'Thank you. Very kind. I must bid you farewell.' He turned away and said to Deedes, 'I will ride. Please instruct the stables accordingly.'

He turned back to Cecily and said, 'Goodbye.'

'Goodbye.' She wanted so much to tell him that she loved him, but clearly she could not say it in front of Deedes. And, really, it wasn't at all appropriate at this moment. 'I will pray for you.'

'Thank you.' And then he turned to walk round to the back of the house in the direction of the stables.

And in that moment Cecily knew for certain that she had lost him.

# *Chapter Fourteen*

*Felix*

As Felix rode hard through Wimbledon in the light of the moon, he couldn't escape his thoughts. The only other time he'd ridden this hard and with this much fear in his heart had been when Aurora had gone into early labour with Robbie, while Felix was out hunting, and he'd received word that she had delivered safely of a healthy, although small boy, but that she was fading.

He had arrived in time to hold her in his arms as she died.

And he had vowed that he would never again let down his loved ones, his dependents, his sons.

And here he was: a failure. He had let his sons down so that he could spend time with Cecily. And apparently spending time with her was not compatible with his vow to look after his children on behalf of Aurora. He'd been selfish, self-serving.

Also. The fear that he was experiencing now in regard to James was reminding him extremely forcibly of how he'd felt when he lost Aurora. Could he really cope with remarrying, loving someone as much as that again? He *did* love Cecily that much, but could he really be happy married to her, or would he be constantly terrified of something happening to her? What if *she* died in childbirth?

He'd been so stupid.

He'd told her he loved her. Many times. The first time he'd said it had been after the first glorious night they'd spent together in his library in London. He'd been planning to return to Garth the next day, but somehow, when she'd taken control of their lovemaking like that, he'd suddenly realised how very much he loved her, how much he'd loved how she was with James and Robbie, how much he enjoyed her company, how much he cared about her, not to mention how much he enjoyed doing what they did together and wished to have a lifetime of engaging in the full act together…

And he'd told her he loved her. He hadn't known what to do with that thought at first, but then in Richmond Park he'd realised that he really did want to marry her, be with her forever.

He'd been on the point of proposing properly to her. The only reason that he hadn't done so when they were in the park was that he'd wanted to make the proposal a glorious, romantic, wonderful gesture.

And, damnation, here he was again, even as he rode to James's bedside, thinking about Cecily, rather than about his son.

He should put Cecily out of his mind until James recovered. He *would* recover; he had to.

And when James was better and Felix had the time to attend to other affairs, he would ask his man of business to begin immediately to look for a cottage for Cecily, to provide her, as agreed, with a list of properties to choose between, so that she could leave his London house and begin her new life there sooner rather than later, which would be better for everyone.

He could tell his man of business that it was to house a relative of his. Cecily had mentioned that she would like to live quite near to Sussex, but not *very* near, so they had agreed that the search for her house would be concentrated in Kent and Hampshire. He didn't want to think too hard now about the fact that that would mean that she was living some distance away from him and that it would be difficult for him to visit her very often without occasioning talk amongst her neighbours. He would miss her horribly, of course he would. And worry about her greatly.

But he had to think of his sons.

If he *had* proposed to her, would she have accepted, he wondered. Perhaps, perhaps not. She'd only ever told him she loved him in response to him saying it first. And she had been very excited at the prospect of becoming a lady of independent means with her own house.

Perhaps she wouldn't have *wished* to marry him.

And, damn, he *had* to stop thinking about her and focus on his boys.

The ride felt long but he was home by midnight; it was fortunate that tonight the moon was almost full, and he knew the way very well.

Having handed the reins of his horse to a groom, he strode straight up to the nursery, where he encountered the horrifying sight of his red-cheeked, sweating son thrashing around in his bed, crying for his mama, with his grandmother trying desperately to soothe him.

Two steps took him to the bed.

'Thank you,' he said to his mother-in-law, taking James from her. 'Thank you for being here. You should get some rest now.'

And then he said to James, 'I'm here now. It's Papa.'

'He needs to drink this.' His mother-in-law indicated a mixture in a glass on the table next to the bed. 'The doctor left it for him. I have been unable to persuade him to drink it.'

Felix nodded and then turned to James. 'I need you to be a strong man,' he told him, in his sternest voice. 'I expect you to drink this immediately.'

James, fortunately, just nodded meekly and drank it.

'Oh, thank God,' his mother-in-law cried. 'How very fortunate that you were able to come so soon.'

'And how very unfortunate that I was not already here,' said Felix grimly.

James was gravely ill for many days. Felix nursed him himself, other than taking the occasional break to sleep, when his mother-in-law pointed out that he would be no use to anyone, especially James, if he became ill from fatigue.

On the third day after Felix arrived home, a letter addressed to James was received.

James had no interest in opening it, but when his grandmother opened it on his behalf and told him that it was from Cecily, he suddenly found the strength to try to sit up and ask if someone would read it to him.

'I will leave it to your father to do so. I will be back shortly, my darling.' She closed the door behind her, leaving Felix holding the letter.

He really didn't want to read some words from Cecily; it just felt too…well, he wasn't sure what.

Uncomfortable, that was it. He'd already been thinking too much about her. He had no choice, however; he hadn't seen James this animated since the start of his illness.

He cleared his throat and began.

*Dear James,*

*I was so sorry to hear that you're feeling ill.*

*I hope that you are feeling a little better now. If your doctor recommends you to take medicine, you should make sure that you do. Even if medicine doesn't taste very nice, it's still better than feeling ill.*

*Separately, just in case you might be a little bored during your illness: remember the stories that I composed for you over Christmas? I have written the first instalment in another one for you, which I enclose. It involves a serious crime—the theft of a diamond necklace—a boy detective and some turnips.*

*I send you all my love and best wishes for a fast recovery.*

*Cecily*

'Please could you read it?' James said, struggling to sit up and sounding suddenly stronger.

'Of course.'

The story sounded just like Cecily; it was almost

as though she was in the room with them. Felix loved her more with every word he read to James.

'I want to know what happens next,' James said when he'd finished. 'Could you ask her?'

'Of course.' So, when he was sure that James was asleep, Felix wrote to Cecily to thank her for what she'd written and to tell her that James had loved it and to ask her—if it wasn't too much trouble—although, actually, he said, if it *was* a lot of trouble he would still be grateful if she would do it; James was the most important thing—if she could possibly complete the story. He concluded his note there, because now wasn't the time to be thinking about his own personal affairs.

The doctor, who had been visiting twice a day, was very pleased the next morning by James's condition, and it became apparent that Cecily's letter had marked a turning point in his illness.

Each evening, as he was flagging, and sometimes his temperature increasing again, Felix read the next instalment of the story.

And each evening, it perked James up, and caused Felix to feel intense longing for Cecily.

He wrote each day to thank her for her latest instalment, but never found the words to say anything else, too overwhelmed with worry and exhaustion.

* * *

Eventually, after ten long days, the doctor confirmed that James had now been fever-free for two days and two nights, and they could assume that the worst was now over and that he would now recover.

Felix waited until the doctor had left, excused himself, leaving James with Laura for a few minutes, and took himself to the privacy of his own chamber, worried that he was going to become tearful, and not wishing his son to see him like that.

He sat down on his bed with his head in his hands, and was then woken some time later, having, he realised, fallen into a deep sleep.

'What time is it?' he asked.

'Six o'clock,' Martin, his valet, replied. 'We thought you should eat.'

Good God. He must have been asleep for three or four hours.

'I will eat in the nursery,' he told Martin.

When Martin had left, he stretched and realised that this was the first deep, untroubled sleep he'd experienced since he got back from London, the first time he'd woken not feeling terrified.

He'd literally done nothing except care for James, worry and take short bursts of sleep to enable him to keep going. During that time he had read Cecily's story to James every evening; it was as though she'd assisted him in caring for his son. He would never be able to thank her enough.

He would also never be able to forgive himself for having been away and so wrapped up in Cecily when James became ill.

He should write immediately to Cecily to let her know that they believed James to be fully on the road to recovery now, and to thank her for all the instalments of her story—and to beg her to finish it for them, because they were all quite agog to discover what would happen at the end.

And then…well, he didn't know.

He couldn't let his boys down again. Although Cecily had been wonderful through James's illness, as close to them and as helpful as someone nearly fifty miles distant could be. But—if he *did* marry her—what if something happened to her? What if she got ill in the way that James just had? Or worse. Could he cope? Could the *boys* cope if something happened to her? They had already lost their own mother. Another loss would be terrible for them.

He didn't know what to do.

He stretched again and rolled his neck, very weary now that he'd had a few hours of proper sleep, his body nudging him to rest further now that the ordeal was drawing to a close.

He should think carefully about things. Maybe after dinner.

James joined him and Robbie at the table for dinner, and, while tired, was in good spirits and asked when he would be able to go outside and run around.

'Doctor Beech says that you might do so as soon as Thursday or Friday,' Felix told him, 'as long as you wrap up very warm and only stay out for a short time initially.'

'But I'm bored,' said James, which made Felix very happy indeed; James had been too ill for boredom until now.

He was less happy later on, sitting in his library, unable not to think about all the blissful time he had spent in this same room with Cecily.

He wanted to write to her again—he missed her hugely—but he didn't know what to say.

He *should* address the fact that he had implied so strongly that he intended to propose to her. Not in writing, though. He should speak to her in person.

When his man of business had made his list of houses for her to visit, he would find a way to speak to her then.

And perhaps his decision about whether or not he wished to marry her would be made for him by then. Perhaps she would not wish to wed him.

He just didn't know.

He did know that he needed to stay with his boys for the time being, and that they should be here together without Cecily.

He wrote to his Aunt Davinia to explain that he

would be unable to return to London for the foreseeable future because he needed to be with the boys, and to ask that she might ensure that Cecily enjoyed herself as much as possible. That wouldn't eat into Cecily's capital at all; as her host it would naturally fall to Felix to cover any expenses incurred, without in any way patronising Cecily.

And once he'd done that, well, that was that.

Cecily would make an excellent mother, he suddenly thought, nursing a glass of whisky in his hands and watching the embers in the fire before him die. Thank God no one had caught them when they had been together and thank God they had not had full relations. If and when they ended their engagement, they would make it very clear that it was she who was jilting him, and, in due course, if she wished to marry a local squire, for example, a previous engagement to a duke would weigh less heavily than the attraction of her independence and home ownership.

He was looking forward to receiving the final instalment of her story even more than James was, he thought; it would allow him another opportunity to hear Cecily's written voice, experience her humour, her inventiveness.

Damn, he missed her.

They received the final instalment the next day.

It made them all very excited, it made them all gasp,

it made them all laugh; and when Felix was alone and re-read it, it gave him an enormous lump in his throat.

The accompanying note was upsetting too.

*Dear Felix,*

*Thank you for your letter. I was so pleased to hear that James is so much better and will recover fully.*

*Here is the final instalment.*

*Thank you so much for everything.*

*Yours,*

*Cecily*

It sounded hurt. It sounded as though she'd accepted that he was not in fact going to propose to her and that she was deeply wounded.

Or did it? Perhaps he was being arrogant and patronising, assuming that she was waiting for him to propose and would have immediately said yes had he done so. Perhaps he had been a mere flirtation—temporary liaison—for her and she was looking forward very much to living independently.

He just didn't know.

He did know that he was very sad that her story had come to an end and there would be no further reason for them to correspond until he heard from her publisher again or his man of business had found some suitable houses for her to consider.

* * *

Entertaining a bored child still recovering from his nasty bout of influenza was very time-consuming.

Once James was able to go outside, however, and tire himself out running around with Robbie—the two of them had been very happy to be reunited after their enforced separation for reasons of quarantine—Felix began to have far too much leisure to think, many of his thoughts again centred on Cecily.

He wrote several letters to her asking if she was enjoying herself in London, before putting them all on the fire.

He wrote to his aunt to ask if all was well and then consigned that one to the fire too, not wishing to raise suspicions as to why he would write to her rather than to his supposed fiancée.

He did supervise James writing a number of short notes to Cecily, and helped him decipher her responses, which made him far more nostalgic for her presence than he would have liked.

He sent an extremely specific list of requirements for Cecily's house to his man of business, because he didn't want her to live anywhere that wasn't perfect for her, and received a slightly exasperated reply.

When he received the list of suitable houses in Kent and Hampshire, he went to visit them himself, returning in between each visit to Garth, to check on the boys.

And then, when Cecily's publisher wrote to say that he was releasing her funds, he finally wrote to Cecily to say that he was enclosing details of the houses his man of business thought would be suitable, all of which he had visited himself, and told her that if she wished to visit any of them herself in advance of making her choice he would arrange for such a visit.

Cecily replied to ask which of the houses he had preferred, and they went backwards and forwards with their correspondence.

Each time he wrote another formally polite letter to her he felt his heart crack a little, and each time he received one of her politely grateful missives his heart cracked a little more.

Finally, they established that she was happy to go with his recommendation of a house—a well-maintained and very attractive six-bedroomed manor house, built in the time of Queen Anne, in pretty gardens in a small village in southern Kent, within striking distance of Tunbridge Wells. Felix's man of business would ensure that the house was supplied with servants and sufficient initial furniture.

Felix would travel to London to collect Cecily and take her to the house, after which they would both write to Lady Bradstock to explain that Cecily had decided that she did not after all wish to marry him. Cecily had already obtained confirmation from Holly that she would like very much to live with her as her companion and would join her immediately.

The anticipation he felt as he drew closer to London to collect Cecily was almost painful. He looked forward very much indeed to seeing her again, to confirm for himself that she seemed in good health and, he hoped, happy. He also, however, could hardly bear the idea of seeing her again because it felt as though it would be like re-opening an old wound that might not have begun to heal but might at least have started to crust over and reduced from extreme pain to a dull ache.

He didn't have any choice, of course; he had committed to taking her to her new house and that was that.

Cecily and his aunts were assembled in a ground-floor drawing room when he arrived just in time to dine with them.

Cecily was attired in a very becoming blue dress that he didn't think he had seen before. As he walked towards her, holding out his hand in his best imitation of a fond fiancé who had not seen his betrothed for far too long, for the benefit of his aunts and cousins, he saw her smile in a way that he realised was certainly not genuine but her own imitation of a doting fiancée.

'Perhaps you might like a moment alone after so long apart,' his Aunt Davinia suggested. 'We will assemble in the dining room and you may join us when you are ready. There can be no need for you to change for dinner, Garth, unless you are particularly desirous of so doing; we shall be quite informal this evening.'

'Thank you,' was all Felix could say, as he watched his aunts file out of the room.

'Thank you for coming to collect me,' Cecily said as soon as the door was closed.

'Have you told them anything?' asked Felix, relieved to have something practical about which to converse.

'I have merely told them that you had suggested I join you in the country, and that you were coming to collect me. Your aunt assumed that that meant that we were planning to marry sooner rather than later, and noted that your mother-in-law would be an excellent chaperone until the date of our wedding.'

'Excellent,' Felix said.

'Yes,' Cecily agreed.

And then they sat in silence for a few moments, while Felix thought how very much he loved her and hoped that she would be happy in the future, and wondered whether she would have accepted a proposal of marriage from him, and Cecily looked at her hands in her lap.

Eventually, Cecily said, 'Perhaps we should now join the others.'

'Yes, I think we should.'

The conversation at dinner was somewhat stilted and entirely soul-less.

Afterwards, Felix for once sat for several minutes by himself with a glass of port, before deciding that he might as well just get the rest of the evening out of the way and going to join the ladies in the drawing room.

They all made further desultory conversation for a few more minutes until Felix pleaded fatigue after his—not particularly tiring—journey and said that he thought that he ought to retire now for the night given that they would be leaving early in the morning.

Cecily smiled a goodnight at him but did not even twitch; she clearly had no intention of leaving the room at the same time as him.

Felix's aunts clearly held Cecily in great affection; there were many very genuine-looking tears when they bid each other farewell the next morning, his aunts obviously assuming that Cecily would be residing with Felix from now on as they would shortly be wed.

'Thank you so much for all your many kindnesses,' Cecily said as she hugged Felix's Aunt Davinia. 'I am so very grateful to you; I will never forget the time we have spent together.'

'Not at all.' His aunt returned Cecily's hug fiercely. 'The gratitude must be entirely on my side; I have very much enjoyed taking you about London and all our conversations and shopping trips. I look forward very much to the next time we see each other.'

Cecily sniffed hard and said, 'Thank you,' in a very wobbly voice, before climbing quickly into the travelling chaise.

Felix was travelling inside the chaise with her, to avoid arousing suspicion until they had left, so that there would be no awkwardness for Cecily now. When he closed the carriage door behind himself and sat down on the seat opposite her, he felt himself entirely at a loss for words. He didn't, he realised, usually feel this way. One could always find a few platitudes in any given situation, and when one was a duke others seized on one's platitudes and treated them as though they were extremely interesting conversation—something he had only really thought about properly since spending so much time with Cecily.

So that was what he should do now. Say…*anything.* Because this silence was unpleasant.

'Today is a beautiful day to travel,' he observed.

Cecily had been looking out of the window. She turned her head and gazed at him for a moment.

'I hope so,' she said, before resuming her study of the road outside.

Felix nodded and folded his arms across his chest and began to study the interior of the chaise.

After a few minutes, he began to wonder whether they were genuinely going to sit in silence for the entire journey.

This might be the last time that he and Cecily were going to be alone together for an extended period of time.

He wasn't really sure how and why they had reached the point that they were at now.

Before James's illness, Felix had told Cecily many times that he loved her and she had replied in kind.

And then James had become ill and Cecily had been of a great help to his family.

And since then neither Felix nor Cecily had said anything beyond platitudes, of the kind that one might offer to anyone.

And, while in theory one might assume that it was he, Felix, who had decided that he did not wish after all to marry Cecily, for a number of reasons—he still wasn't certain whether or not it would be a betrayal of Aurora's memory; he should be focused only on his sons; and, perhaps foremost now, he was *scared* of loving again—he had the sense that it was Cecily who had made the decision that she didn't want to marry.

He looked at her perfect—and quite adorable—profile for a moment as she stared out of the window. He had no idea what she was thinking.

'I'm so very sorry,' he suddenly said.

Cecily turned to look at him, her eyebrows shooting up.

'For what?' she asked.

'For… I don't know.'

She looked at him for a long moment and then said, 'I am also very sorry. You rescued me from a horrible fate. If I had married the Earl, it would undoubtedly have been terrible. And if I had succeeded in refusing to marry him without this fake engagement, my aunt and uncle might very well have asked me to leave their home and I might well have become destitute. And if I had not become destitute, they might have treated me even more poorly.

'And I do now realise—since living with your aunts and attending your Christmas house party—how very poorly I *was* treated by them. You have rescued me from all of that and I will be forever grateful to you. And I…if I can speak frankly…we…perhaps we engaged in things we ought not to have done. I hope that you don't feel any discomfort in that regard. I would like to apologise in case you do.'

Felix shook his head, confused. It was almost as

though she was dismissing him, telling him that they had enjoyed an obviously scandalous interlude, and she was apologising for it.

'I presume that you are looking forward to seeing the house?' he asked.

For the first time, she became animated. 'Indeed I am. I am most excited. I feel extremely fortunate to have gained my independence. Very few ladies have this opportunity and I must make the most of it.'

And there it was. She was clearly informing him that she *wanted* her independence and she wanted to *retain* her independence.

'I am of course sad,' she continued, 'to leave London and Lady Bradstock in particular, together with friends I have made, but I am looking forward to living with Holly and to making new friends, and of course continuing with my writing.'

'I am so pleased for you,' Felix said, which was true, of course, but also not true, in that her words stung somehow.

He hoped it was true that she would be happy. Well, of course it was. She would make friends wherever she lived, he was sure, and of course enjoy her writing. But would a quiet country life be right for her? She had visibly enjoyed the London balls and parties and crowds so much. She'd been so wonderful with his tenants. And with his aunts.

He was going to miss her so much.

'I told you I loved you,' he suddenly blurted out. It felt as though they had unfinished business.

Cecily nodded. 'And I told you I loved you. And I do. Very much. I wish you every happiness and I am so very, very glad that James recovered so well from his illness.'

And then she turned her head away from him to look out of the window again and apparently the conversation was closed.

The only thing worse than sitting in the carriage saying nothing other than the occasional banality to each other was sitting opposite each other over luncheon in a private parlour saying nothing other than the most mundane observations about the food—and the surprisingly pretty candles on the table, as commented on by Cecily.

Eventually, after what had felt like possibly the longest journey he'd ever experienced, they arrived in the village in which was situated the house that Felix had selected for Cecily.

'I am really quite nervous,' Cecily said.

Felix was nervous too. He would feel tremendous guilt if she didn't like the house. He was certainly not going to mention his own nerves too; this moment should be entirely for Cecily. He hoped desperately that when she saw the house and went inside she would feel only excitement and pleasure.

'I'm not surprised,' he said.

'I should remember how very much worse my alternative was.' Cecily peered out of the window. 'The village certainly looks very pretty and well kept. The church is a very attractive one. And these houses here are delightful looking.'

Felix exhaled in relief. At least she liked the exterior of the house, even if the interior didn't meet with her expectations.

'We're here,' he told her, as the carriage drew to a halt before one of the houses she had just said she very much liked. 'This is the house. I should say now that, if you don't like it, it will be very easy to find another one instead for you.'

'Thank you.'

Felix moved past her, opened the door, got out and turned to hold his arm out for Cecily.

She placed a hand on her chest and drew a deep breath, before leaning on his arm lightly for a moment to descend.

'It's so pretty,' she breathed.

As they walked up the gate together from the path to the front door, the door was opened by a smiling woman attired in housekeeper garb.

'Also, if you would prefer different servants that can be arranged,' Felix said in Cecily's ear.

'Thank you.' Cecily was smiling at the housekeeper.

'This is Lady Cecily Carlow,' Felix addressed the woman. 'I understand that you are Mrs Gibbs.'

'Yes I am.' The woman bobbed a small curtsy. 'I am very pleased to welcome you to your new home, Lady Cecily. I trust that you will find everything to your satisfaction and will be very happy to change anything as you see fit.'

'Thank you so much, Mrs Gibbs.'

Cecily and the housekeeper exchanged smiles and Felix relaxed a little; this seemed a promising start.

And then they walked inside. Cecily looked all around the hall and turned to Felix with what looked like her first genuine big smile of the day.

'I think I'm going to love living here,' she said.

'I'm so pleased,' he said.

And then he watched Mrs Gibbs show her into the reception room on the left.

He would have liked to show her the house himself, watch her—happy, he hoped—reaction. But he wasn't going to be part of her life here and it didn't seem right for him to be part of her exploration of the house.

So he stood by the front door while she began this next part of her life without him.

# *Chapter Fifteen*

*Cecily*

The house was beautiful. Cecily had immediately loved the look of it when she'd seen it from outside, before she'd even known that it was *hers*. And on further exploration she still loved it.

Its design was very neat and tidy; it was built from honey-coloured stone with two windows either side of its front door on the ground floor and five windows along the front above. It was the perfect size. She would have a sitting room, a writing room and a dining room in addition to the kitchen. Above stairs, there were chambers for her and Holly, two guests and Mrs Gibbs, with two further chambers in the attic for two maids. Felix's man of business had also employed a man who lived locally to act as gardener, footman and any other position that might be required of him.

It was all wonderful.

The only disappointment in fact was that Felix did not appear to wish to be a part of her exploring the house.

But that was actually perfect; she shouldn't be disappointed. This was *her* house. She was going to be happy here and she was going to be happy without him. So it *was* better to explore it without him.

The sound of a carriage drawing up outside distracted her as she re-entered the bedchamber that was to be hers. She saw from the window that the person alighting from the carriage was Holly and almost flew out of the room and down the stairs to hug her tightly as she entered the house.

'Oh, Holly, I am so pleased to see you,' she almost sobbed.

The tears that did then come arose from a mix of emotions: joy that she and Holly finally had their home and that it was so lovely; delight to be reunited with one of the few people who had ever truly cared for her; and, if she was honest, deep sadness that this would be perhaps the last time that she would spend a day with Felix.

She needed to dry her eyes and be happy. Immediately.

Mrs Gibbs had told her that she had dinner prepared for them.

'Would you care to dine with us?' she asked Felix.

He had told her that he would be staying in the village inn overnight so that he would be available in the morning to help should she have encountered any problems, so he must obviously be available this evening.

'I...'

'We would like you to do so.' Cecily suddenly wanted to have a pleasant dinner, involving civilised conversation on non-contentious topics, as her last memory of this interlude with him. 'I would very much like you to meet Holly properly.'

'I would like that,' Felix said, clearly having no other option.

In the event, the three of them had a very pleasant dinner, Holly's presence easing the constraint between Cecily and Felix.

Holly had an excellent knowledge of geography and history, and their conversation touched on many interesting topics.

Felix stayed for an hour after they had finished eating, before removing to the inn, and by the end of the evening, Cecily felt almost at ease in his company.

He bid her and Holly goodnight together, so she had no further time alone with him.

'I will return in the morning to confirm that everything is in order here, before I leave for Sussex,' he told them as he left.

'How very kind of the Duke to have rescued you with the fake engagement,' Holly said as they watched him go—Cecily had told her all about it, although had not, obviously, included any of the more intimate details of her stay in Garth.

'Indeed. We plan to write to the newspaper and his aunts tomorrow to inform them that I have concluded that, while he is everything that is amiable—' Cecily temporarily lost the use of her voice, before recovering herself '—the life of a duchess is not to my taste and for that reason we should not suit.' She stood up, to disguise any oddness in her demeanour, and said, 'I think we should perhaps both retire for the night after such an eventful day of travelling and moving into our new home.'

When Felix came to see them in the morning, Cecily and Holly were able to confirm that there were no apparent problems with the house.

Cecily and Felix then set out for a short walk, on Felix's suggestion, to agree exactly what wording they would use when writing to Lady Bradstock and placing the relevant notice in the papers.

They stayed about a yard from each other at all times during the walk, and were extremely polite, each agreeing almost entirely with anything the other said. Their conversation was entirely business-like, concerned only with the specifics of the wording they would use. There were no jokes, few smiles, no laughter.

It only took a few short minutes for them to conclude that they were in full agreement as to what each should say in regard to the termination of the engagement.

'Let us now return to the house, then,' Cecily said, 'so that you might begin your journey to Sussex while you still have much of the day before you.'

Felix nodded.

'This is a delightful walk,' Cecily observed, to cover the fact that—yet again—she had somewhat moist eyes. 'I am sure that Holly and I shall very much enjoy living here. Thank you very much for finding it for me.'

'I certainly think it is a particularly nice part of the world,' Felix said as the house came back into view, signalling the approach of the end of their walk. 'I should like to visit you here from time to time if I may.'

'We should be delighted to see you,' Cecily told him.

'I am pleased to hear it. Well, goodbye for now. I won't return inside; I will walk back to the inn directly from here and then leave in the chaise from there. I have already bid Holly farewell.'

'Goodbye. I wish you a safe journey.'

'Thank you. I will write to you with any details

from the publisher.' Felix looked into her eyes for a long moment and then said, in a low, hoarse voice, 'I love you very, very much.'

And then, without waiting for any response, he turned and walked away very fast.

Cecily stared at his departing back, filled with the most intense sense of desolation. She was glad that, when she had sensed in the chaise that he might be tempted to propose to her, she had told him that this was the life she wanted. It *was* the life she wanted. She *needed* to do this, be independent. Felix had made it very clear that he would always put his sons' needs above hers, and that was the way it should be, but it meant that he was not the right husband for her. And perhaps he felt that way because of something about her; perhaps her aunt had been right that she was unlovable. Or perhaps it was his unique position as a widower.

Whichever, this was the right thing for her. However sad it was to see him go.

She sniffed, trying not to cry as she watched him.

After a long few moments, she shook her head. She *would* be happy. She *would* make a good life for herself here. Having been able to buy this house and live independently with Holly and to have servants she already liked was tremendous good fortune. She had been very lucky. She *would* recover from this feeling of despair. She would write another book. She would make friends in the village. She *would* be happy.

Felix, though. She felt as though she would never recover from this time they'd spent together; it would leave a permanent and indelible mark on her.

She mouthed *I love you too*, at his disappearing figure, and then stood with tears rolling down her cheeks, watching until she could no longer see him.

# Chapter Sixteen

*Felix*

*August 1815*

Felix grinned at his boys as they strode back towards the house together following a long walk around the estate. He couldn't be prouder of them.

He couldn't be happier, actually, that he had the opportunity to spend so much time with them and was playing such a big role in their childhoods.

He couldn't be happier in any way, actually.

Well, almost any way.

There was one thing—one person—whose absence he found it hard not to think about.

There had been a moment this morning, when he was visiting one of his most elderly tenants, when he'd been asked—again—about Cecily. And at that moment—again—he'd questioned his own sanity, frankly.

He missed her. Other people missed her.

She was happy, now, though. He knew that because they did correspond quite regularly. Her book was doing extraordinarily well, surpassing all expectations, and the publisher had just said that he very much liked her second manuscript. In addition, from what she'd told him in her letters, he knew that she had a very full life now, with many new friends. It sounded, indeed, as though the local vicar spent a great deal of time with them in her house. Perhaps she might marry him. That would be a great thing, actually; she would make a wonderful vicar's wife and a wonderful mother.

She'd probably be very happy married to the vicar. If Felix *did* have a quibble at the idea, it was that from the way she'd described him he did sound a little prosy, and perhaps a little too old for Cecily. But she did seem to enjoy his company. Felix wanted her to be happy. The vicar would probably be a perfectly adequate husband for her.

He stamped his feet particularly hard as they trod up the steps and encountered surprise in the form of an infinitesimally raised eyebrow from his butler.

Felix ignored the eyebrow, shook his head at his own thoughts, sent the boys up to the nursery, and took himself to his library to go through today's correspondence. Perhaps he would find a letter from Cecily waiting for him.

It wasn't just a letter, in fact: a large parcel had arrived, addressed in Cecily's hand, the sight of which, pathetically, made his heart beat a little faster.

An accompanying note informed him that, as promised, she had copied out her third novel and had sent it to him in the hope that, as a trusted adviser and only the second reader after Miss Holland of her first two books, he might read it and provide her with his opinion on it.

He was engrossed within five minutes and the rest of the afternoon disappeared as he read the manuscript without stopping.

It was as though he could hear her voice speaking as he read. It was wonderful. It was romantic. It was *adorable*. He loved it. He loved *her*.

He would write to her this evening and tell her how much he liked it. He would *not* tell her how much he loved her because, well, it wouldn't be helpful.

He placed the manuscript carefully on a side table and went up to the nursery to see his boys for half an hour before he and their grandmother ate an early dinner with them.

He wrote to Cecily that evening, to say how very much he had enjoyed the novel and to ask whether she would like him—as her de facto agent in the process—to take it to her publisher. He included in his letter, as he always did now when writing to her, the latest news about the boys' exploits—including a fall into a lake and some extremely reprehensible but also very amusing rotten fruit throwing—and a mention of how some of his tenants were getting on, as well as comments on the events from Cecily's life that she had mentioned. They exchanged very regular comments and indeed advice; and, being truthful, he would have to admit that he cherished their correspondence very highly.

After luncheon the next day, his mother-in-law asked him if he had a few moments to spare, and led him into the library.

'I'm so sorry if I intruded,' she said without preamble, 'but I began to read this story, not realising that it must be something sent personally to you. In some ways I hesitate to ask, because it does feel as though I am continuing to intrude, but in others I feel that I *must*.'

'What is it that you hesitate to ask?' asked Felix, not sure whether or not he should feel alarmed.

'Was it written by Lady Cecily? Her voice shines through very strongly, I feel.'

Good heavens. He nodded. 'Yes.'

'And the hero—while of course a sailor rather than a duke—is of course you?' she continued.

'I…' What? Really? He had not expected her to say that.

'I hope that what I am going to say can be forgiven and forgotten if it is wrong.' She looked at him more severely than he'd ever seen her look before.

'Certainly,' he said meekly.

'I loved my daughter. I love you as a son. You are thirty years old. You are a young man. My daughter would not have wanted you to grieve forever. And your boys loved Lady Cecily when she was here. If you love her and she loves you—which, from the way that first chapter reads, she certainly does, not to mention the way you acted together at Christmas—you should not feel that you are betraying Aurora's memory. She lost her life. You still have yours. One might say that you would be betraying her memory if you didn't live your life to the fullest.'

Felix blinked at her. Her words chimed with something Cecily had said when they arrived in London together, when she had said that having been fortunate enough to have the opportunity to have the experience of visiting his house she should make the most of it in recognition of those who did not have the same opportunity.

'Think hard about that,' Laura said.

'I am.' He couldn't actually think at all. Was the sailor *really* based on him? He had certainly recognised Cecily in the—quite adorable—heroine, but…

His mother-in-law looked at him even more severely. 'Are you really thinking about it?'

He shook his head.

'Sit down now and think.'

He sat down.

She sat down opposite him.

'I do understand your point,' he said eventually, 'and I have never thought of it like that before.'

'Why don't you just tell her you love her?' she asked.

'It isn't as simple as that. I don't *want* to love anyone else. It's too dangerous. It hurts.'

'Does it hurt now?' She was still being severe. 'Living apart from Lady Cecily, never seeing her? Missing her? Worrying about her?'

'Yes,' he admitted. 'But also, what if something happens to her? What about the boys? How would they cope?'

'I'm not sure that children should be taught not to love just in case it hurts one day. That is to teach them to exist rather than to live.'

Felix nodded slowly.

'I think you should perhaps re-read that manuscript now in light of what I just told you,' she said.

By the time he'd finished the story for a second time, he knew that his mother-in-law was right. About everything.

## *Chapter Seventeen*

*Cecily*

Cecily read Felix's letter for about the eighth time before placing it carefully in the box in which she kept all his letters.

She missed him still, very much, but she was learning to live without him, with many wonderful things in her life now. This time last year, she could only have dreamt of being this fortunate.

She had some good friends here now, as well as many acquaintances, and very much enjoyed walks, the occasional outing further afield and evening entertainments with them.

Her writing was also continuing to go well. Her second book was now selling extremely well, the publisher had accepted the third, and she had a fourth well under way.

Holly, of course, was an excellent companion.

It was all so much better than she could ever have hoped. So she really shouldn't be silly enough to hanker after a handsome, kind, wonderful duke, who, for a brief moment in time, had seemed almost to belong to her. He had in fact *never* belonged to her. They were still friends, and that was good enough, *more* than enough.

She would perhaps go for a walk to the shops to buy some ribbons to distract herself.

The walk to the haberdasher's *was* distracting—she encountered two of her particular friends when she was there, which was very nice—and by the time she returned home her equilibrium was almost entirely restored.

Except, when she entered the house, she gasped out loud at the sound of a masculine voice, which, in that moment, sounded extremely reminiscent of Felix's. It obviously *wasn't* him; she clearly hadn't put him out of her mind as well as she'd thought she had and was imagining things.

The voice was coming from the direction of the parlour, in conversation with Holly. Who *was* it? It really did sound like Felix.

'Oh,' she said faintly when she opened the door to the room.

It *was* Felix.

'Hello,' he said very cheerfully, springing up from

his chair and immediately making the room look considerably smaller than it usually did. 'Would you like to go for a walk?'

'Yes, do.' Holly nearly pushed them out of the front door.

'Oh,' Cecily said yet again as the door closed behind them.

'Where do you like walking?' he asked.

'I don't know,' she said weakly.

'This way, perhaps?' He held his arm out and set off at a great rate along the road and then down a side path until they were entirely out of sight and earshot of the road, at which point he stopped and said, 'I hope you don't mind, but I have something extremely important to say to you.'

'Is it about my book?' Cecily asked. 'Or…your boys? Or Lady Beaulieu or Lady Bradstock?'

'No. It's about us.'

'What?'

'I love you to distraction and I have missed you terribly.'

'Oh.' Cecily had not been prepared for this at all.

Felix was looking much less sure of himself than usual. 'I appreciate that you might wish to maintain your independence, but each of us only gets one life and we should make the most of it. I would regret it forever if I didn't make one last attempt.'

'One last attempt to…?' Cecily queried.

Felix suddenly knelt in front of her on the grass.

'Lady Cecily Carlow, will you do me the very great honour of becoming my wife?'

'Oh.'

Felix waited.

'I… I don't know.' She could barely stand up, let alone think. This had been the last thing she'd expected. 'But you don't want to marry me,' she said weakly.

'I *do* want to marry you.'

'Really?'

'Yes. I thought that it would be a betrayal of Aurora's memory, but I now realise that that isn't true. And then I was scared because I didn't want to grieve again. But then I realised that my life was very empty without you. I love you and I would like to spend the rest of my life trying to make you happy, and I would like you to be part of my family with James and Robbie. You complete me. You complete us.'

Cecily shook her head, almost stunned. 'But I am not someone who gets married.'

'Why not?' asked Felix, still kneeling there.

'I am not… I am not someone who others love like that.'

'What? Yes, you are. *I* love you like that. I love you to distraction.'

Cecily shook her head again. 'No. My own aunt and uncle lived with me all the way through my childhood and couldn't love me. I am not a lovable person.'

'They are stupid, unpleasant dolts,' Felix said. 'You are extremely lovable. You know, they treated you *so* badly. It's surprising that they didn't have a greater effect on you. Do you remember that your aunt told you that you were clumsy and that sometimes you *were* clumsy then? But you aren't any longer, from my observation. I feel that she *made* you like that. I feel that it is only because you are such an adorable, kind, interesting, *wonderful* woman that you survived that experience.'

'Oh. Maybe.' Cecily had never thought about it like that before.

'*They* are the unlovable ones, not you.'

'Thank you,' she said.

'In addition,' Felix continued, 'Lady Beaulieu—my late wife's mother no less—holds you in very high esteem and recommended that, if I love you, as she suspected I do, I marry you. My sons love you. All my aunts love you. My tenants love you. A great many readers of your book love you, and, let me tell you, your books sound *exactly* like you, and if they love your written word, they certainly love *you*.'

'Oh,' said Cecily uncertainly. His words all *sounded* as though they made sense.

'I'm not sure I want to get married, however,' she

found herself saying. 'I like my independence. It is a wonderful thing for a woman to be independent.'

'It is.' Felix nodded. 'I would hope that if you were to become my wife you would continue to write if you so wished and I would settle this house and a large sum of money on you so that you would always have your independence.'

'Felix, you are a very good man.' Marriage would be so much easier for all women if all husbands would do the same.

'Thank you. More to the point, though, I wondered—' Felix suddenly sounded diffident '—whether *you* would be able to find it in yourself to love *me*? We have not actually established that point very recently.'

Cecily sniffed and tried to blink back tears. 'Yes, of course I love you.'

'Not the vicar?'

Cecily laughed through her tears. 'I think a match might be made between the vicar and *Holly*.'

'Oh, very interesting. Although not now because we have more important things to talk about, I hope.' Felix gripped her hands more tightly. 'If you do love me and you think you could be happy living with me, please would you marry me? Because there is a very big hole in my life without you at my side.' He looked hard at her. 'Do you quite understand that it is not *you* who are unlovable, it is your dreadful aunt and uncle who had no love to give you? It was *them*, not you. *You* are infinitely lovable, my darling.'

'Oh, Felix.'

Felix shifted slightly on his knee. 'Is that a yes?'

Cecily sniffed very hard but a tear still plopped onto their hands. 'Yes, it is.' Then she smiled. 'Yes, please. I would very much love to marry you.'

'Thank heavens.' Felix stood up and pulled her into his arms and kissed her delightfully hard on the lips.

'I love you so much,' he said a long time later.

'I love you too,' Cecily said, beaming at him.

'*This* time,' he said, 'I would like to be married as soon as possible, tomorrow or the day after, by special licence, because I would very much like to show you the natural conclusion of everything we did together at Christmas and I feel that we ought to be married first.'

And then they kissed and kissed and did lots of extremely pleasurable things that unmarried people were probably not supposed to do.

# *Epilogue*

*Cecily*

*Christmas Eve 1817*

Cecily smiled as she watched her stepsons take their little sister's hands, a boy on each side of her, and lead her over to where the head gardener had brought in evergreens and seasonal leaves and berries so that they could make wreaths with the addition of oranges, apples and ribbons.

Her daughter, Isabella, was now eighteen months, and a *very* busy toddler. Her brothers adored her and the nursery was a very happy one. It would be further augmented next year, but only Cecily knew that at the moment. She had realised a week ago but hadn't yet told Felix; it would make the perfect Christmas present for him.

Last year they had had a quiet Christmas here at Garth, but this year they had decided to host a large house party, as they had done three years ago during their fake engagement. The castle was full of guests, including Laura, Felix's late wife's mother, who had now very happily remarried herself and lived about ten miles away—so was fortunately still able to see her grandsons very regularly—and Holly and her newly-promoted-to-bishop husband who had managed to delegate Christmas Day duties this year, not to mention all Felix's aunts.

It was wonderful, and Cecily still couldn't believe her good fortune in bumping into Felix on her walk that fateful day just over three years ago when she might otherwise have ended up married to the Earl of Steed—who had subsequently wed a nineteen-year-old young lady and promptly died a week later. The widowed Countess was now a good friend of Cecily's and had confided in her that she *loved* being a wealthy widow.

Her thoughts were interrupted by Mrs Jarvis asking if she might have a quick word to discuss some of the arrangements for the guests.

'Of course.' Cecily smiled at her. She and Mrs Jarvis were now on extremely good terms.

The rest of the day passed in a whirl, with the completion of the decorations, the welcoming of final guests and their annual party for the tenants and their families.

By the time the gentlemen joined the ladies after dinner, Cecily was very ready to retire to bed.

Felix had come straight over to where she was enjoying a comfortable cose with Holly on a sofa at the far end of the room.

'May I join you?' He sat down on the sofa next to Cecily, and she, as always, felt a happy shiver at his touch.

He took a close look at Cecily, and then said, 'You look a little fatigued. It has been a very busy day. Shall we perhaps retire now?'

'I think that might be a good idea,' Cecily told him, 'as long as it doesn't mean that others feel they ought also to retire. Perhaps we could organise some Christmas carol singing around the pianoforte and then we could slip away.'

'I would be very happy to accompany the singers, should you so wish,' Holly suggested.

'Thank you; that would be perfect,' said Cecily gratefully.

A few minutes later, under cover of a raucous rendition of 'Deck the Halls', Cecily and Felix stole to the door of the drawing room and then made their escape.

'I think—' Cecily put her hand through her husband's arm '—that I would like to choose a book to read.'

'Oh. I thought you were enjoying *Emma*?' asked Felix, apparently oblivious to her true intent.

'I would nonetheless like to go to the library,' she said.

'Oh,' he replied. '*Oh.* Certainly.'

When they got there, he held the library door open for Cecily and then locked it behind himself.

'Just as a precaution,' he said. 'One never likes to be disturbed when choosing books.'

'No, indeed,' Cecily agreed, before wandering over to the nearest shelves.

As she stood looking at what appeared to be Virgil in the original, Felix came behind her and wrapped his arms around her and leaned down to kiss her neck.

'Mmm,' she said. And then, 'Mmm,' again, as he lifted her and carried her to the nearest chair before kissing her on her lips.

She kissed him back, before pulling away.

'I have something to say.' She smiled at his look of disappointment.

'You wished to come in here to *talk*?' he asked.

'I wished to come in here to give you one of your Christmas presents.'

'Would that be a...*pleasurable* present?'

'I should hope,' said Cecily mock severely, 'that you find *all* my presents pleasurable.' She climbed off his lap and made her way over to a side table. 'I placed a present for you in here earlier.' She opened a drawer and took out a wrapped gift.

'That is very kind. I also have a gift for you but had not thought to secrete it in here.'

'Open it,' she said.

Felix's face when he had finished his unwrapping made her laugh out loud.

'Thank you,' he said, clearly trying very hard to look happy.

'I embroidered it myself,' she said.

'I…see that.' Felix held up the *terribly* embroidered nightcap that she had hurriedly made and wrapped for him. 'Thank you. I am…honoured.'

'You do *look* honoured,' she said, still sniggering.

'I really am. Thank you.'

'I have something else for you.'

'You do?' His look of near terror made her laugh more.

She pulled him up from the chair where he was still sitting and took the nightcap out of his hands and placed it on the table.

'I have a secret,' she said.

'Is it an embroidery-related secret?'

'Well… No.' She stood on her tiptoes and kissed him on the lips and then wound her arms around his neck.

'This is very nice,' said Felix as she pulled back for a second.

'I have a little dance for you,' she said.

'You do?'

'Mm-hmm. Sit down.' And then, very masterfully, she pushed him back into the chair, before she began to undo her dress.

Felix was smiling. 'I think I'm going to enjoy this dance,' he said.

'I hope so,' she said, as she allowed her dress to fall to her ankles and then stepped out of it.

Felix reached for her, and she danced away from him, fully naked now.

'You're killing me,' he groaned.

'In a good way, though?'

'In a *very* good way.'

When she had danced her way around the room, Felix following her very closely with his eyes, she danced back to him, and sat down on his lap, pleased to feel the immediate evidence of how much he'd enjoyed the dance.

'That,' he said, allowing his hands to roam most pleasurably over her body, 'was the best dance I have ever seen, and a wonderful present.'

'I would like you to look at my body,' she said.

'I have been looking at it,' he said, 'and I have very much enjoyed doing so.'

'Do you notice anything different?'

'I wondered…' He stroked her stomach very gently, and then bent to kiss her breasts. 'Are you…?'

'Yes,' she said, sighing at his touch. 'We are going to have another baby.'

'That,' he said, running one hand up her inner thigh while he kissed her gently, 'is a wonderful present.'

Felix had been terrified throughout her pregnancy with Isabella but—once she had delivered the baby safely—had told her that he had come to the conclusion that Aurora's loss was something that one had to regard in the way that one might regard a riding accident, or influenza; it was usually safe and it was unlikely that the same misfortune would occur twice in one family, and they couldn't live their lives in fear. And since then he had been open with her about his hopes for an extremely large family.

'Happy Christmas,' Cecily said. 'Oh, *Felix*!'

'If you can undress in here, so can I.' He lifted her and carried her to the chaise longue at the far end of the room that they had more than once made use of most enjoyably, kissing her as he walked. 'I intend to make the beginning of this Christmas Day a *very* happy one for you, my perfect wife.'

* * * * *

*If you loved this story, you'll be sure to love Sophia Williams's other captivating reads*

How the Duke Met His Match
The Secret She Kept from the Earl
When Cinderella Met the Duke

*Look out for more stories from Sophia Williams, coming soon!*

MILLS & BOON®

Coming next month

A MARQUESS TO REMEMBER
Jenni Fletcher

Florence's nostrils flared, as if she were restraining her temper with an effort. 'I still think there has to be a way out of this marriage.'

'There isn't.'

'So that's it?' She stared up at Leo with an appalled expression. 'You're just going to give up?'

'Yes.' He sighed, feeling very tired all of a sudden. This whole argument seemed to have been revolving around his head for weeks. Ironically, tonight was the first time he'd involved her in the discussion, but every time, he'd come to the same disheartening conclusion, that there was no way out. The marriage trap had well and truly closed around him. 'Now I think that's enough of a tour for tonight. I suggest that we both retire and get some sleep.'

'Well, that explains it.' She rose slowly to her feet, her gaze still fixed on his. 'That's why you look at me like so coldly, like you despise me. It's because you do.'

'What else did you expect?' He didn't deny it. 'This marriage isn't what I wanted.'

'Me neither, no matter what you think.' She wrenched her shoulders back. 'All I know is that there has to be some reasonable explanation for what happened and I'm going to find out what it is.'

He looked her up and down, impressed despite himself. With her chin in the air and a fierce glare on her face, she looked magnificently, almost regally defiant. If he weren't still so angry, he thought he might have been tempted to reach out and haul her against him, to stop her mouth with his own.

'Then I wish you luck.'

*Continue reading*

A MARQUESS TO REMEMBER
Jenni Fletcher

*Available next month*
millsandboon.co.uk

# COMING SOON!

We really hope you enjoyed reading this book.
If you're looking for more romance
be sure to head to the shops when
new books are available on

## Thursday 18th December

**To see which titles are coming soon, please visit**

**millsandboon.co.uk/nextmonth**

MILLS & BOON